Social Murderer

by

Ian Cummins

PROLOGUE - EXCERPT FROM "THE BOOK"

BY JOHN JACKSON

Having laboured for so long over the decision, once it was made, Bruno found it easy to start planning its implementation.

He needed to find six girls' first names that would fit the pattern and form the answer to his puzzle. The pattern would then create the key that would unlock the reward.

He downloaded a list of the top one thousand girls' names from the internet. The puzzle needed the names to be five letters long, so he quickly pared the list to two hundred and twenty-eight names of this length. It took him half an hour to write a simple program to find six names that could be combined to fit the pattern. He felt sure that there would be multiple possibilities, but, having run the program, he discovered that it produced almost a hundred possible answers – but many would be unsuitable.

There were less than six months to find these women and deal with them, so the task needed to be achievable. The first set of six names contained Ettie, Elana, and Elara – these names were, he believed, relatively unusual and it would take him far too long to find suitable subjects from that list. The next set included Ffion, Amely, Raine, and Honey. Again, completely impractical.

He went back to the list of names and removed the ones he thought were likely to prove too difficult to find. There may well be plenty of babies and small children with some of these exotic names, but he would need to find adult women. Maybe one unusual name in the list would be OK, but no more.

Re-running his program against the reduced list of a hundred and twenty-two names produced a handful of possible groups. Looking through them, he decided which one he would use. There was only one relatively unusual name in the list, and two of the names were in very common usage. As a bonus, there was one name that he already identified as a potential target. She was very old, and her death would not be suspicious. Her murder would be easily accomplished, and it would give him a head start by completing the first link in the puzzle quickly.

She was local, which was a distinct disadvantage since it might alert the police to his presence. He would prefer to put distance between himself and his victims but was reasonably sure that he could make her death look like it had resulted from natural causes. If this was not how it was presumed, and an investigation was held – he was still confident he could get away with it. And it did not matter that one of the six murder victims was local – the rest would be scattered all over the country. Even if they were linked by the police – which he thought was distinctly unlikely, there would be nothing to pinpoint his location.

These would be the six women who would be the victims of the six murders that one intelligent person would connect. Eventually. And that person would then be able to solve the puzzle and collect the reward – which was enough money to be life-changing. And if they had connected the names and solved the puzzle, they would deserve the reward.

It was getting late, but Bruno was on a roll and was not yet ready to stop.

He now needed to find the women. He set about Twitter with renewed vigour. He initiated searches from his account, as well as the two additional accounts with fake names that he had purposefully set up. He was searching for five of the names – one he didn't need to look for was Nelly. He already knew her, and it would be all right for one of the women to be known to him. None of the others would be – yet.

He would follow the accounts of these women with the names he had chosen, interact with them, find out about them and, he was sure, ultimately be able to locate them. One of each name on his list. Carol, Emily, Gerri, Macie, Megan and Nelly. They would become famous in a way – unwillingly and unfortunately so.

And if a moment of worry about what he was doing passed across his mind, he dismissed it. These people were, after all, not that important. Their lives were so empty that they could squander a significant portion of their time interacting with strangers on social media. They would not be missed.

1. John Jackson's Blog (1)

Saturday, May 6th

OK, here goes. The start of my blog, online diary, or whatever. My first thought was to call it a journal, but that sounds more like something written by a nineteenth-century spinster than the thoughts and feelings of a twenty-first-century computer programmer. So, I'll go with blog. I don't expect anyone to read it – apart from me and Denis of course – but since he recommends creating it as part of the process of writing my first book, I'm going to go along with his suggestion.

There are no plans to publish this – it's just for my benefit at present. If you are reading this, then something has gone wrong. Maybe there will be some clues as to how and why it did go wrong buried in this background detail.

I'm thinking hard about the title of the book. It needs to have the element of murder and mystery in the title, and a link to computers and social media. And it must be concise. I've thought about "The Twitter Murders", but I'm worried about infringing copyright by using the name of a specific product/company, as well as being concerned about linking to a name that might have negative connotations. I'll have to broaden the title to cover the whole of social media.

Death by SM would confuse people who think that SM stands for Sado-Masochism rather than social media, and I would not want to misrepresent the book. There are more catchy titles like "Program of Murder" and even "Death@Unknown_Hands" (or maybe "Deaths@... to be more accurate.) I quite like "The Social Murderer Mystery" but my favourite title at the moment is just plain "Social Murderer".

Funny, I'd always imagined that an author would think of the title first, and then write the book. But one of my first lessons from the online course was that the title is one of the last things you decide - since you cannot be sure where your story might go until it gets to its conclusion.

Anyway, there are a few months before I need to make that decision, and in the meantime, it's just going to be called "The Book".

Denis says that writing a regular blog will help me to develop my skills. I'm sure I desperately need to do that. and he seems to know all about the subject. And maybe this is an auspicious day on which to start it. We have a new King and Queen being crowned today – and I feel like this is the first day of my official retirement, so it fits well.

Despite my lack of writing experience, he said that the plot I outlined for my book was extremely promising. I'll tell you more about that later, but Denis's words were "It's going to be difficult to write and you'll need to do more research - but it has terrific potential. And the part you've already written shows real promise. But before you attempt to write a whole book, John, describing what has happened to you and expressing your feelings will provide invaluable assistance in describing what happens to other people and how they feel."

And I trust him, so I'm willing to take this advice. "Besides," he added – in jest, I'm sure - "when you become a successful writer, you'll be able to call this blog your memoir, and sell it as your second book!"

I don't know if he realised how encouraging his words were. I've not written more than a page at a time since I left school! So, suitably encouraged, I've promised to give it a go and to send him frequent updates on this blog and "The Book" as it progresses.

Having explained why I'm writing this; I'll expand my explanation to include the reasons for wanting to develop my writing skills. Then I can get on with the blog itself.

I'm taking early retirement. I've checked my finances and I can afford it and recent events make it necessary. Besides, if I do run short of funds, I've got something to fall back on. When I handed in my notice to Ralph, after he'd finished trying to find out why I was leaving and begging me to stay on, I did agree that if he was stuck at any time in the next few months, and the job wasn't too big, I'd do it for cash.

Even though I'm only fifty-five, I've worked hard all my life, earned well, and put more than enough into a pension fund. And there were jobs over the years that paid bonuses and I've always put that money to one side. So, I'm comfortably off, and I can focus my efforts on doing something that will be rewarding in other ways than monetary measurement.

But since the accident, I'm finding it more difficult to work at the pace at which I've worked all my life. They tell you to go out at the top of your career, don't they? That's what I'm doing. I'd hate to hang around, being given all the shit jobs because I'm no longer able to complete everything quickly and accurately. Having filled such a huge part of my life with work, I'll have lots of time on my hands, and they tell me that creative writing is a good way to fill it. So, I signed up for the creative writing course, met Denis online, and am now doing what he suggests.

When I first thought about writing a book, I had doubts about my ability. Because writing must come, at least partly, from your experience - and my life experience is rather limited. I've been to lots of places, so writing about different locations will not be a problem. And if the plot necessitates me going somewhere, I have the time and the funds to make the journey. But I have limited experience with people – for reasons which will become clear. So, creating and developing characters is going to be a challenge.

And then I thought some more and realised that there is a rich, ready source to create a range of different characters. It's called social media.

It never ceases to amaze me how many details people reveal about themselves to total strangers on social media. And I'm sorry if this comment appears sexist, but this does seem to be truer for women than men. This suits me down to the ground because almost all the characters in my story are women – so I'm confident I can get all the input I need without leaving my chair.

That concludes the introduction –the description of the task, to use the terminology of my trade. Now I can get down to telling my whole story. the only way I know how – to start at the beginning and work through to the present day. But I'm not going to include every detail of my fifty-five years on this planet – only the interesting and relevant bits. The events in my life which have determined my current situation.

This will be like one of the computer programs I've spent my life writing. It will begin at the beginning and end at the end, but hopefully, there'll be enough loops, branches, and conditional statements to keep you interested and entertained. And I'll try to make that the last reference to computer programming. I can't promise, but I'll try.

Sunday, May 7th

I was the second child of my parents' marriage, Tom having arrived three years earlier. My dad, known as Jack - presumably because his real first name was too difficult to pronounce - worked in the local coal mine, and the whole family lived in the same house that I'm in right now.

Back then there were coal mines in this part of the world. I won't go into whether it was Maggie Thatcher's fault they were closed, or it was caused by poor management or the unions, or if it was just the natural end of economic viability that caused them to close. That's not the purpose of my story. What's relevant is that my dad's job and the stay-at-home opportunity it gave my mother were key factors in my upbringing. Ones that influenced the rest of my life.

I had a happy childhood. As a kid, you don't think about whether you're happy or not – you just get on with life as best you can. But my first clear memory is not a happy one. My father was one of several miners killed in an underground explosion at the local pit. I must have been about six years old, and my first clear memory is of a policewoman and a policeman arriving at our house in the middle of the afternoon to tell my mum what had happened. I remember her crying at the time.

I also remember that the weeks that immediately followed the disaster were filled with a seemingly endless parade of friends and neighbours bringing food for the family, toys for my brother and me, and sympathy for my mum.

As a working-class child, I was not expected to attend the funeral. This was something that only adults did. Unless you were royalty or posh, then maybe kids attended. But we were neither posh nor royalty, so Tom and I were looked after by a neighbour when they buried Dad.

It was a huge affair as most of the victims of the disaster had a shared service and were buried at the same time and in the same cemetery. After that, life returned to near normal. Mum got compensation and she didn't have to go to work. I'm guessing she drank a bit more often than previously – she certainly smoked a lot more. And she seemed shrunken by the experience. But what made her much worse was when Tom died.

He had gone on an activity week organised by the school. In typical big brother fashion, in the weeks leading up to it, he had worked hard at making me jealous, describing all the wonderful activities he'd be taking part in. I remember being fifty percent jealous of him and fifty percent happy in a strange way. While he was gone, I'd have a whole week of just me and mum, and I was looking forward to that – but it was not the sort of thing that I would ever have admitted. To him, to mum, or anyone else.

At the activity centre, he was in a canoe that overturned, and he was the only boy who wasn't saved. There was quite a fuss about his drowning, of course. Inquiries were conducted into the supervision of the children by the staff and teachers. No doubt they produced their reports and 'lessons were learned.' To be honest, I can't tell you what the outcome was – and I don't think that my mum even knew back then. It didn't seem to matter - she had lost her first child and I didn't have a brother anymore. That was all that mattered.

You can guess the impact it had on her, and it was not good. For me, the effect was to make me withdraw more into myself. I know we got the same kind of neighbourly help as when dad went – but afterwards, I found it a lot harder to get on with other kids. I think that they also started to avoid me. There's a fear that people have of a family that has been the victim of multiple tragedies. It's as if they might have some disaster-inducing virus that might be contagious. So, people don't go near.

It also left me with a lasting feeling of deep discomfort with the police. Not their fault, at all. But the only two times I had encountered them they had brought disaster (or to be more accurate, the news of disaster) to my home. To this day I have a strong negative reaction when I see uniformed police, especially if I see a policeman and a policewoman together. I expect it's too late to change that, and I just have to live with it.

I became a quiet, bookish child, and Mum became an even paler shadow of her former self. I learned how to cook myself a basic meal on the days when Mum wasn't feeling well or was too sleepy to wake up when I shook her. She was still my mum – sometimes distracted, often a little over-protective (and who can blame her) but I like to think that I was the reason that she stayed (relatively) sane and (relatively) sober. She just about kept it together.

She must have done something right because when I finished junior school at the age of eleven, she told me that I wouldn't be going to the same school as most of my classmates – I'd qualified to go to Grammar School in Nottingham. I can't remember taking any specific test to get there, but she had evidently made it happen because I know that you only got admitted to a Grammar School if you passed an entrance test.

So, I took the one-hour bus journey to and from school every day with a dozen other kids who had also qualified. But they didn't become my friends. They were from different backgrounds - the semi-detached part of town, not the terraced houses.

I can only really remember Stephen. He was the son of the local solicitor, and the only reason I can remember him is that we bonded because we were both bullied. Nothing nasty – and certainly back then it was almost expected if you were the only working-class kid in a class of middle-class kids (which I was) or if you had a surname that easily lent itself to being mocked (which Stephen had).

We've subsequently become friends. But back then we would speak to each other on the way to and from school – but that was as far as it went. (His surname is Crapnell).

Even though I was often alone, I enjoyed my time at Grammar School. I loved the way that the classes were always quiet, and you could hear what the teachers said. And if you asked a question – during or after class, the teachers would take the time to answer and make sure you had understood. A mixture of respect (and perhaps a little fear) made sure that homework was always done on time, and I progressed well. And I loved the school library. Two large rooms, full of books on every subject imaginable to a teenage boy back then. Even a few about computers, which by my mid-teens were becoming an obsession for me.

There were some computers at school – but I knew even then that they were outdated. And I wasn't interested in playing games on them the way that most of my friends were. I joined the school computer club, and it was the period of my childhood when I came closest to having real friends. We worked on some interesting projects, and I got a reputation as a whiz kid since I was able to diagnose and fix problems. But, fed by the many stories of science fiction that I devoured at every opportunity, I wanted to get my hands on the big powerful computers that I knew were out there. I wanted to change the world.

Friday, May 12th

When my school days came to an end, I had to go away to college to have any hope of following my dreams. But first, I had to make sure that my mum was safe and could manage without me. By now she was an alcoholic – I believe the term used is 'functioning alcoholic', which she was – just about functioning! But I was worried that if I left home to go to college, she might not be able to cope.

Using every trick in the book, I got her to join a local group that assisted addicts, and the effects were all that I hoped. Partly through the effectiveness of the programme, and partly through the friendship she developed with her mentor, Billy. She mentioned him a lot when we talked, and I suspected that he was becoming more than just a mentor to her. At that time, I thought that was entirely a good thing, although I was to have second thoughts later. But I'll come to that in due course.

Cutting a long story short, I felt it was OK to leave home and I successfully applied for a place at Manchester University and enrolled in a B.Sc. course in Computing.

I came home as often as possible – several weekends during the terms and throughout every vacation. I easily got a job in the local pub as I was such a big lad. (I was – and still am – over six feet tall, just like my father.) What's more, while at University I had taken up sport and started fitness training. I played rugby for the first fifteen and spent a few hours every week in the gym. Exercise and fitness have been part of my life ever since. I discovered how much better I felt about myself when I put on some muscle, and I've stayed that way from that day to this.

But (coming out of my programming loop) back then it made me easily employable, and I hoped it would be a way to bond with Billy Rodriguez, who, as I had long suspected, had become my mum's new partner and moved into our house during my first term at uni. But him being a big man, and the fact that we both loved Mum, were not enough to enable Billy and me to get close.

He was significantly younger than Mum, which might have been one of the reasons he did not get on well with me. Our ages were dangerously close, and he must have felt awkward about that. But I tried to be friends and hoped we had enough in common. We certainly both wanted the best for my mum. I'm guessing that his physical size was part of his appeal to my mother. After all, my father must have been a big feller too. Where else did I get it from?

I didn't (and still don't) know too much about Billy. I suspected that Mum didn't know too much about him either. I was never sure whether the reason she clammed up whenever I asked about him was that she didn't know that much about him, or she knew more and didn't want to tell me.

I thought that bonding with Billy was important for many reasons. I owed it to my mother to check him out as much as possible. She didn't have a fortune to be scammed out of – but she did own her own home, so maybe that was attracting him. And as she aged, it would be good to feel sure that she was in good hands. And when I found out that his job was something to do with computers, my selfish interest kicked in. Maybe he could help me with my career.

But he was terminally tight-lipped, so I learned very little and had to rely on my gut instincts. He certainly seemed to be very fond of her. Maybe I was not as easy to get on with as I thought and that was why we weren't connecting. Anyway, he and I did not become friends, but I was content that he made Mum happy and more importantly, kept her safe, so it was OK for me to be so far away for much of the time.

Friday, May 26th

When I finished university, Billy was still with Mum, and there was still tension between us – entirely on his part I felt - but on the plus side, I had complete freedom to get a job away from home, which is what I did. I started as a programmer at a large insurance company which, unusually, had its headquarters in the north of England and not in London like most do.

But I've omitted a step. Before I moved away permanently, I had to make sure that Mum had no objections to me changing my name. Apart from my height, one of the other things I inherited from my father was a last name that was long, Polish, difficult to pronounce, and impossible to spell.

My dad's father had come to the UK during World War Two as a mechanic in the RAF before being demobbed, getting a job as a mechanic at the mine, and marrying an Englishwoman. Looking at my father's date of birth, it seems that they married just in time!

I was proud of my Polish heritage and considered Grandad to be a hero – but the last name was a problem. I'd accepted the ribbing I got at school and the need to spell the name out to every member of officialdom and every shopkeeper or tradesman. But I wanted to avoid any possibility of discrimination when job hunting and I was getting increasingly frustrated.

With the growing use of computerised systems, a wrong spelling of your name could mean a failed delivery or a screw-up on a financial transaction that could take ages to put right. Mum had reverted to her maiden name after Dad died – possibly for the same reasons that I wanted to change, or maybe to signify a new beginning. Anyway, she had no problem with me doing likewise, and I took the good old-fashioned English name, Jackson.

It meant I kept the same initials, and the few friends I had could still call me JJ. I was also being true to my father and following the ancient process of naming, as my father was always known as Jack. So, I was Jack's son. In job interviews, it was an interesting topic to discuss when the interviewer discovered that I had changed my name.

I found a tiny studio flat that I could afford to rent (another good reason for living up north rather than in London, where property prices would have condemned me to further years of sharing accommodation). A month after acquiring my university degree I started work at the insurance company.

There was plenty to learn and to do as their computers needed constant reprogramming for new types of insurance, changes in actuarial tables, and so forth, and the first couple of years sped by. I did my best to get home to see Mum as often as I could, but my visits became less frequent and the deterioration in her health became more obvious. She continued smoking and drinking to the end, and it was no surprise when she was admitted to hospital with breathing problems. What was a surprise was how steep a slope she went down, and how short a time she was on it. She died within three weeks.

I took time off work for the funeral and was comforted by the large numbers that turned out – the sense of community in the village had outlasted the mine on which that community was founded. But then I faced a new set of problems.

Billy and I visited the solicitor for the reading of her will and discovered that apart from a one-off gift to Billy, Mum had left everything to me.

He was livid. Discovering that he had no ownership of the home he had shared with her all these years produced a lengthy rant. Right there in the solicitors' office. He threatened both me and my 'friend' Stephen, the solicitor, accusing us of collusion, corruption, and worse. He stormed out of the meeting, telling us we had not heard the last from him and that he would be taking legal action.

At this point, Stephen and I were not close friends, we had only just reintroduced ourselves having not spoken since our school days. But Billy's rant and the fact that we had to work together to prepare ourselves for any problems he might cause, helped us to build a friendship. A friendship that has grown steadily since that day until now, many years later.

He assured me that Billy in legal terms did not have a leg to stand on, and (with the aid of a strong drink from a bottle secreted in his office cabinet to help us over the shock of what had just happened) we discussed the steps we needed to take. We agreed on a strategy and drafted an exceedingly polite letter informing Billy that he could remain in the house as long as he wanted, subject to signing a tenancy agreement. In recognition of his special position, the rent would be extremely low – covering only the estimated upkeep costs of the property. Stephen told me he thought it was an exemplary offer – but it did not elicit a reply from Billy.

I'll edit what happened over the next few months. Dealing with all the normal administration involved in the death of a close family member was more difficult than I had expected. I had never imagined that the death of a woman who had lived such a simple life would necessitate contact with so many different branches of officialdom. The utilities, the local council, the post office, the pensions office, the list seemed endless; but when you add into the mix the presence of a sitting and uncooperative tenant in your property, it was not easy. My friendship with Stephen was forged in these trying times.

Friday, June 2nd

I'll fast forward a few months - to when Billy Rodriguez puts an envelope through Stephen's office door telling us that he was leaving town and had no plans to return but (this last part of the letter being all in capital letters) we had not heard the last of him!

Stephen accompanied me to the property the following weekend and we found it to be extremely run down, with the garden overgrown and the furniture worn and filthy. But no wanton destruction or vandalism had occurred. Now that we had a complete picture of the situation, he insisted that the police needed to be told about Billy's threats, and reluctantly I agreed, on condition that he would inform them. I still found it very difficult to deal with them since the events of my childhood. The threat had been made against both of us and Stephen, being a solicitor, had some standing in the eyes of the law, so he agreed to inform them. Thankfully that marked the end of my dealings with Billy Rodriguez.

I'm not sure at what point I decided to move back into the family home. With Billy gone, I visited on several weekends, spending my spare time and spare money putting it back together. Originally, I'd intended to sell it, but there had been developments in my career that changed my mind.

The insurance company embarked on a project to build one of the first computer-based price comparison systems in the UK. The internet was not yet widespread enough for this to be aimed at the public, so their system was built for insurance brokers. Its aim was for brokers to bring the business to my employers when the customer could be shown that we offered either the best deal or one that was imperceptibly different from our competitors. And the system would gather important data for future business growth.

As one of the in-house computer staff, I was not part of the project – we had to get on with the day-to-day work while a team of contract programmers did the more interesting and challenging stuff around the new system.

I did my best to interface with them both professionally and socially, and quickly learned that they were getting paid way more than the in-house staff. I was as helpful as possible (the older employees made this easy for me as they refused to talk to the incomers unless forced to). At the end of the project, I contacted the boss of the contracting company to see if they had any vacancies, and with good references from the team members I'd been interfacing with, I got a job with them.

Friday, June 16th

It's been a couple of weeks since I last added something, and when I reviewed what I've written so far, I thought I needed to explain more about the nature of the work involved in my new employment and the reason this helped me decide to move back into the ancestral home.

Ralph Borshell ran Premier Programming, a high-grade computer programming task force that he hired out to large companies that needed projects done quickly and were prepared to pay for it.

At that time the number of computers being installed in businesses outstripped the number of people skilled enough to get them to do what was needed, so there was a lot of demand for skilled computer programmers. And I could do the work and had the hunger for it.

But the work involved moving to wherever the need was. Being footloose and fancy-free it suited me fine. Nights in cheap hotels, cooked breakfasts served buffet style, and evening meals at steak bars were no hardship. And if the project was super urgent or was falling behind schedule, I was the first to volunteer for extra hours. The pay was based on hours worked, and continued employment was based on being able to deliver quality code quickly.

The variable location of the work meant that it didn't matter where I lived, so I gave up the studio bolthole and moved back here. Gaps between projects were short – and I spent them fixing up the house, having the occasional drink with Stephen and other locals, and reassuming my love of the Bees – the local football team. Throughout my childhood I'd attended their home games with religious frequency and fervour, accompanied by my father when he was alive. But more of that thread in a moment.

My increased income meant that I could hire professional help for the home renovation. I didn't get carried away – but made sure the place suited me and my lifestyle. An expanded kitchen and large living space downstairs, with a bedroom, an office, and a small exercise room upstairs. Within a few months, I had the house looking the way I wanted it and got on with life.

Saturday, June 17th

The lack of any partner or any relationship in my life needs addressing. I'd had a few brief relationships while at university. And while not averse to female company, I found that I didn't need it. I was, and still am, quite simply happy on my own. I don't rule it out, but at the time of writing it would now seem to be exceedingly unlikely to ever happen. I had – and still have – a few female friends. But I'm still on my own.

The female friends that I do have are ones that I've met either in the local pub or while following the Bees. The pub, especially the monthly quiz nights, is one cornerstone of my social life, and the football team is the other. And since virtually all my work companions are male, the only women I meet are quiz team members and fellow Bees fanatics.

As I said earlier, I'm still friends with Stephen. And we joke that he owes me a huge favour since I solved a major business problem for him over a jar or two in the local. He was complaining about some of the outdated business practices that he had been lumbered with when his father finally retired.

What bothered him was the habit of people depositing their valuable documents with a solicitor for years. Usually. the document set was a will and the deeds for the family home. His father had almost certainly helped the client draw up the will – for a small fee – and agreed to be an executor for the estate – for another small fee. In return, the client expected his firm to keep the documents secure for dozens of years, and to be allowed to access them for occasional updates, and eventual use when the client passed on. All for a very small annual fee.

He had to maintain a storage room and keep it secure, clean, and dry, all for a minimal return. It was not a profitable business, and he was keen to get out of it, but wary of upsetting (and losing) clients. I told him the obvious solution was to do what my employer did when asked to take on responsibility for the update of installed computer systems. A different business admittedly – but the same problem. Clients wanted a forever guarantee that their system would function no matter what else in the universe changed. It just isn't practical and so he offers the service but quotes such a high price that nobody ever takes it up. I suggested to Stephen that he do the same.

"But I can't go back on those people to whom we've been offering the service for years," he said. So, I suggested he tell them that the circumstances had changed. Mention GDPR security requirements and new government legislation. In case anyone asks, GDPR stands for general data protection regulation, and it governs data security for just about everyone and everything. But you don't need to be specific. Keep it vague. You can say that GDPR has become part of the law, and then in the next sentence say that your charges are going up. You don't have to make the false claim that the former had caused the latter – just put them in consecutive sentences and your clients will conclude that the one caused the other.

The penny dropped and he agreed to do what I suggested. I told him that there would be no charge for my professional consultation, but I'd make sure that one day I would ask him for a big favour in return. I now know what it's going to be – but there's a long way to go before I ask it.

My recent accident has not only made me take early retirement but has also reminded me that I need to put my affairs in order. I've drawn up a will and twisted Stephen's arm so that he agreed to be my sole executor. Its complications will no doubt have him (or his successor) cursing me long after I've gone! I haven't drafted the requirements yet – I will have to do so soon, but I've extracted the promise that he'll do it.

Apart from the local pub, the other key component of my social life is the local football team, the Bees (so-called because of their traditional playing colours of black and yellow). They draw a weekly attendance in the (very) low thousands and spend their time bouncing between the two lower divisions of the English Football League.

Since I moved back home, I've attended almost every home game (except those played midweek when I am working away) and I follow them on away matches across the length and breadth of England. I either join my fellow fans on the club-sponsored bus – or when the fancy takes me, I extend my trip if the away team is in an interesting or remote part of the country. Visits to the likes of Exeter and Plymouth in Devon (and, more recently, Ipswich in Suffolk) allow me to take an extended weekend break which I thoroughly enjoy. I stay at a nice hotel and enjoy the local sights and the local cuisine.

Which brings us up to date. In programming terms, it completes the first loop, I suppose. I now need to cover a little more about the book I'm writing and the advice that Denis gave me. Assuming I follow that advice, it will fill a lot of my time in the next few months.

Friday, June 30th

The plot of the book concerns an ageing computer geek (write about what you know, they say) who goes bad when he learns that he has only months left to live. He's a bit of a cliché. A loner, overweight, living on takeaways, and pale-skinned from endless hours in front of the computer screen. He has very few friends and no living family, owns his house, and has a comfortable bank balance but faces the prospect of departing the world without having left a mark on it.

His mind becomes twisted (maybe it's the as-yet-undetermined disease eating away at him, maybe he's just a bad person, I haven't made up my mind yet) and he resolves to use his death to indulge in his one real passion – setting and solving puzzles. The only place where he will be missed is in the online world of puzzle setters and solvers, in which he plays a key role. He decides to set one final puzzle, with the prize being his inheritance. His estate will be worth well over a quarter of a million, so it should leave a mark somehow. His puzzle will involve six unsolved murders, which he will commit. When the names of the victims, all women and all with five letters in their first name, are arranged in the pattern determined by the puzzle, it will reveal a password that will unlock the money.

Denis gave the plot his thumbs up – but wanted to know how the main character was going to find these women. If they had to have specific names and, assuming (quite correctly) that this guy did not have too many females in his life, finding the six victims in such a short time would be difficult – and hence maybe make the plot unbelievable.

I assured him that finding them would not be difficult – the modern social media world was full of people willing to reveal amazing amounts of detail about themselves to total strangers. But Denis insisted that I prove it to him. He felt quite strongly that since the main character was somewhat of a cliché, it would be essential for the book to focus on how real the women victims were. The centrepiece of the book should be the victims, not the perpetrator.

He set me the challenge of proving that they could be found, and I accepted the gauntlet he had thrown down.

I've ruled out any thought of Bruno (the name I've given to my main character – I do think it is suitably dark) using a dating app. It would leave too much of a 'footprint' and anyway, he would struggle to find that many dates in such a short time, especially when the names of the women had to be from such a restricted list.

Facebook too was not going to be a great help as a source of suitable women. It might help him find some information on the women, but interacting with these women would be difficult without either making himself known or creating several fake identities, each with a 'back story', and photographic evidence, and he did not have the time for that.

The main tool for Bruno would be Twitter. It's all about the written word with very few pictures involved. Many participants do not even have their real photo on their profile, and much is taken on trust. Although Denis has his doubts, I'm going to see if I can make it work. If I can show him that a named victim can be found and contacted from this platform, then he says the outline of the book is sound.

I set up three profiles on Twitter. I was, of course, not going to use my own, that's reserved for chatting about the football team and other personal matters. But I already had a profile set up for Tom (I'll explain more about that soon) and so I added one for Dick, a young financial worker who lives in the West Country. Dick connects to the network via a customer site of mine so his profile would be difficult to trace back to me. And then I added a third profile for Harriet. I thought that a woman's profile might help get some interactions with the women who will give me the details that I'll use to assemble the characters in the book. Harriet lives in London and connects via a different portal. Each of the three will connect with each other, and can look for different women, interact with them, and (hopefully) provide the information I need to write the book. Tom, Dick, and Harriet – I like that.

Dick found a waitress in a Greek restaurant in the Northwest of England who had one of the names I needed. Without any effort, he discovered by reading the history of her tweets, that she was single, had a daughter who was away from home in her first year at university, and a son who was living at home and doing his A Levels at a local college. She also had a boyfriend.

She used the term boyfriend, which to me implied that he did not live with her and was not the father of the children. If he lived with her, she would be much more likely to call him her partner. She must have cared about the place she worked, and when she posted the name of the restaurant and gave it a little review to drum up some business, I had all the information I needed to complete the profile and make contact.

I'm not going to write loads about her here because I'll only have to write it all again in the book.

I sent a few paragraphs describing the woman to Denis, but he was not happy. He told me it needed more details to make her a real person that the reader could believe in and sympathise with. So, I took the obvious action and went to the restaurant for a meal. I chose a Monday evening, quite late, as she worked evenings, and this would be the least busy part of the week. I'd hopefully be able to chat with her and get more of the details that Denis wanted.

It was a very useful visit, which I'll describe briefly. She was certainly as attractive as the pictures she'd posted on social media – she had not needed to apply filters and hadn't done so. As soon as she opened her mouth it was obvious that she was a Geordie – and it was easy to assume that she had followed the since-departed father of her children to this part of the world. (At least that is what it will say in the book).

I could smell drink on her breath, so she obviously enjoyed a glass of wine (or two) during her shift. But the key discovery was a significant tattoo on the back of her right hand. It was the tail of an animal that evidently continued up her arm because it emerged at her neckline and curled around the back of her neck. A snake, I assumed – after all, the girl with the dragon tattoo was in an entirely different book.

Her tattoo could have posed a problem because I hate tattoos on women. I can barely abide them on men, but on women, they are a complete turn-off for me. Don't get me wrong, I acknowledge that every woman has the right to do with her body as she wishes, but anything more than a little butterfly or dolphin discretely placed would prevent me from ever getting close.

Luckily, I did not need to get close, but I also could not let my feelings be known. Telling her I hated tattoos on women would not have been the best conversation opener, and it might well have ended any discussion there and then. I wanted to talk to her to find out more about her for my book, so of course, I spoke admiringly about the tattoo and flirted mildly when I asked about where else she might have some ink on her. And the flirtation was seemingly welcomed.

This made me wonder about how Bruno might react in the situation. Would he be tattooed? I'd prefer not. So, I came up with the idea that he was a great admirer of tattoos, which would prompt the question as to why he had none (visible) himself. The answer was that he had once tried to get a tattoo, but it had produced such a violent allergic reaction that he could not proceed. Another reason for him to be angry about the world. I also used this same excuse when talking to her myself. And I got a sympathetic response.

I completed my research by sitting in my car outside the restaurant until it closed and noting that the waitress did not leave for half an hour after closing. The tables had been cleared and reset, and both I and the young couple who were the only other customers had long since left. Unless there was some wrangling over the split of tips (which I thought highly unlikely, even though I had, out of guilt, left her a significant tip myself) my obvious conclusion was that she was staying for one more drink with the kitchen staff.

Discrete observation of her ten-minute walk home to a nearby end-of-terrace house, which was dark when she reached it, completed the profile and confirmed my assumption that her boyfriend was not a permanent resident at the property. I conveyed the additional details I'd discovered about her to Denis - and included them in the book.

He was extremely complimentary about my first real piece of work and assured me that if the rest of the book was up to this standard, I would have something to be proud of!

2. "A Routine Murder"

Detective Inspector Linda Evans   Sunday, October 8th

"It's a bit of a messy one, ma'am," was the greeting I received from Constable Tweedie as I approached the front door. He was looking decidedly green about the gills and had obviously been the one who had discovered the body. Thankfully he was now getting plenty of fresh air as he stood at the front door, preventing unwanted entrants. He was trying to raise the strength to glower at the group of concerned citizens (or rubberneckers as some would call them) gathering on the pavement just outside the front gate.

I entered the house and could immediately hear that the action was taking place upstairs. Crime scene personnel were already at work when I entered the bedroom where the naked body of a young woman was lying – in an unnaturally straight and neatly arranged position - across the bed. Beneath her, the sheets, pillowcases, bedding, and floor were heavily stained with the blood that had poured out when her throat had been slashed.

"I won't bother to ask the cause of death. Anything else you can tell me?" I asked, directing my questions to George Woollard, the pathologist. I followed unofficial police procedure by refusing to enter into any small talk with him before asking him the crucial question.

If ever the phrase 'We must stop meeting like this' was justified, it was now, I thought, but refrained from using it. But we had met so often that I immediately recognised George, despite him being dressed in a white forensic onesie and having his back towards me as he placed plastic bags into his large case on the bedside table. I must be dealing with too much violent crime if I can recognise him that easily.

"She was not in this position when she was killed," he began. "From the location of the blood splatter, she was probably lying along the bed with her head here", he continued, pointing to a point in the centre of the bed, about thirty centimeters from the headboard.

"She was lying face down when she was killed, possibly restrained, but if so, it was voluntary because there are no marks on her wrists or ankles. And there's no sign of anything that might have been used to tie her, so the killer may have disposed of it. He probably pulled her head back and slashed her throat with a single cut from right to left." George helpfully mimed the gestures of pulling back and slashing to make my experience that little bit more real.

"So, he's left-handed?" I asked, feeling the need to say something. Even in these times of political correctness, I felt it safe to assume that the perpetrator was male.

"Yes, and above average strength. Not just to cut so deeply, but also because he then moved her so she would be lying across the bed. And even though she's not that big, lifting a dead weight is not easy, and there's no sign of the bedclothes moving, so he must have lifted her off the bed."

"I can't see any reason why he moved her like that, can you?" I asked and got a "no" and a shake of a wise head in reply.

"Anything else you can tell me about him?" I asked.

"Other than the fact that he's obviously a callous bastard, no. He would have had a lot of blood on him, and it looks like he took a shower in the bathroom before leaving."

"Anything else?"

"Signs of recent sexual activity – no surprise there, but our murderer took care of any deposits he had made, so there's nothing to go on there."

"Time of death?"

"Best guess I can give right now is about forty-eight hours ago, so sometime late Friday afternoon or early Friday evening. I may be able to improve on that when I do a full exam – but that's the best I can give you right now," he answered, not even bothering to look up from his grisly task.

I walked over to get a closer look at the victim. Pretty enough, make-up still in place, and very, very dead.

Footsteps on the stairs told me that Detective Sergeant Roger Holden was on his way up. He'd been the one who had called me about half an hour earlier, but he must have been downstairs when I arrived. He was immediately able to impart the key information.

"Her name is Megan McCormick," he began. I noted that he also followed unofficial procedure and didn't bother with an introductory 'Good evening'.

"She's a prostitute – probably more correct these days to call her an escort or a sex worker. Works under the name of Suzanne. There's no sign of a break-in and there's plenty of cash in her purse, so it wouldn't appear to be a burglary. And there's a knife missing from the set on the kitchen work surface, so I think we can guess what the murder weapon was."

"Any diary or calendar with clients' names on it?" I asked hopefully.

"Looks like she did everything online," he replied.

"Well, obviously not *everything*," I interrupted. I felt that a bit of levity would remind him that he didn't have to dance around the messy details, just because I'm a woman.

He smiled with just a hint of relief before continuing. "We've got her mobile phone and her laptop, so hopefully they'll reveal plenty."

"Yes, important to reveal plenty," I said, glancing at the body. "Let's go downstairs to talk – no need to spend any more time in here." I was hoping that I would be permitted just a slight amount more squeamishness, allowing for the fact that it was a member of my sex who was lying brutalised in front of us.

"I guess it's OK to move the body?" George asked.

"Yes, it's OK to move her," I replied stressing the final word. 'Let her be *her* for as long as possible before she becomes *the body*', I thought.

Sitting in the neat, tidy cosy downstairs room, DS Holden and I went through the list of the first tasks that needed to be done. There seemed to be little chance of much forensic assistance. No doubt the bedroom would reveal the fingerprints of many of her clients, and the untouched state of things downstairs did not offer any promise of providing helpful information.

"Our murderer took a knife from the kitchen – which shows he probably didn't intend to kill her when he arrived. Or he knew her so well that he knew there were sharp knives in the kitchen ready for him to use", I added with just a touch of late-evening irony. "And the absence of any signs of a struggle and her being naked point very much towards this being done by one of her clients," I said, at the risk of stating the obvious.

"Get uniform to search the immediate area. We can always hope that he was careless and just tossed the knife immediately after he left. But somehow, I don't think we're going to get that lucky."

We decided that DS Holden would go back to the station and start finding out as much about Megan as possible – starting by pushing the tech people to get her phone and laptop opened ASAP. Meanwhile, we would see if my friendly female face and womanly intuition could extract anything useful from the neighbours.

Before we left, I returned to the bedroom and asked the forensic team, still beavering away, if they had found anything of interest. "Just this," one of them replied. He held up a transparent evidence bag containing a neatly folded black and yellow knitted scarf. "It's a supporters' scarf for the local football team. Seemed a bit incongruous, draped across the back of the chair in the middle of the bedroom."

"Women are allowed to be football supporters too," I replied. Possibly an over-defensive feminist remark, but quite understandable from a woman who's been in the police force for more than ten years.

"Well, we haven't seen any other evidence of her being a football fan – and all her clothes are neatly put away, so this seemed oddly out of place."

"Quite right. Thanks, that's possibly a good lead. Can you put that at the top of the list for examination for any DNA?" I asked.

"Certainly ma'am," he answered, confidence restored by my compliment. "But woolly material like this is a bit of a bugger. Not likely we'll find anything."

-

Two hours later I joined DS Holden at the station. All I had been able to find out was that Megan kept herself very much to herself. There were frequent male visitors to her house, but only ever one at a time. There were occasional problems when one of her guests parked inconsiderately ('probably in a rush to enjoy their time with her,' I thought). But otherwise, she would appear to have been the perfect neighbour.

Nobody in the area had invested in a doorbell with a camera attachment, and there was nothing nearby that was worth enough to warrant the installation of CCTV cameras, so there was no evidence from that source. I felt that another ninety minutes of my life had just been wasted.

A reporter from the local paper telephoned, and the call was put through to me. Gone are the days of a reporter dashing to the scene of the crime and talking to neighbours and witnesses. Nowadays they just call the police station, take down the details, and type it onto their computer screens.

I confirmed that there had been a suspicious death of a young woman but could not yet confirm her name as her relatives had not been informed. The reporter asked if I was heading the case, but I simply replied that we would be releasing full details the following day. I guessed he might have been trying to be clever. If it was a suspicious death, then I could head up the investigation. But a murder would normally have a Chief Inspector to head it.

Of course, we already knew it was murder, and DCI Tony Lancaster was officially heading up the inquiry. But he had informed me earlier that evening that his time was totally taken up with a multiple death in Nottingham town centre which had racial overtones. I would have to handle this one without the benefit of his help. As he put it, it was a perfectly routine murder. And of course, I would keep him fully informed.

Don't get me wrong – I have no gripes about how I'm treated as a woman in today's police service. And the same goes for most of my female colleagues that I've spoken to on this subject. We need to remember that a police force as we know it has been in existence for over two hundred years – and we women have only really had a role in it for the last thirty or forty of those. At least as far as having a role in the front line or management. Before that, we were largely there to deal with kids, do the filing, make the tea, and hold the hands of victims or their wives.

But now we're punching our weight – with the caveat that our weight will always be slightly less than that of our male colleagues. And we've penetrated the glass ceiling. Even if our most famous sister – put in the prestigious role of heading the Met – didn't totally cover herself in glory. Maybe she just had exceptionally bad timing. I fear that she's most likely to be remembered as the woman who was in post when several solids hit several fans. Or maybe she'll just be remembered for the unfortunate mistake of the TV quiz contestant who called her Caressa Dick.

I let DS Holden go home to his family while I spent a couple more hours at the station dotting i's and crossing t's and starting all the necessary paperwork – or computer work to be more accurate – that's involved in setting up a murder inquiry. The board had to be prepared with the key details of the incident for tomorrow morning's team briefing, and I had to complete all those mundane boring tasks that get edited out when they show a murder inquiry on a TV police drama. You know – the one where at least one murder is solved per hour. Sometimes I wonder why it takes us so long in the real world!

Eventually, I went home to get the good night's sleep I'd need because the next few days were likely to be very busy and very trying. But first, I had to eat and suddenly a microwave casserole for one looked surprisingly appealing. Then, the dishes had to be washed, dried, and put away. I cannot abide the thought of dishes, even clean ones, lying around. They have to be put back in the cupboard or I'd never get to sleep.

The unsolved clues of a murder investigation were like dirty dishes as far as I was concerned. It was awful having them lying there in plain sight for everyone to see. I had to get them cleaned up and put away as soon as I could.

The first dirty dish that concerned me was 'Why Now?'. Our murderer must have been known to his victim. He had to have been a regular client for her to allow him to tie her up. Why did he choose to kill her on this particular visit? What was the trigger? Something she said? Or some external factor? And then, why the knife? Whatever it was that he used to tie her wrists – and presumably her ankles too – didn't that present itself as a far more suitable weapon? Why did he have to take the trouble of going to the kitchen and fetching a knife, and then go through the messy business of throat cutting when a simple strangulation would have been so much easier?

He may have brought the material with him – or, more likely, she kept some suitable material for her special clients. I believe that the preferred material for such activities is silk rope. Normal rope is unsuitable since it is so coarse that it chafes the skin of the wrists and ankles, but the stuff that was originally designed to tie back expensive curtains turns out to be ideal for human restraint. Whether he brought it with him, or she provided it, surely it had to be easier to use it to kill her than the method he'd chosen. And this did not seem to be a man who did things without having a good reason.

We were obviously dealing with an unusual person. A man for whom the most intimate of human interrelation – sex – was regularly (and possibly exclusively) performed as part of a commercial transaction. Not only that, but a man who found it possible to move swiftly from sexual congress to violent murder. With the calm demeanour to ensure that no forensic clues were left - and then to take a shower in the victim's bathroom!

My boss had described this as a routine murder. I had a nasty suspicion that we were going to discover that this was not going to be anything of the sort.

I could look at the situation as an opportunity to prove my credentials for eventual promotion to Detective Chief Inspector. Or I could look at this as another example of overstretched police having to adapt to manpower shortages necessitating a Detective Inspector handling a murder – but I'm not that cynical.

2. John Jackson's Blog (2)

Friday, 7th July

If my blog was the journal of a nineteenth-century spinster, or, even better, a Victorian Novel divided into chapters, then this chapter would have a subtitle something like "In which our narrator makes confessions which may yet have consequences."

Having had such good feedback from Denis about the first chapter of my blog, I'm going to keep going in much the same style and will soon fulfill the promise in the suggested subtitle.

My work life progressed steadily. I was rarely in a period of unemployment of any significant length between two projects and was well rewarded for the ones I worked on. They were varied and, except where they deserve mention because of their impact on the greater narrative, I'll not bore you with any details.

The first confession? Well, I have re-read what I've written so far and realised that you might think that I am ascetic and have forsaken all forms of female company. Well, I'm not and I haven't.

I know from brief experiences while at university that I'm straight. Perhaps I should say something like 100% heterosexual just to make it clear, and I apologise if using the word 'straight' offends.

I do feel the need for close female companionship from time to time, and I take a commercial approach to the issue. There's an establishment nearby where there are several women available for hire by the hour, and I visit when the need arises. You may wonder how such an establishment can exist in our small town – but we are only a few miles from the intersection of one of the UK's main motorways and a major trunk road. There is a substantial amount of 'passing trade'.

I visited the place about once a month, right up until I had my accident there. After that, I didn't feel inclined to return, so I looked around the internet and discovered a lady who offered the same services and worked from her home – about three miles from where I live. Her name is Suzanne and I've become one of her regular customers.

But back to the present. I've received another email from Denis Fittaley and the questions he was asking worried me. The detail he wanted to know about the waitress that had been the subject, (or the victim), of the first chapter of my book was, in my opinion, excessive. It seemed prurient. He was asking for far too many details, I thought.

I'm no expert, but I have read quite a few books in my time, and I have a reasonable understanding of what needs to be included and what does not. Were the details he was asking for necessary to improve my novel? Or were they for his satisfaction, or some other nefarious purpose? It caused me to go back over the email trail of my correspondence with him and question several issues.

I also was beginning to feel unhappy about the whole experience of the online writing course. The first couple of lessons had been fine enough and contained a few useful pointers, especially for a novice like me. But after that, it seemed that what was happening was that the people attending the course were providing all the course content. Fair enough for us to be asked to raise our issues, and for a course leader to include some of them in the course if they thought it would be an experience that might be shared by other attendees and thus useful. But the whole course was becoming an extended "readers' letters" column. I felt that I had been conned and was seriously concerned that the material I had created and shared with Denis might later become part of somebody else's book.

I also noticed that Denis's email address was not the same as the email address of the company organising the course. I thought about sharing my concerns with other people who were on the course but decided not to. What I did do was to put the whole of Chapter One of my book on a secure website, making clear the date on which it had been uploaded. So, if any of the material should ever show up somewhere else, I would have proof of plagiarism.

I might have had a bit too much to drink on the evening in question, but I worked myself up into a bit of a rage. I was concerned that I'd been conned. Me! Someone who in most people's eyes would be considered a computer expert being conned in this way. Falling for the most obvious ruse of being flattered, in this case by reference to my writing. So, I went a bit berserk.

I deleted every piece of correspondence I had ever had with either Denis Fittaley or the course organisers, and every reference to them on my system and in my records. And then made sure that their email addresses were screened from my email system.

Once I had calmed down the following morning, I did think that maybe there was a slight element of 'The cobbler's children being the worst shod' about the episode. I've always been very careful about data security when working on clients' systems – sometimes setting up an extra level of VPN just to make sure. But I had done little or nothing about security in my new venture. So, I set up an extra level of password encryption on my laptop and server. And to make sure my book was safe from any prying eyes I dragged out an old extra-safe security system.

I've always felt uncomfortable about anyone reading my book before it's finished. So, I've decided to do what I should have done from the start and make it virtually impossible for someone to read it.

The hardware was in the cupboard where I kept all my electronic gadgets. I knew what I was looking for, but it took some finding. I've acquired all kinds of stuff over the years – technology moves fast enough to obsolete items before their useful life is finished, and anyway, I just hate throwing stuff away. I've accumulated so much – special stuff for certain projects or just general junk for my use. There's a walk-in cupboard in my room that was probably intended to be a wardrobe, but for me, it's an electronic warehouse.

Eventually, I found it. It's a disk drive that was available a few years ago and has become obsolete because it was not easy to use, but I believe it's the best way to secure my book. It has 256-bit security implemented so that you write to the disk in the same way as you would to your C drive or any server – but it encodes the content as you write. You then store the key anywhere you like – on your PC, a server, or a memory stick, whatever - and use it when you read it back.

It fell out of fashion because it had a relatively low capacity – only a few Megabytes if you can believe such low-capacity storage devices were ever sold – and it takes quite a long time to read or write. But I don't mind that. I can afford a few extra minutes every time I open the book when I'm writing, and a few more to close it when I've finished. So that's where my book now resides. With a backup copy stored on a secure remote site that only I know the address of. And unless you have the key to my black box, there's no way you're going to read any of the files that are stored on it. Nothing is ever totally secure, but this is the best that I can come up with. I've also stored five other small files on the box. They are files that I probably need to keep - but do not want to have them lying around for the wrong eyes to see.

Friday 14th July

The good news is that the book is progressing far better than I had ever hoped. I am constantly surprised, even amazed, at the amount of detail that people share about themselves with complete strangers. Especially women.

With the eradication of Denis, I no longer need to please anyone other than myself, so I've decided to do the research that I would write about as if it were Bruno's research. I've listed five names and am now following a few women who each bear one of these names. There's a database record for each of them in which I enter the information they published about themselves, and I've built up a picture of each person.

Gradually I've whittled down the numbers in the database as those that were not communicating frequently have been dropped and those that were more revealing have become the subject of my focus. When I have what I think is enough information about a particular person – aided and abetted where necessary by a little prompting in the form of correspondence between the woman concerned and one of my alter egos, I complete the record.

Of course. I don't have to be quite as meticulous as Bruno. I'm writing fiction after all – so I can sometimes combine or invent details on the different women, change their names, etcetera. But I don't want to do too much of this – I have to have some experience of how difficult Bruno's task would be, and how fast he could realistically complete it. So, I can invent stuff about their backgrounds – Bruno wouldn't necessarily know most of this stuff anyway. But what I'm trying to stay truthful to is the way that they let their guard down. How they make a vital slip and reveal just too much information about themselves. Information that lets someone find them and make physical contact. And, in the case of Bruno, that contact is very physical indeed. And terminal.

I have now completed the profile of Bruno's second victim, and I am moving on to the third and fourth – both of which are showing promise. I've also decided to cheat a little and allow Bruno something of a head start. He is going to be allowed to have one local victim – someone he already knows – just to make it a little easier. To get him started, so to speak. After all, the rest of his victims will be scattered across the whole country, and provided he chooses his local one and the method for her demise very carefully, I think that's all right.

Tuesday, August 1st

The perils of writing anything that involves current technology have struck my blog. Elon Musk, having bought the company a few months ago, has decided to change the name of his latest toy from Twitter to X. For the moment I am going to do nothing about it as far as my blog is concerned. It seems everyone is still calling it Twitter, so I shall too. There's even the chance that the name might have to be changed back. It would not be the first time this sort of thing has happened.

If I must change how I refer to it, then I will, and you will notice. But until then just consider that when I use the term 'Twitter' I am referring to 'X: The Application formerly known as Twitter.'

With apologies to Prince, of course!

Friday, September 8th

There's been a long gap between my last entry and this one because I've been so busy.

The third and fourth victim profiles that I mentioned in my last entry were completed much more quickly than I'd imagined. I had to convert each of them into a chapter in the book, and I'm a slow writer. I type with about four or five fingers and try very hard to get it right – but usually find I need to go over it again before I'm even moderately satisfied with the result.

I either write in my office or, on sunny days, in the garden. It's about the only use my garden table and chairs ever get. I have the radio on in the background (I've always hated silence), usually tuned to the local radio station just for background noise. I only actually listen to it when I stop to think about something.

Some woman was being interviewed earlier today and giving tips for new writers, so I stopped completely and listened to her. It seems that I have at least got one thing right in my book. She said that every story has a beginning part, a middle part, and an end part. And that you should start your novel at the beginning of the middle part of the story. Well, my novel (for which I still can't decide on a title) begins when Bruno is selecting his victims. The middle bit covers the killings. I'll then have to fill in the beginning part – which will be loosely based on my own life, but with some hints as to where he 'went wrong' that I'll have to invent. And the last part will cover the detection of his crimes – because, of course, he will have to be found out and caught.

I've now written the story of four of his victims – invented their back-stories, amalgamated their lives from the postings of multiple women on social media, and described how they revealed just one piece of information too many which led to their death at his hands.

As I write each one, I then delete all parts of the database referring to that name. So, I am now down to two that need completing. One is an unusual name, which I always suspected was going to cause me problems, and one is, surprisingly one of the most common names on the list. I've got several entries in the database for that name, but none of them have yet given me that vital break.

The only event of any significance in my recent life marked another step along my path to retirement. I sold my car. A couple of bills came due for payment, and I realised I wouldn't need a prestige car any longer. I don't do the work mileage and for my personal needs, which are mostly football-related, I can easily use something much less flashy. I've caused myself a problem because the car sold much more quickly than I expected and the cash is now sitting in a holdall in the loft, waiting for me to find a replacement.

Friday, October 6th

Quite a long break again. But it was fruitful. Number five is now done! It was one of the more complex chapters of the book and one I'm quite proud of. I thought it important that Bruno should take more care about the murders as he progressed – he could probably afford to be careless with the last one because by then it would not make much difference if he was caught. But before then, he would want to take more precautions to avoid detection before his game was complete. Like a batter in cricket who is nearing the completion of his century, he would want to ensure he was not caught out in the nineties and would therefore play more carefully.

He also took some steps to throw the police off his trail - just in case they were getting closer.

Back in the real world, I've been seeking solace with Suzanne more frequently of late. I harbour no delusions about our relationship – I am, and always will be, nothing more than a good customer, but we are very comfortable with each other. This is probably why, on my most recent visit, when she teased me yet again about how vanilla my tastes were and asked for the umpteenth time "Surely, John, there must be something a little bit kinky you'd like to do," I finally admitted it.

"I've always wondered what it would be like to tie a woman up and have sex with her," I blurted out.

She laughed a little, paused for a moment, and then said, "You know there aren't many men I'd trust to do that to me, but you are lucky enough to be one of them." And immediately jumped out of bed and left the room. Moments later she returned carrying some ties in her hand. Men's ties that she told me she kept in her wardrobe for when she had to dress up as a schoolgirl or a butch secretary. I don't need to go into detail, do I?

I tied her up, she playacted perfectly, and yes, it was just a little bit more enjoyable than usual.

Afterwards, she was talking to me about something mundane (I can't remember what it was, but that's not important) and in the course of her dialogue she said, in that strange way she sometimes talked, "I said to myself, Megan, this is not a good situation..."

It caught me by surprise. Of course, I realised that Suzanne was probably not her real name. Most women in her line of work change their name to a different, usually more exotic, name for their work alias. But I was suddenly, inexplicably overcome with the strangest of feelings.

In the previous hour, I had totally relaxed my defences. I had admitted and then enacted, my most secret desires with a woman and I didn't even know her name. I cannot explain how shaken I felt, and even now as I write it down it looks stupid to have been so upset about how exposed I felt and how much of a stranger to me she really was. But that was how I felt, and I had to get out of there as quickly as possible. I'll have to apologise when I see her again for being so rude, but I departed unnaturally quickly, leaving her speechless on the bed.

I can only say that I have never experienced feelings quite like it before – and I sincerely hope never to again.

My day was made even worse by the vagaries of the British weather. I always walked to Suzanne's house. It was good exercise and since it took the best part of an hour to get there, it made every visit into a bigger event, filling a whole afternoon. Unfortunately, what had been a bright sunny afternoon when I left my house became a very showery one for my journey home. I got absolutely drenched on my way back.

I was wearing a light jacket – dark blue in colour, but light in weight – jeans and a polo shirt. When I got home, I saw that my shoes were ruined and the polo shirt was stained (presumably because dye had run from the jacket, I didn't bother to look too closely). So, they were both thrown in the bin immediately. Everything else I was wearing went straight into the washing machine and I spent half an hour in the shower. Dried and dressed, I sat down with a large mug of cocoa and pulled myself together.

Saturday, October 7th

I stopped writing the blog yesterday much sooner than I had planned because I have another confession to make – and this is the one that is probably more serious since it involves me breaking the law. And I promise, once again, that these confessions will be connected shortly, and you'll understand why I've needed to make them. I've tried several ways to ease my way into the story, but none were successful, so I stopped writing. And even now I notice that I'm procrastinating A fault I'm often guilty of, dithering before putting something difficult on record. So here goes!

My major confession is that I have kept my older brother alive illegally.

Before you get worried by visions of an embalmed body sitting in a rocking chair or something similar (I assume that everyone has seen the movie 'Psycho' so that remark is understood), I'll quickly explain that it's nothing like that. I have only kept him alive in an administrative, commercial, financial, and legal kind of way. I could have confessed even more luridly, because, in a way I have not just kept him alive, I have brought him back to life.

It all started just over five years ago. I had enjoyed a particularly successful (and hard-working) year which brought my total earnings into the six-figure bracket. In fact, there had been two consecutive such years.

At the risk of boring you, I'll explain a small but important wrinkle in the British tax system. Everyone has a tax-free allowance – a sum of money you can earn each year before you start paying income tax. At the time this all occurred, the annual tax-free allowance was about ten thousand pounds, although it's gone up a bit since. But, once you earn a hundred thousand pounds in a tax year, you start to lose your tax-free allowance – at the rate of one pound for every two pounds you earn. So, for every extra two pounds you earn, you not only pay the standard tax, but you also lose an allowance of standard tax on one pound. This means that your marginal tax rate is sixty percent, for the next twenty grand you earn.

Now, I have no problem with the principle of higher tax rates for higher earners. I believe it's fair for the higher earner to pay more. But when the government wants to take more than half my pay, I think it's fundamentally wrong and since there's nothing I can do about the law, I'm going to take steps to avoid this trap.

When this happens to you, the first year is not a problem, you just ask your employer to delay some of your pay – he's hardly likely to refuse since the money stays a bit longer in his bank account. You keep your earnings below a hundred thousand, he pays you the excess the following year, and then Bob is your proverbial uncle. But then you have a problem the following year if you exceed a hundred grand again, and you've made it worse by moving part of your previous year's income into this year. And even if your boss is willing, you are going to present him (and yourself) with an ever-growing problem.

I discussed this very issue with Ralph.

"You don't have a wife, do you?" he asked. "You see, some of the guys employ their wives as secretaries and offset some of the money this way. Have you thought of getting married?"

I knew he was kidding.

"Seems like that would be a good way of spending a grand to save a ton," I said in response, illustrating my opinion that marriage would probably cost me more than it would save me. But he set me thinking of a way I could mitigate the problem, and I began to work on the solution as soon as I finished my call with him.

Once I thought about it, the solution was not far away. When you do as much programming and testing as I do, you need a set of information that you can quickly call up to test programs. (Speaking of which, I know I'm branching off from the main thread here but bear with me – it'll become clear soon enough.)

I had always used my late brother's information for the first test of any system which concerned people. There was nothing mawkish or macabre or reality-denying about it. It was just my way of commemorating him. So, he had a Facebook account, a Twitter account, and so on – all giving my home address as his address - and he was the first person through the door on any system I was working on. Which did result in him receiving junk mail and spam, but that was easy to file appropriately. I also have a full set of other records for bulk testing, but he was first – and if the system needed to differentiate between men and women, my late mum would be second through the door.

It occurred to me that with a bit of cooperation from Ralph, I might be able to let my brother help me save some tax. And I had an unhealthy itch just to see if it was possible. I had his birth certificate – even his National Health number. So, I went online and tried to get a National Insurance number for him – as this should be all that was necessary for him to be employed.

It was ridiculously easy. He was allocated an NI number, and when I approached Ralph to see if he would be willing to pay part of my income to Tom, he made it possible.

"I can't have him as an employee, there are too many checks and balances for that," he said, "but if he submitted a claim for work done as a self-employed contractor – and you testified that the work he had done was up to your standard...." A wink accompanied this remark. "Then it will not be a problem."

So, Tom started to submit claims for work done each month. Strangely enough, at the same time, my work hours diminished by almost identical amounts to those claimed by Tom. I changed the name of the person responsible for the utility bills on my house to Tom's name and opened an online bank account for him so that he could be paid. He paid the gas and electricity bills and figuratively drew a few quid each month from the cash dispenser, which he passed to me as rent.

Of course, he submitted an annual income tax return – he didn't claim any travelling expenses since he worked from home – and he always paid the amount of tax assessed promptly and in full. It all worked perfectly well as far as I'm concerned. I have had five happy years of paying much less tax than I would otherwise have done.

But this is the reason I'm so worried about getting involved with the police. If they start to probe into my affairs, how long is it going to be before they find out what I've done?

But I've got to call them, now I've heard the news.

Sunday, October 8th

I had to pause before continuing. Partly because the news had such an impact on me and partly because there's such a change in the mood of what I'm writing.

Suzanne, (or Megan as I suppose I'll now have to call her) was murdered sometime soon after my most recent visit. It was on the local news yesterday. It can only be a matter of time before they find out that I was one of her customers, and then they'll want to talk to me. So, it's much better if I call them first and let them know.

I guess that I'm one of those people that the police always say they want to hear from. They say anyone who knows anything that they believe will be helpful should contact them. And maybe I know something that might be helpful. I certainly want them to catch the bastard who did this to her. There's just the worry about my using Tom's name with the Inland Revenue.

And the fact that when I had my accident, I gave my name as Tom Jędrzejczyk.

I'll call them first thing tomorrow. This gives me all today and tomorrow to write up the stories of Bruno's last two victims (yes, the final details all came through at last) and to complete the 'middle part' (as the lady on local radio referred to it) of the book. And to delete the last remnants of the database of women's names and their profiles, now that it's done its job.

If I am going to be interrupted by the police, then it makes a good time to have a break before writing the remaining chapters of my book.

4. Police Inquiries Are Progressing

Detective Inspector Linda Evans   Monday, October 9th

The day after the discovery of Megan's body, I held my first briefing and organised my small team. Police resources, like so much else in life, were not as plentiful as they once had been. I let everyone know what we knew – which did not take long - and allotted the routine tasks. I reminded them that we were looking for what the pathologist had so succinctly referred to as a 'callous bastard' who had murdered a young woman for no apparent reason, probably shortly after having had sex with her. I reminded them in my subtle way that the life of a prostitute was just as valued as any other young woman, and I would not tolerate investigations being performed with anything less than full rigour.

The day brought us two pieces of vital information that enabled us to progress the inquiry. Firstly, the tech people unlocked her phone. Now, all we had to do was wait for the network provider to give us a list of her calls, hopefully by the end of the day. Megan's parents were contacted and informed. They knew very little of their daughter's life and, as expected, were unable to assist our inquiry in any way.

A press conference was called at which the media were provided with the minimum necessary details and informed that this was now officially a murder inquiry. I confirmed that DCI Lancaster was leading the inquiry but added that I would be handling all interactions with the press. I made the usual call for anyone who knows anything to come forward as soon as possible and reassured them that confidentiality would be respected.

The second piece of potentially vital information came as quite a surprise. Following my remarks at the press conference, someone actually came forward. A phone call was received from a John ('by name and by nature,' I thought) who admitted to visiting Megan on the day she died. DS Holden and I arranged to see him at his house to find out what he could tell us.

The house was in the middle of a small terrace in Mansfield, a town some fifteen miles from Nottingham, where Megan had lived and worked. John lived in one of the larger types of miners' houses which had three bedrooms, a real back garden, and even a small space between the road and the front door. An estate agent might call it a front garden, but I'll stick with my description of it as a small space.

We were shown into the front room by John Jackson, a seemingly comfortably off man whom I estimated to be in his mid-fifties. A big guy, not just tall but with muscle definition that spoke of plenty of gym work. The house was neatly, if a little simply, furnished and almost unnaturally tidy. Expecting that the coffee offered might be real, we both accepted his offer and settled down for a friendly chat.

He admitted to being a client of Megan and having visited her half a dozen times in the last six months. Being a single man, he told us, there was no need for him to be embarrassed or coy and he also openly admitted to working with her on her web design (making an atypical use of his computer skills). His last visit had occurred on Friday afternoon.

"I left her lying in bed at about four o'clock and got home about an hour later," he confirmed. Unfortunately, he lived alone so nobody could verify this. He suggested, and obviously hoped, that someone had seen him on his walk between her house and his.

DS Holden asked if he knew anything about any of her other clients.

"You've probably never visited a prostitute, have you?" he asked in response to this question. Having not received an answer, he continued by saying, "I can assure you that one topic of conversation you never have in those circumstances is who else she's *seeing*. He paused slightly before saying the last word, probably considering whether to use a more earthy alternative. But he then seemed to remember a valuable additional detail.

"I can tell you she got a call from one of her other customers just before I left because she remarked that she would have to delay the start of her weekend", he said.

"So, this would be about what time?" I asked.

"I left her about four, so this would have been about ten to four, I guess", he answered.

DS Holden said nothing, so I assumed that this agreed with the information he had received from the mobile phone service provider earlier in the day.

"And are you able to tell us anything about this call, by any chance?"

"I can only assume that he was a regular client because she wasn't on the phone with him for more than a couple of minutes."

"And you didn't overhear anything that was said?"

"Sorry, no."

"And you didn't perhaps catch the name of the caller?"

"No, she left the room to take the call, so I heard nothing at all."

He was dealing far too comfortably with our questions for my liking. I felt it was time to see if I could disturb him with some more direct questioning.

"Did your activities with Megan ever involve you tying her up?" I asked.

Predictably, John paused before answering. I believe he had been caught a little off guard. He turned towards me and gave me a look that I found disturbing. For a brief moment I was, not an investigating police officer, just a woman, and I got the feeling that he was juxtaposing me and Megan. Then he blinked and his gaze resumed normality.

"Megan was very good at her job," he said almost wistfully. "She was able to take one to areas of experience and pleasure that might not have happened otherwise. I shall miss her. But I feel it would be very wrong of me to discuss our specific activities."

There was a pause and I decided to fill it by saying simply "I'll take that as a yes, then."

"I notice you're a Bees supporter," DS Holden interrupted. (I later found out he had noticed a black and yellow scarf hanging in the hall and I was impressed with his observation skills. Despite my earlier remark to the scene of crime team, I had no real interest in football. The big premier league games, internationals maybe. But lower league kickabouts? Not for me.)

"Yes, for my sins," John replied in what I believe is the completely normal way of expressing one's support of a minor football team.

"Do you go to the games?"

"Yes, I get to almost every home game and a few of the away games too – if the place we're playing at is interesting enough. There are a few – even in League Two, you know."

"Do you think we've got a chance of promotion this year?" my football-supporting colleague continued.

"Maybe, if we don't fall apart in the run-in like we did last year. I think we're a good bet for the playoffs."

"Do you know if Megan was a Bees supporter?" I asked, desperately wishing to move from the lad-bonding between the suspect and my DS and back to the mundane topic of a murder inquiry.

"I don't think so. At least she never said anything about it, and I guess I would have seen her at a game – the crowds are quite small you know."

DS Holden nodded knowingly.

"Why do you ask?" John asked.

The reply from my colleague was probably not the textbook way of responding. You're not supposed to reveal anything to an interviewee that you don't have to – but it turned out to be the right thing to do.

"We found a black and yellow scarf in her house," he replied.

John might well be a highly intelligent man and a careful one at that, but he could not disguise his reaction to this revelation. It appeared to be a surprise to him. Neither DS Holden nor I said anything, and we decided to change the direction of our questioning.

I asked John if he lived alone, which he confirmed. He added the information about his inheriting the house and that both his father and brother had been the victims of tragic deaths. We already knew this from some brief background research before leaving the police station but said nothing.

I questioned him about the ex-partner of his mother - since their difficulties were on our files from the complaint against Billy lodged by Stephen Crapnell. John assured me that despite Billy leaving a threatening letter when he departed, he had neither heard nor seen anything of him since.

"Do you mind me asking what you do for a living?" I asked.

"I'm a computer programmer," John replied.

"And where do you work?" seemed the natural follow-on question. I was not aware of any nearby companies that would be paying top dollar for such skills.

"Mostly I work from home," John replied. "But I sometimes go onsite for a few days. It's a contract programming company I work for, but the actual company that I'm programming for could be almost anywhere."

He let us have the details of his employer so that we could verify that he had been working for them for many years. We were drawing close to the end of the interview and asked if John minded if we had a look around the house.

"Actually, I may well have left some sensitive information about some projects lying around, so I'd rather you didn't," he replied.

I used my friendliest possible tone when adding "We could always get a warrant, you know."

"No problem," John replied, with the same amount of friendliness – and probably the same amount of honesty – as I had shown. "That'll give me the chance to tidy up and make sure anything confidential is secure before you come back."

We also asked if he would permit us to take a saliva sample for DNA testing.

"It's just to help eliminate you from the inquiry you understand," DS Holden asked, giving the standard spiel.

"I'm not under arrest, am I?" was the unexpected reply.

"No, of course not", I replied – suddenly interested in John's unexpected response.

"It's just that I've worked on a few police systems, and I don't want to run any risk of my information leaking from one database to another, so I'll politely say no,", he replied.

"You are aware that if you are arrested, we have the authority to insist that you give a sample," I replied and immediately regretted it. He'd verified he wasn't under arrest for a good reason.

"Yes, I believe I understand the implications of being arrested, what you can do, and the risks you run and the limitations it imposes," he continued, smiling with his mouth but not his eyes.

He was, of course, right. There was no way we could arrest him now as it would open up the chance of false arrest claims and limit our options – we would need additional grounds to perform any re-arrest at a future date. I could understand that a freelancer like himself would sue and sue heavily for wrongful arrest as it could have a detrimental effect on his record. So many employers were insisting on DBS checks these days, and an arrest on his record could reduce his employability. We were going to need some evidence before treading down that path.

But his lack of cooperation raised a warning flag.

-

DS Holden and I discussed the interview on our way back to the station. We agreed that he reacted to the information about the scarf found at Megan's house, but neither of us could exactly say what that reaction meant or what might have caused it. And his polite refusal to let us look around or give a sample was also not entirely normal – but could theoretically have been for the reasons he had stated.

I asked DS Holden if he thought John could be the callous bastard we were looking for, and he thought for quite a while before answering. "He's not the sort of person I imagined we'd be looking for, but there's something definitely 'off' about him."

I was pleased to have my feelings confirmed.

"He's left-handed," he said.

Unfortunately for DS Holden, we had a half-hour drive and not much to say.

"Glad to know you're paying attention," I replied with a smile. "You noticed my clever piece of police work in getting him to have coffee with us, then. With him being male, between eighteen and eighty, and left-handed that means he is definitely one of the high-rated suspects for this crime. Let's see, with eleven percent of the UK population being left-handed that means we've cut the list down to about one point eight million people. I find it's good to adopt a positive frame of mind at the start of an investigation."

"And what about the scarf?" I asked, after a brief period of silence, to bring us back from my sarcastic rant because I couldn't yet work out its significance.

"Well," he asked, choosing his words carefully. "There must be some significance. It doesn't seem likely that it belonged to her. And the murderer was very careful at the scene, which makes it highly unlikely that he left it behind by accident."

"Which opens up the possibility that it was left there deliberately ", I continued for him. "And that would imply that the murderer may be leaving us a false trail to follow?"

His "Hmm" as an answer seemed to agree with my summation. Possible but somewhat unlikely.

Since there were no other avenues open to us to check up on John and he was the only person of interest we had, we arranged an appointment with Ralph Borshell, the Managing Director of Premier Programs, John's employer.

-

Later that evening I updated DCI Lancaster on our progress, and he asked what I thought of Mister Jackson.

"Well, there's no obvious motive," I replied, "but there is something about him that just doesn't ring true," I answered.

"Are you sure it's not just that a good-looking, well-built, well-off guy seems to be able to live happily without a woman to look after him?" he asked.

"Or a man to look after him," I answered, establishing my PC credentials. (And I don't mean police constable).

"No, it's not just that, something is definitely off-kilter. The way he reacted to the fact that we'd found a football scarf at her place was odd. Maybe we'll find out more once we've got the forensic report. And tomorrow we'll be going through the phone records. We received her call history from her provider a few minutes before we visited John. She did receive a call late on Friday afternoon, just as John said, but it was from a burner phone, so I doubt we'll get too far with that. But something might come from her other customers."

-

The next couple of days provided entertainment of a sort for DS Holden as he called all the men whose phone numbers had been on Megan's call list. The numbers were all mobiles - I guess that even if you do still have a landline, calling an escort is not likely to be one of the occasions on which you would use it. So, there was never the chance for that classic movie situation of calling the punter's wife. Nonetheless, he had a good few very embarrassed men to speak to. He also spoke to a couple of disappointed clients, who had turned up at Megan's house on Monday and not received an answer when knocking at her door.

The exercise may well have entertained, but it produced no useful information. We received her unlocked laptop from the techies and accessed her diary. There was no entry between John's acknowledged appointment on Friday afternoon and the first of her disappointed clients on Monday. She presumably had either not bothered to enter her last-minute booking or had not had time to do so.

Forensics drew a blank so far as the scarf was concerned. The bedroom had several sets of prints, a couple of which were identified as belonging to gentlemen who had previously crossed our path in other matters, but neither had any record for violence nor could be deemed as suspects. And the search of the garden and nearby area did not turn up the murder weapon – or anything else useful, either.

We gathered as much information about Mister Jackson as we could, but with him having no police record – in fact, not much record of anything – and no living family members, there was little to be found.

I spoke again with DCI Lancaster, and we agreed that we could bring John Jackson in for further questioning. Nothing too heavy, but we would see how he reacted to a little more pressure, the unusual surroundings of a police interview room, and the actual presence of the scarf.

I said I'd do it in a couple of days, once we were sure we had as much on him as possible.

-

Premier Programs was based in one of those multi-office facilities on the outskirts of Birmingham. It presumably allowed Mr. Borshell to pay only for a small cubicle as an office, but to make his callers believe he was a much larger organisation and to use the prestigious boardroom when he had to meet important visitors – or investigating police officers.

We were shown in by a telephonist-receptionist with a Black Country accent that was so thick you could probably slice it and sell it. "Mr. Borshell will be with you soon", is what I think she said.

Mister (call me Ralph) Borshell confirmed that John Jackson had worked for him for over twenty years and that he had been one of the superstars of the organisation. He'd worked long hours on the projects where he had been employed and had displayed remarkable programming skills that had helped the company gain a reputation for delivering difficult projects in record time. And as such, John had earned well for the whole time.

I noticed the way that he used the past tense when saying that John had been one of his star performers and asked if he was still employed.

"Yes, he's still employed," he answered somewhat hesitantly, "But since his accident, he's been winding down a lot, and I think he's seriously considering retiring early."

This was new information and I asked him if he could tell us more about this accident.

"All I can say is that it happened about six months ago. He had to take a few days off work at the time. I think he might have been in hospital for a couple of days, and I know he told me he was suffering from headaches for a few days afterwards. But he didn't seem to be willing to share any information about exactly what the accident was. And as I said, ever since then he's been slowing down. But John likes to keep most things close to his chest and he obviously didn't want to talk about whatever it was that happened, so I didn't push."

We asked a few more questions. What John said about sensitive client information could well have been true, since his clients included large companies and even some government departments, but noticeably Ralph confirmed that John should only ever be working on one project at a time, so there should not ever be paperwork from multiple clients lying around his house.

He was able to provide plenty of information about John's work – but knew next to nothing about his personal life and told us even less.

On our drive back we agreed that the accident might be significant and that once again, John had not told us everything. In other words, Mr Borshell and Mister Jackson were both, in our humble opinions, as they say, hiding something. This thought was confirmed when inquiries with the local hospitals were unable to uncover any information about a patient called John Jackson, either attending an A&E department or as an inpatient at any time in the past twelve months.

Our inquiries might have stalled there, but the following day we received unexpected and welcome assistance and a promising additional avenue was opened for us to pursue.

I received a call from Detective Inspector Widdowson of the Kent Murder Squad. He told me that they were pursuing an inquiry into the murder of a young woman that had occurred on a deserted stretch of the Kent coast two weeks previously. In a nearby car park, they had found an abandoned car that had forensic links to the murder, and they had traced its owner but had then come up with a problem.

"According to the DVLA, the car was registered to a Mr Richard Horsnell in Swindon, but when we followed up, there was nobody of that name at the address given, nor does there ever seem to have been. And to all intents and purposes, it seems that this Mr Horsnell does not exist."

Despite my natural interest in spending my time to help someone else's murder inquiry when my own was making almost no progress and I had a list of a hundred things I needed to do, I interrupted DI Widdowson to ask what relevance this might have to me.

"The previous owner of the vehicle was a Mister John Jackson, and I believe he is listed as a person of interest on a current inquiry you are running", he replied, instantly gaining my full and undivided attention.

I quickly established that John had sold the car via an advertisement on a popular online forum managed by a well-known car magazine group. Kent Police were, not surprisingly, very interested in speaking to Mr Jackson to see what light he could shed upon the transaction and the purchaser. When I told him that we were considering bringing Mr Jackson in for further questioning concerning our inquiry, we agreed to set up a meeting at Nottingham Nick the following day at which we could both question him. DI Widdowson would send one of his team – he would have liked to have accompanied him, but police resources meant that he could only spare one officer. We spent a few minutes agreeing that things weren't what they used to be - before ending the call.

With DCI Lancaster's approval, I arranged to bring John in for questioning the following day, and now that he was linked to two murder inquiries, we had enough justification to execute a search warrant on his house at the same time.

5. John Jackson's Blog (3)

Tuesday, October 10th

I knew the police would visit me. And thankfully I kept my calm. The presence of a policewoman and a policeman caused me a bit of discomfort, but they weren't in uniform which would have made it worse. There was no mistaking that they were police. It must be something in the way they hold themselves, the way they stand, or the way they speak. I don't know what it is, but there's certainly no mistaking it. I knew they were police before I opened the door.

But the chat was friendly enough. I hope they didn't find me too blasé about my relationship with Suzanne, or Megan as I now must refer to her. I expect they're more used to dealing with married men who are embarrassed to be found visiting an escort. I'm not like that, never have been, and never will be.

I felt I answered their questions as thoroughly as I could and gave them every assistance. I know they didn't like me refusing to give a DNA sample, but I was being honest. The security of their databases is generally awful. And I have no wish for an error to occur that attaches my DNA to anything it shouldn't be attached to.

I rather liked the woman detective. She was smart, in every sense of the word. She seemed to be what they call 'at home in her skin'. Quite attractive too – and unmistakably sexy. I also got the feeling that, like me, she is a bit of a loner – but probably unlike me, she doesn't want to be. If only I were twenty years younger!

Everything was going very well until they mentioned finding a scarf at Megan's house. I know I reacted to that, and I think that once I've explained something, you'll understand why.

Let's loop back to my discussions with Denis about the plot for 'The Book'. I'd said that the killer would not always use the same method of dealing with his victims. If he used the same method, it would make it too easy for the police to link the killings and maybe even easier for them to solve the crimes. He wanted to make it more challenging for them. But Denis made the point that there had to be something that linked the killings – some 'signature' that might not be obvious at first but would be revealed upon deeper examination.

Since the killings were planned to happen in random parts of the country, none of the investigating teams would be aware of the other killings. The women would be of different ages and there would be nothing in their profiles to connect them – apart from the fact that they were women and their names had five letters. Nobody was going to link them for that reason. Almost two hundred women are murdered in the UK every year, so there's not much chance of them being linked if you don't have some sort of signature, he told me.

I must have had the Bees in mind when I came up with the idea – maybe I was looking at something at home at the time or thinking about the next game or the last game or something. The idea came to me that Bruno would see himself as some form of cartoon villain. Possibly something influenced by the recent glut of superhero films, and the fact that watching or reading comics has now become an acceptable adult pastime. It was always reserved for kids when I was one.

Anyway, he might see himself as a killer insect – a wasp, a bee, or even better, a hornet. He might even give himself the name 'The Hornet' or 'The Stinger'. Perhaps he'd seen a nature documentary on TV about these insects and he loved the fact that some insects even disguise themselves by having yellow and black stripes to make other animals think they were more dangerous than they really were.

So, to reinforce this image of himself, and to give the person who eventually investigated the killings a clue, he would leave something at the site of each killing. A different object, but something else black and yellow.

Denis liked the idea – and it became part of Bruno's signature in the book.

So, I think you can understand why I reacted as I did when the police told me that they'd found a black and yellow scarf at Megan's house. I was being totally honest when I told the police that I didn't think she had any interest in football. I didn't tell them how much time she and I had spent together – when I was doing the stuff for her website, we often had a chat about things in our lives. I'm sure I must have said something about my interest in the local football team – and she would have responded if she had any interest in it. And I was equally sure that I would have seen her if she'd gone to any games. The crowds at Bees' games are not that large, after all.

I guess that one of her other clients must have left the scarf behind by mistake. The alternative explanation is too bizarre and too scary to contemplate. Can I even speculate that someone has read the draft of my book, stolen the idea of a clue being a black and yellow object, and then left just such an object at the murder site of a woman who is known to me? No, I refuse to contemplate that.

And I'm sure that the reaction I gave, plus the fact that I have admitted that I was there shortly before she died will mean that the police will be back to interview me again – unless they find her killer very soon.

If the scarf was the only issue, I wouldn't be too worried. But there's something else as well. Another reason for me to be very unhappy about the prospect of police searching my house. Which means it's time for me to explain something else. Another confession, I'm afraid. This one is probably the most serious of the lot, and definitely the last one I will be making.

I've never been able to hold my drink, which is why I try to never put myself in a situation where large quantities of booze are going to be consumed. But sometimes it's unavoidable – you can't walk out early from a business gathering, a celebration or a 'works do' without alienating your colleagues. And sticking to soft drinks makes you seem such a wimp.

It was at one of these get-togethers that I'd had one or two too many and I took on a stupid bet. I'd told some of my colleagues that I had a foolproof way of getting a handgun and he challenged me. I took the bet, which was stupid – as most of these things are. Particularly stupid as I was about to break the law. Not only was it stupid, but also proving myself right was going to cost me more than the amount I stood to win. But I did it.

First, I waited and watched. I paid particular attention to a couple of the chatroom sites that are frequented by people in my line of work. I was waiting for one of the many programmers in the USA that I've had contact with over the years to report a problem on the site and ask for help. This, after all, was one of the main reasons the chatroom exists, so I didn't have to wait too long before a suitable opportunity arose.

Jim from Texas raised a tough technical question on one of the forums. It concerned a tricky use of indexed files, and he got some bits and pieces of advice from other forum users, but I knew he needed more help. I'd faced – and overcome - the same problem a few months previously, so I emailed him and said I'd give him a full solution to his problem, but he would owe me a huge favour in return. I can't remember exactly how he responded but it was along the lines of being desperate for help and being OK with doing anything legal in return if I could help him out.

I sent him the full solution to his problem and waited a few days for him to confirm it had worked. He was very grateful, so then I asked him for the promised favour.

I knew a little about Jim. We had other things in common, besides our line of work. He was also keen on exercise and bodybuilding, and we spoke online about this from time to time. He was also a keen sports fan – but only his American sports. He tried to get me excited about American Football (with limited success) and I in turn tried to get him interested in real football (or soccer as he insisted on calling it). I had no success in this. But we had chatted several times and so our relationship had some foundation, and I felt comfortable asking him a favour.

Knowing Jim was Texan and borderline redneck I used an explanation that would suit him, as I thought he was more likely to agree to a plea that acknowledged every man's right to protect his property. If I had told him the reason that I wanted it was to help me win a bet, he probably would have refused.

I've deleted the email I sent him, for obvious reasons, but I believe this is an accurate reproduction of it:

> Jim
>
> You've been telling me for years that it's crazy for us Brits to be unable to protect our family and property in the way that real men do by having a firearm. I'm now ready to concede at last that you're right. A few nasty incidents

have recently occurred close to where I live. I don't have any family to protect but I have some expensive electronics in my home and some gym equipment that might be very attractive to a potential thief.

I could get myself a shotgun legally and easily – but that is not really what I want at my bedside at night. A handgun would be much more practical. Which is where you could do me a big favour.

I'll admit that I'm breaking the UK law – but it's a stupid law so I'll face the music if anything ever happens. God forbid that someone should ever break in – but if they did, I know that the police would do nothing if I called and said, "I think someone is breaking into my house." But if I said, "Someone is breaking into my house, I've got a gun and if I find him, I'll shoot him," they're likely to be here in double quick time.

So, I'll absolve you from all responsibility. You can keep this email to show that it was all done at my instigation if you ever need to. I'll be dealing with everything at my end. And I believe I've found a foolproof way for you to get the gun to me.

Here are the details of some stuff I'd like you to order and ship to me. It's the full set of components for an authentic cowboy costume – let's say it's for a fancy-dress party or a Halloween event, whatever.

(In the original email there was a list of websites for cowboy boots, Stetson hats, authentic period Levis, personalised holsters for the guns, and replica Colt 45 revolvers. Together with the necessary ordering details, product codes, sizes, and so on.)

What I need you to do is substitute a real Colt 45 for one of the replicas when you ship it to me. I know you can lay hands on one easily as you've always told me. Include a few bullets and let me know your bank details and the price of everything including shipping costs and I'll wire the money to you before you buy any of it.

I promise that this will be the end of the matter – and we will both hope never to see the thing ever used.

After he received the email, there was a little back-and-forth correspondence before the package arrived, just as I had asked for. Absolutely no problems. I showed the gun to my work colleague and won the bet.

And ever since then, I've kept the gun, together with all the rest of the outfit, in a rucksack in my wardrobe.

It's a useful story, one that I can use in my book. Denis liked it and Bruno will be able to use a handgun to kill one of his victims. But, in anticipation of the possibility of the police crawling all around my house soon, I went to the wardrobe recently intending to dispose of the illegal firearm and discovered that the gun, and the bullets that came with it, had disappeared. The rest of the cowboy outfit was still there, but of the gun, there was no sign.

I know that only Denis and I know of its existence – unless Jim in Texas had told someone, or my email had been hacked. And I'm very worried.

I've already deleted all references to Denis everywhere (except in this blog) and I will not be mentioning him to the police. I know next to nothing about him, anyway. And it's not that I feel I owe him anything, but if it ever emerges that the gun was used to commit a crime, I might be charged as an accessory or something, so that whole episode will be kept secret. The only good thing that seems to have come out of it is, as Denis suggested, writing it down has helped me address my feelings. And any time I think about Denis or the way I reacted to the whole situation concerning him, I get deeply embarrassed.

I thought long and hard about how someone might have gained access to my house. I've hardly left the house for the last few months, so it must have occurred earlier. I've double-checked all the doors and windows and there's no sign of a forced entry. Then it came to me. It must have happened while I was in hospital after my accident. I was out for the count for a good couple of days. When I woke up my keys were in the hospital bedside cabinet with the rest of my things, but they would have been easily available to almost anyone of the hospital staff for a couple of days.

So naturally I toured the house to see if anything else was missing. The thieves hadn't stolen my laptop or any of my TV or audio equipment – and my watch (which is the only thing I possess that is worth stealing) was with me in the hospital. There aren't any valuables, I thought, and then I remembered that I'd bought a few sovereigns from a customer a while back. I'm no collector, but my customer happened to tell me he was keen to get rid of them, so I checked the current buy price he would get from a dealer, and he sold them to me at trade price. I thought they'd make a good long-term investment.

I'd kept them in a small box in the top drawer of my bedside table. Stupid, I know. But now they were gone, and I can't even report them missing or claim for them on insurance. The insurance company will want a crime reference number and if the police find them, they may well find the gun at the same time, and I do not want anything like that to happen. Bugger!

I've implemented increased security on all my systems. I know that no system is ever totally secure, but I'm confident that routine police forensics will not be able to read my laptop or server. Some people could crack my passwords, but they are not likely to be involved even in a murder case.

I assume there's a possibility that when the police return – which I expect they will do at some point in the future - they'll come armed with a search warrant. There's no chance I'll let them poke around if they haven't got one. But if they do, I need to be ready. And in case they start confiscating my computers, I'm going to have to finish my book before this happens – just in case.

There are a couple of tasks I need to complete as soon as possible. The final pieces of research. I need to find out how Bruno is going to create a will that leaves his entire estate to the winner of a contest. It's got to be possible. And luckily, I know just the man who will tell me how – Stephen. It's also occurred to me that I need to put my financial affairs in order. I need to write a will because otherwise, I know that the money would go to the Treasury – as does all the money from people who die intestate. And then it just gets added to the pile of money for those wastrels in Westminster to squander in the same way that they misspend every other penny that they lay their hands on. I'd rather leave it to a good cause.

If I time my appointment with Stephen correctly, say five o'clock, we should be able to go for a drink afterwards – that would be nice.

Unfortunately, my other piece of research will not be so much fun. I need to find out how Bruno will spend his last few days on Earth. He has a terminal disease and will want to be comfortable. There's nobody to look after him and he has enough money to pay for the best care, so I'm assuming he is going to go into a hospice. I need to find the address of the nearest one and discover how a patient gets admitted. That will cost me a small donation – which I have no problem with. I could also let them know I'll leave something to them in the will, which ties it all together neatly.

I will have to take care at my appointment with Stephen to make sure I explain which part of my inquiry is true and which part is fictional.

I tend to get a bit excited when I talk about my book. I'm quite proud of having written one (and I nearly have completed one, now). And, as I approach the conclusion of the book and spend more and more time not only writing but re-writing, it takes over my mind. I think about plot twists just before I go to sleep, and sometimes the story features in my dreams. And I do read the book aloud to myself – I was told that's a good way to perfect your prose. You sure as heck notice when a sentence is so long that you can't read the whole thing without pausing for breath. And that's the time you must break it in two.

I've still not settled on the title – I'll have to give that some more thought.

Tuesday, October, 10th

Why are solicitors so damned awkward? I suppose it is because their training, all their experience, almost the reason for their very existence is to deal with things going wrong. Or to take action to prevent them from going wrong.

So, when I told Stephen that I wanted him to help me with the book I was writing, I thought that he would be able to give me a nice set of guidelines for how Bruno could word his will. I didn't tell Stephen the whole story. I just told him that the main character in my book was going to die and had nobody to leave his money to, and, being an eccentric, he wanted to leave it to the winner of a competition. I even reminded him about Kit Williams and his golden hare – which Stephen either remembered or pretended to out of politeness.

But then he started coming up with all sorts of complications. Would the winner of the competition be alive at the time of my main character's death? Because he or she would have to be, to benefit from the will. I admitted that it could be a long time after the death that the puzzle was solved, but that it was highly unlikely that the person who solved it was not alive right now. This led him to remind me that the job of a solicitor is to guard against all events, even the unlikely ones. "What would happen to the money if the puzzle never got solved? Or it was such a long time after it was set that the firm of solicitors had ceased to exist?" he asked.

I raised the possibility of the money reverting to a charity or good cause in such an event and he advised against it. He reminded me that all wills (except those of the royal family) become public information once probate has been applied for. Charities and similar organisations have departments that check all published wills of any size and if they were a potential beneficiary and the alternate beneficiary was an unnamed competition winner, the will might be challenged.

He was able to provide some help with how this fictitious will might be worded. The words to use to appoint the firm of solicitors as executors and trustees of the estate, instructing them to sell the assets and place the funds in trust. He reminded me that the will must include a charging clause, that two partners (and their successors) should be appointed as trustees, and that the senior partner of the firm should apply for probate.

His final words on the subject were to remind me that there were companies known as 'heir hunters' who might well attempt to find relatives that this unfortunate man did not know he had. And those relatives might challenge the will. It could not be watertight and might well experience some 'enforceability issues.'

I had no choice but to thank him for his help and assure him that I would try to include as much of his advice as possible in the finished book.

Thankfully, my inquiries at the hospice were much more straightforward.

Early hours, Wednesday, October 11th

An important update: I've finished the book at last. I just could not get to sleep, so I took the unusual step of writing late at night. And then once I'd started, I could not stop. It took me longer than I thought – I had to write up the whole story of Bruno's online puzzle and the instructions for whoever solves it. And then there was all the stuff from my conversation with Stephen yesterday. Thankfully the bit about the hospice was much easier. A referral letter from an appropriate specialist and a small donation would be enough to guarantee admittance. So I've made sure that Bruno has 'all his ducks in a row'.

And then I had to put the final twist in (to the book). And it's done. One copy is secured locally and one remotely. I sincerely doubt that anyone will ever be able to crack the local copy – and the remote copy should only become available once the puzzle is solved, so it's as safe as it could reasonably be. If the police do take the device containing the local copy, I will have to wait until they return it before I have any chance of revising the text of the book. But until then it will have to do.

I also destroyed all that remained of the database I'd been using while I was writing the book – the one with the details of the women with the six chosen names and the information they'd revealed on their web chats. To be honest I'd been destroying it bit by bit as I wrote the book – once a victim had been written up, all references to anyone with that name were deleted. But now I've thoroughly checked that every last shred of information has gone.

It's kind of sad, parting company with it. That book has been my constant companion for the last six months. I've worked on it almost every day. And now I've got to wait until this current issue blows over before I dare touch it again. Oh well!

6. A Man Has Been Brought in for Questioning

Detective Inspector Linda Evans   Morning, Friday, October 13th

We called at John Jackson's house at eight-thirty the next morning and asked him to accompany us to the station to answer further questions concerning the murder of Megan McCormick. He asked if we were arresting him, and we confirmed that it was not an arrest, just a request to assist us in our inquiries. Something about the way he asked the question made me believe he was aware of the differences between assisting with inquiries and being under arrest. Or at least he thought he was. I said nothing but filed away the thought.

We also informed him that we had a search warrant and that a team of officers would be searching his house for any evidence they thought might be relevant.

"Some of the papers in my office belong to my employers," John said. "I'm not sure I'm allowed to let you look at them."

"I understand," I replied in the nicest possible manner. "Why don't you check with Mister Borshell to see what he says?"

I was following my instinct here. There was a possibility that both John and his boss were hiding something. If they refused to cooperate, I'd be convinced that this possibility was more likely. His boss would know that this could only result in us digging deeper, so I was confident of his full cooperation. After a brief telephone call, John told us that he had received the OK to let us look through the files.

He handed a set of keys to DS Holden. "This is the front door, and this is the filing cabinet," he said indicating the relevant keys. "You shouldn't need anything else."

He asked us to take care, especially as his office contained a lot of expensive computer equipment, and we assured him that we would search very carefully later that same day. I didn't tell him that I wanted to wait until we had completed our first session interviewing him so that I might be able to give some hints to the search party about what we were looking for. But that was how it was going to happen.

Once we arrived at the station, we put him in the interview room. Having previously tasted the quality of coffee he was accustomed to in his own home, I complimented him on his decision to refuse the cup of police coffee we offered him. It was probably better for him that he stayed with tap water – even the police can't ruin that.

Having left him waiting for fifteen minutes, DS Holden and I joined him in the interview room.

Our first line of questioning concerned his accident. He confirmed that he had had an accident about six months ago. A fall that necessitated some time off work. He also reiterated that since then he had suffered from repeated headaches and felt unable to concentrate fully which had led him to plan an early retirement. When DS Holden asked him if he could provide more details about the accident, he said that his memory was a little fuzzy, and there was a good reason for this, since he had incurred a head injury in the accident. But when this line of questioning was pursued a little further, John went off into a story about working on computer programs for sports betting.

I can think of very few other combinations of three subjects that are more likely to make me switch off than computers, sports, and betting. But DS Holden seemed interested, so I let him continue the discussion, while I took the chance to look through John's file one more time. The fact that he was talking was good. Once he started talking, he was unlikely to stop and was therefore more likely to let us know something he didn't intend to.

What is it about men that makes them so interested in sports, especially those that involve teams of men and a ball? It must be something rooted in our primitive behaviour patterns. A need to be part of a group of fellow humans hunting the same object (or objective) together, I suppose.

Don't get me wrong, I have no objection to football or rugby per se. What's not to like about watching healthy young men clad in shorts and tight shirts running around? To be honest, I quite enjoy it. But just talking about it? Or betting on it? No thanks.

Anyway, I tuned in enough to note that immediately before his accident, John had been drinking with colleagues and had then gone on to a club, where he had fallen down some stairs. More crucially, he refused to give details of the club where it had happened. He told us that he had received some minor injuries, and these had necessitated a short stay in hospital. I made a note to check up on this information later.

Thinking about John's health led me to become aware that he did not look too good today. Perhaps it was the harsher light of the interview room compared to the gentler light in his home. Maybe it was the understandable stress of being in a police station – which was an unusual and probably unique experience for him, as it is for most first-time offenders. Or maybe he had just had a rough night the night before. But he certainly did not look well. When I first saw him, my main impression was that he was big and strong, but now I would add that he also seemed to be underweight and unnaturally pale.

DS Holden paused his line of questioning, and we asked John to go over his visit to Megan the previous Friday. His story contained no significant differences from the first version he had given us a few days earlier.

"Can you remember what you were wearing when you visited her?"

He thought briefly before answering. "Jeans, a light brown pair of shoes, a polo shirt, and a blue jacket," he replied.

"And would these items be in your house currently?" I asked.

"Why do you want to know that?" he replied.

The standard police procedures tell you that you should avoid answering questions from a suspect, but if you do answer, you must not give an untruthful reply. I broke these rules when I answered.

"We've not been able to find anyone to confirm your departure time. Seems that nobody saw you anywhere on your walk home either. If we were able to tell people how you were dressed, maybe show them a picture, perhaps it could help prompt their memory."

Of course, this was not the reason – we wanted to know which garments of his to take from his house for forensic tests. We didn't have the resources to test everything in his wardrobe, and I thought the reason I had given for the question would be more likely to get the truth from him.

"The jeans and the jacket will still be there – but the rain ruined my shirt and my shoes, so they went straight in the bin when I got home."

I made a note of his reply and passed the information on to the search team at the next break in the interview. I told DC Priddis that we were looking for a lightweight blue jacket and a pair of jeans – presumably a smart pair, not the gardening ones. Apart from that, it was all the usual stuff we were looking for. Paperwork, anything that looked out of place, etcetera. I also told them we wanted any items of memorabilia related to the local football team that he supported – we had already spotted a couple of black and yellow scarves – so anything else they found that was in those colours should also be brought in.

I also reminded them that he was a computer geek and worked from home, so there would be at least one laptop and one server that he regularly used. We would want to see them, but they should be very careful to disconnect everything carefully. And make sure that if they decided to take possession of any pieces of computer equipment, they should bring the right power cord and connectors in with it.

DC Priddis told me that there was a single filing cabinet in the office, with three drawers full of paperwork. "It seems like rather a lot to bring in, and we'll probably have problems because it will stop him from working," he said.

"Just make a note of the titles of each folder, take a quick shufti through it, and make a note of its contents. If anything looks out of place, bring it in", I replied. DC Priddis obviously understood or worked out the meaning of the slang of my father's generation because he didn't ask what 'shufti' meant.

-

I'd like to say that the interview was fruitful and moved our investigation forward significantly. But I can't lie. We got next to nothing. The only highlight was half an hour later when I received a call from the search team which caused me to leave the interview room.

"We've had to stop the search, ma'am," I was informed and naturally asked why.

"We've found a gun. We need someone from the firearms team to come over and make sure it's safe."

"And what sort of gun is it?" I asked and was told it was a revolver, which, being a type of handgun, made its possession by a UK citizen illegal.

This was an unexpected development and an obvious avenue for further questions.

Returning to the interview room, I didn't know what to expect when I asked John why he had a firearm in his house, but his outburst of laughter certainly was not high on my list of anticipated reactions.

"It's not real," he said. Then, realising that we were not exactly sharing in his amusement, he ceased smiling and continued, "If you ask your search team what they found alongside the gun, they'll tell you it was a full cowboy outfit. My employers ran a serious fancy dress party a while back, and I put together the outfit as accurately as possible. The replica gun was the final piece."

I was still not amused, and I knew that my lack of hilarity would be shared by the search team and the firearms officer who was already on his way to the premises. The waste of time would not improve anyone's mood.

So, as lunchtime approached, we left John alone again for a few minutes, and DS Holden and I left the room and agreed that we were getting nowhere, but we hoped to get something from the possessions, particularly the computers, that the search team was now bringing in.

Once we had that information, we might well speak to John again, but we had no evidence to hold him in custody.

I then returned to the interview room in the company of DS Riaz Khan of Kent Police, who had arrived later than expected courtesy of a delayed LNER train. For me. it was good for once not to be the shortest person in the room. At five foot seven, I know I'm shorter than most people in the police service, but recently I'd spent so much time with John and DS Holden – both well over six feet tall – that I was beginning to get a complex. Riaz, however, was barely five six.

I introduced him to John and to the recording machine in the interview room and informed John that we had some questions regarding the sale of his car. John was understandably surprised.

"You sold a white BMW three series recently, I believe," my new fellow interviewer began.

"Yes," John replied a little hesitantly.

"Can you talk us through the sale?"

"Well, I'm doing a lot less mileage now, and I'll probably be doing even less when I'm fully retired, so I thought it would be a good time to go for an electric car. Help save the planet, and all that."

This was not the aspect of the sale that interested either Riaz or me, and he got in first with a response.

"Tell us about the actual sale."

"I put an ad on the Autocar website, and I got an immediate response from a guy in Swindon. We exchanged a couple of emails and then he arranged to come and see it."

"And can you remember the exact day he came?"

"It would have been Saturday the twenty-third of last month," John replied after a slight pause for thought.

"And what can you tell us about the person who bought the car?"

"He was a tall guy. I remember that because he immediately said something when he saw me. Along the lines of 'if it's big enough for you, then it'll be big enough for me.'"

"Did you get his name and address details?"

"Yes. I had to fill in the transfer document for the DVLA. His name was Horsfield or Horsenell or something."

"And his address?"

"Something like Hillcrest Road or Avenue."

"And can you describe him for us?"

"Well, tall, like I said. About my age, I'd guess, but maybe a bit older. He had grey hair and a grey beard but wasn't that old."

It appeared that DS Khan had as much (or as little) faith as I did in photofit pictures provided by the average member of the public ("worse than fucking useless" was how I believe he described them) and so we did not ask John to provide one. And John's description coincided with the very limited description they had received of the suspect in their case.

"How did he pay you for the car?"

"Cash. I put it in a holdall in the loft – never know when a bit of extra cash might come in handy."

Until now, all the questions had come from Riaz, but I wanted to add a couple of my own.

"Would anyone else have known the car was up for sale?" I asked.

"I told the guys down at the pub – the quiz team, you know. And of course, I put a sign in the car's window, so anyone passing would have known if they'd taken the trouble to look."

I asked what condition the car was in when it was sold.

"Oh, I made sure it was in excellent condition. I took it to that place on the Chesterfield Road. They're Polish guys, I believe. They do an excellent job – and I gave them an extra twenty to give it a really good going over, and they did. It was spotless. Even blacked the tyres for me."

John asked why we were so interested in the car, and I thought it reasonable to let him know that it was suspected of involvement in a crime – but I left it at that, and he did not ask for any more details.

DS Khan asked John if he could account for his movements over the previous weekend. While I quietly pondered the thought that the phrase 'account for your movements' must be in the top ten of police-speak sayings, John gave us an overview of his weekend.

"I went down to London that weekend," he said. "The Bees had a game at Leyton Orient on Saturday, so I decided to make a weekend of it. I took the train down Thursday evening and checked in to the Holiday Inn near Euston station. I've got a lot of Holiday Inn points from my work trips, so I decided to spend some of them. On Friday I went around a couple of museums – the Science and Natural History ones, and then on the Saturday morning, I did something I've been meaning to do for years and went to the Tower of London. Joined a group and had a guided tour from one of the Beefeaters. You know, those guys really know their stuff – and they've got a great line in patter. It was a very enjoyable way to spend a couple of hours. I went to the game, we got a draw, I had a couple of beers with some of the guys I knew and a nice meal that evening in a Greek restaurant that the hotel recommended, and then came back home on Sunday."

It was a useful alibi, of course. A comprehensive list of activities, but without anything specific during Friday when the murder occurred. DS Khan made notes – but I guessed it was pretty useless. Only the hotel and the restaurants he had eaten at would be able to give us any confirmation. And possibly the tour guide at the Tower. Nothing would corroborate where he claimed to have been on the Friday when the murder was committed. And of course, his story still placed him much closer to the murder than he would normally have been.

We left John alone in the interview room and held a brief conference between the three of us. DS Holden and I updated DS Khan with brief details of Megan's murder, and he gave us an overview of the killing of Macie, the young woman whose body had been found on the shoreline in Kent.

Although there were few parallels between the killings in the list of connections that we usually look for – method, location, and so on – we were struck by one overriding similarity. A young woman had been brutally murdered for no apparent reason by a cold-blooded killer in broad daylight.

'Would it have been any better if it had been a warm-blooded killer acting in narrow daylight?' I mused to myself.

I asked how they had tied the car to the murder and DS Khan told me that the car had matched the description of a car seen near the scene of the crime. It had been left in Ebbsfleet Station car park, and when they had done a follow-up with DVLA they had found out that the details of the owner on the DVLA records were false.

I wanted to know a little bit more about the discovery of the car.

"Just a phone call from a member of the public," he replied.

"Were the details of the caller recorded?" I asked and was told that they had not given a name, and the call had been made from a public telephone. DS Khan in return asked why I wanted to know about this.

"It's just a bit convenient, that's all. The car is found in a station car park, even though it must be quite normal for cars to be left there sometimes for a few days. Isn't that the station that connects to Paris?"

"It used to be, but since the pandemic, the Eurostar doesn't stop there anymore. But you're right, people do sometimes leave their car there for several days because they go from Ebbsfleet to St. Pancras and then catch the Paris train from there."

"Any forensic evidence?" I asked and was told that there had been sand in the driver's footwell that matched the sand near the murder site.

"Anything to link the car to its owner? Fingerprints or anything?" I continued.

"No - that was a little odd. There was not a single fingerprint anywhere in the car. Someone had taken great care to clean it – and to keep it clean," he replied.

"So, in both the crimes we're talking about, there's been a major piece of evidence that points directly to John Jackson. And it has been uncannily easy to find."

"Do you think he should be a suspect for both murders?" DS Khan asked, his voice betraying a little surprise.

"I think we've got to consider that," I replied, "or the fact that someone is deliberately making him look like a suspect for both murders."

I asked him for some more details about the murder of Macie.

"You said she was shot by a large calibre handgun at close range, is that right?"

He confirmed it was.

"And why was she in such a god-forsaken place as you described?"

"She was planning to walk the Kent Coastal Path – she had told her many followers on social media that this was her plan – and she had a friend due to meet her at the end of this stage – about five miles further on."

"Was there anything particularly unusual about the murder?" I asked and silently questioned my sanity.

I was thinking 'You've described how a young woman was shot dead at close range in the middle of the day for no apparent reason and you want to know if there was anything particularly unusual. As if what you've already described was completely fucking normal?'

DS Khan brought me back to my senses by saying "There was one thing. Her body was moved after she was killed."

"Moved how?" I asked, putting urgency before proper grammar.

"She was laid across the path. At right angles to the path itself."

DS Holden and I exchanged a glance. This was something of a "lightbulb" moment and so we explained to our visitor that Megan's body had been moved similarly. All three of us agreed that this unexplained behaviour made it highly likely that we were looking for the same killer for both women. It was either John or else it was someone who was trying hard to point the finger at him. We also agreed that there was very little else we were going to get from him now, and we needed more evidence before we could move ahead with an arrest.

Moments later, I returned to the interview room and informed John he was free to go and that a car would be ready at the front door in five minutes to return him to his home.

One of the many pieces of advice I received from my father – an 'old school' policeman in every sense of the phrase - was that if it was possible, you should always walk a suspect off the premises when you let him go.

"Chat with him as you go, in a relaxed way to reassure him. Change the subject. Let him relax. When a suspect experiences the relief that the ordeal of police questioning was over, it's the time he or she is most likely to let down their defences and say something that they shouldn't." That was how he'd put it.

So, I talked about John's plans for early retirement with him as we walked through the double doors at the front of the station and waited a few minutes until a patrol car turned up. And I'm very glad I did. Not because of anything he said, but because of something that happened as we were on our way out.

Sargeant Mandy Lewis was entering the station, just as we were leaving. She looked at John in a way that instantly told me she recognised him and made a movement as if to speak to him, but noting my presence, thought better of it. I was convinced that he recognised her too, even though he tried desperately to hide it. As soon as he was in the back of the car, I retraced my steps and, as expected, found Mandy waiting to talk to me.

"What's Tom been up to?" she asked, indicating the direction from which I had just come.

"Tom? No, that's not Tom, that's John – John Jackson. He's a person of interest in the Megan McCormick case," I told her.

"No way! I spent a whole week visiting him in hospital. That's Tom. I'm sure of it. I can't tell you his last name – something long, Polish, and unpronounceable," she replied.

Mandy was one of the stalwarts of the station. She had been there longer than almost everyone else on the roster. Mandy knew everything that anyone needed to know about what went on at that station – and everything that no one needed to know too. There was no way I was doubting her word, but there was obviously a story I needed to hear, and I told her so.

Mandy looked around the entrance hall in a way that said she feared telling me her story where someone might overhear it.

"I'm finishing my shift at six, can we talk about this in the pub?" she asked. It seemed an odd request. Why couldn't she just tell me there and then? It confirmed to me that this was going to be an interesting story.

"Sure, see you there just after six?" I replied.

Returning to the briefing room I joined DS Holden and DS Khan to discuss our progress or lack thereof.

I asked him what else they had found out about the mystery man that was their suspect.

"Well, he doesn't exist. The name on the DVLA record was Richard Horsnell. Obviously, someone owns the car, and left it in the station car park - but he's not called Richard Horsnell. We've checked everyone in the UK by that name and eliminated them all. Whoever he is, he was in Swindon the day before the murder, we know that. He parked his recently acquired car in a couple of different places in the town and bought a new mobile phone. We were able to use that to trace his movements.

That evening he travelled along the M4 to a small town called Taplow, just west of Slough. He parked there overnight before driving to Kent the next morning. We've got him on CCTV at Cobham Services on the M25 on the morning of the murder, but it's a pretty lousy image.

We think he may have stayed with a friend overnight, or he may even live in Taplow. But we're relying on the police there doing some door-to-door inquiries because we know he parked close to the station and there are no hotels nearby. So, we reckon he either stayed locally, or he was picked up there and dropped off the next morning."

"Do you have any explanation for why someone, whatever his name might be, should drive all the way from Swindon to a remote part of the Kent coast to kill a complete fucking stranger?" I asked as my frustration began to get the better of me.

"The only connection we've made is that she did once exchange messages on Twitter with someone calling himself Richard Horsenell, but that's not much help because young Macie seems to have spoken to half the bloody population on social media at one time or another. We've also had no joy in trying to trace whoever is the real account holder who presents himself as Richard Horsenell. "

"Anything of interest in the conversation between them?" I asked – the question being as vague as our understanding of what was going on.

"No – he read her posts and saw she was walking the Kent Coastal path so he sent her a link to some information about some people who had walked it recently."

"If you've got a file of his social media interactions, I'd like a copy – to see if there are any other connections we can draw."

DS Khan promised to send it to me the next day.

Apart from consoling ourselves on the main similarity between our two inquiries – which was the fact that we were getting nowhere – Riaz was able to add one small piece of possibly useful information.

When they had liaised with Wiltshire police, they had been alerted to a recent unsolved case in Swindon. A young woman had been strangled in her car on a side street near the care home where she had been visiting her father. The only similarity to the Kent case was that there appeared to be absolutely no motive. The victim had apparently been chosen at random.

There had been a sighting of an old man in her company – a fellow visitor to the care home who had allegedly been a colleague of her father during his working life. But the name and address that the old man had entered in the visitor's book at the home turned out to be false. The house existed. In fact, the victim was found in her car parked a few yards away from the address he'd given, but nobody knew who the old man was, nor had they ever seen anyone matching his description.

"Were they able to get any more information about the suspect from the people in the care home?" I asked.

"No – he only made the one visit and staff barely noticed him. And the guy he visited doesn't know if it's Christmas or breakfast time, so he's not been able to help."

"Anything unusual about this murder that they told you? Was her body moved or anything?"

"No, she was found slumped in the driving seat of her car. There was one thing, though. The old man gave his name at the care home as Stanley, and a screwdriver with the logo of the Stanley Tools Company was found at the woman's feet. The local police think the killer was taking the piss."

"Do you think this could be your, or should I say our, mysterious mister Horsnell?" I asked DS Khan, but he could not shed any further light on the matter. They had nothing else to go on - as the old gag about the stolen toilet went.

Winding up the business for the day, we agreed to keep each other in touch with developments. He promised to let us know about any progress in his case and if he heard anything more from Swindon or Taplow as he was liaising with both forces in those locations. Likewise, we promised to let him know of any progress we made on Megan's killing. DS Holden gave him a lift back to the train station.

I resolved to use the information we had gleaned from the Kent force to ask for more resources for my inquiry. We needed to follow up on John's weekend in London – and see if we could find some holes in his alibi.

I was left to ponder these disparate threads that might connect to help solve three killings which might be closely connected. Or they might have nothing whatsoever to do with each other.

Detection is all about making connections. Two of these three murders were connected by a car. Two had a connection to Swindon. All three were connected by the age and sex of the victim. The theme of false identity ran through all the cases. But the normal connections – something that linked the victims to the killer or each other, or similarities in the method of killing – were missing. And there seemed no single purpose or driving force behind the murders.

At an appropriate time, I intended to remind DCI Lancaster about his description of Megan's killing as 'a routine murder'.

7. Am I My Brother's Keeper?

Detective Inspector Linda Evans   Evening, Friday, 13th October

The pub that Mandy Lewis had referred to was the Black Lion. It's about fifty yards from the front door of the station and is a thoroughly nondescript establishment – typical of the modern town-centre pub. The only reason it is still in business may well be that it has such a regular and heavy-spending clientele – known elsewhere as the Nottinghamshire Constabulary.

The police service doesn't make up its entire customer base. The pub also has a clientele comprised of people who want to bump into members of the Nottinghamshire Constabulary (yes, there are always some) and those who feel that a pub full of off-duty policemen is probably one of the safer places to hang out in the city.

I entered at five minutes past six and beat Mandy to the bar by only a couple of minutes. I ordered two large white wines. I ordered large measures partly because I guessed that her story was going to last at least the length of a large glass of wine. And partly because as far as I'm concerned, wine is only served in two different sizes – large and bottle.

Mandy and I have known each other for a long time and are both dyed-in-the-wool police officers. We knew why we were here. Very little time was wasted on either pleasantries or small talk before she began her story.

"Do you remember about six months ago, maybe a little longer, the uniform section carried out a high-profile raid on that knocking shop just off the M1?" she began.

I nodded, vaguely remembering it and not wanting to interrupt her story this early in its telling.

"There were rumours of some illegal immigrants working there, possible gang involvement in the running of the place, human trafficking, drugs, the works. In the end, it all proved to be much ado about sod-all, but we nicked a couple of illegals, found some drugs, and made a few arrests. It probably looked good on the figures, which is why the super himself came along. We might have got more but for what happened with young Tom or John or whatever his name is."

She stopped for a gulp of wine, and I said, "Tell me more," safe in the knowledge that was exactly what she planned to do.

"Anyway, I was stationed in the waiting room with Neppo," she began, and I had to interrupt. "Neppo?" I asked.

"Sorry, Police Constable Christopher Peake. You know who he is, or at least you must know who his father is?" she replied.

"Yes, he's the Lord High Executioner. But why is his son called Neppo?" I asked, knowing it was an irrelevance, but such a strange nickname just couldn't be allowed to pass.

"Well, when we first heard that he would be joining us, the guys were talking about it and one of them says something like 'Wow, it must be great having a dad who's the Chief Constable. He can use all his power and influence to get you a great job - like a probationary police constable in Nottingham Nick.' And then someone else says, 'Yeah that's what you call real nepotism' and then someone else mishears what was said and asks, 'He's called Neppo what?' which produced a great laugh. So, a few days later when the lad joined us, they immediately started calling him Neppo. It didn't seem to bother him – in fact, I think he enjoyed having a nickname and being one of the lads. He's been Neppo ever since."

Having had my curiosity salved, it was time to get back to the story.

"Meanwhile, back at the knocking shop?" I asked.

"Yes, well there's me and Neppo and a couple of the club's punters. We're expecting more to turn up once they've had the chance to put their trousers back on, so to speak. Our brief is to take their details, call the office, verify that they're not wanted for anything, and if they're clean, let them go. So, the two of us were sitting in the reception area of the establishment – where the punters wait for their erm … companions." She struggled to find the right word and seemed unhappy with 'companions' but left it there.

"Anyway, there were two punters in the room with us. An old guy, trying desperately to make himself as invisible as possible, and the man who had given his name as Tom. I'd taken their details and radio-ed them in and was waiting for them to be confirmed. The old guy was quiet as a mouse, but Tom was getting very edgy.

As you know he's quite a big guy and he would not sit down when we asked him to. He was walking up and down – very agitated. Not threatening – but not exactly making us feel comfortable either. So, Neppo asks him one more time to sit down – he even said please – and the guy refuses and walks towards us. And that's when Neppo warns him again and before I know what's happened, he's tasered him.

I think he gave a warning – and in the inquisition that happened later, he said he did, and I accepted his word. So that's become a fact now.

But what I didn't say – and ain't planning to either – is that he didn't hit him in the torso like you're supposed to. He hit him higher – maybe his neck, maybe his head. Not that it mattered anyway because the guy drops like a stone when it hits him – like they all do. The trouble is, he was standing at the top of the stairs at the time. So, he falls all the way down. Breaks his arm, buggers up his shoulder, and cracks his skull on the floor.

Nobody else saw what happened, but we had to get an ambulance immediately, of course. And the raid was brought to a halt soon after."

She stopped and took another gulp of her wine. "Bit of a shit show," was my considered reply.

"You could say that. Anyway, once the guy was in the ambulance and safely on his way to hospital, the super takes me aside and asks what happened. And I told him just like I told you now."

Realising where we were going, she started to hesitate and slow her speed of information delivery.

"Look Mandy, you know you can trust me not to talk out of turn. But this might just have some relevance to Megan's murder, so you know you've got to tell me," I said.

"I know you won't say anything that'll drop me in it, but I have to be very careful what I say here," she continued.

"Understood. Carry on," I replied, adding "Please" after.

"Well, the boss asked me not to file a report until we knew exactly what the state of this guy in the hospital is, and what he's going to do about it when he comes round. He tells me to go and see how he was getting on and what he was going to say.

So, I went to the hospital to visit him the next day. I spoke to the doctors, and they told me that they were keeping him under sedation for a couple of days. The arm was a clean break, and the shoulder was a straightforward dislocation and they'd fixed both. But they were a bit worried about the blow he'd had to his head. He'd literally cracked his skull, and they wanted the swelling to go down before waking him up.

I went back to the hospital every day for a week. He came round after a couple of days, and we talked for a good half an hour a day. I don't think he had too many other visitors and he seemed happy to chat. He remembered very little of what had happened. He could recall going to the club and having a fall, but he seemed to think that it was all a result of him having had a few drinks before he got there. He couldn't remember me, or Neppo, or the taser, or anything about the raid."

"And that was the end of it?" I asked.

"Yep. The super told me to report the fall, but the discharge of a taser was not to be mentioned. Which it should have been, and if it had been some other poor constable who'd done it, it would have been."

This was an area I had no desire to get into – at least at that point. I asked if she was OK to answer a few questions about Tom (or John) and she gave me an uncertain "yes" in response. I ordered a couple more wines to ease matters.

"So, he gave his name as Tom?" I asked.

"Yes. I checked it up – and I've double-checked since we spoke earlier today." She took a notebook out of her handbag, opened it, and said, "Tom Jędrzejczyk, (spelling the last name one letter at a time). No police record. Gave an address in Layton Avenue, Mansfield and it all checked out." She replaced the notebook.

"That's interesting", I replied. "The address is the same as our suspect, who has the much more boring name of John Jackson. And as far as we can tell John lives alone. Something we need to check up on a little further." I was both giving her my side of the story and speaking my thoughts aloud.

We talked a little more until we had both finished our second glass, but there was nothing more that she had to add to the story. I reassured her once more that nothing would be said about the tasering incident unless it was absolutely necessary, and even then, I'd warn her before doing so.

She thanked me, and I added that I may have to speak to the Super at some point to hear his side of the story, but she was fine with that.

The next morning, I got DS Holden to find out all he could about Mister Tom Jędrzejczyk, while I consulted DC Priddis who had led the search party. There was next to nothing to report from them.

They had taken some paperwork, but nothing seemed relevant. Don gave me the list of files he'd found in the filing cabinet and a brief set of notes under each to explain the contents.

Each file was neat and apparently up to date. The normal stuff – a file labelled Cars containing the purchase invoice for his BMW, its registration documents, receipts for services, and a couple of Speed Awareness Courses. A file labelled Insurance with copies of his policies for his car, his home and contents, professional indemnity, and so on. Our person of interest was obviously a well-organised man.

A few of the files contained only one sheet of paper – and in those files, DC Priddis remarked, the notes were almost always handwritten, and neatly so. The desktop was clear of paperwork except for a few sheets in an in-tray. They had brought those sheets back to the station even though they could find no significance in them, presuming they concerned jobs that John was currently involved with.

Two sheets of plain A4 paper caught my eye. One had simply the name Denis Fittaley written on it, the other was headed with the name Billy Rodriguez and beneath it there were two lines of handwritten notes:

Alcohol event – Church? Local government? Charity?

Date left: 20/09/91 – Where to?

It looked like he was researching two names from his past and had not been able to discover anything about either person.

The search team had also taken some items of clothing which had been sent for DNA testing, and some computer hardware. This was being checked by the IT boys and girls – 'boys and girls' being DC Priddis's term, not mine, but I agree that it was accurate. When I look at the technical staff, I often wonder if they are full-time employees or are here on work experience and have taken a week off secondary school.

We had taken possession of a laptop and a server which were both password-protected and there was no possibility of getting any information from either of them. We had also acquired a strange electronic black box, which had been connected to the laptop by some form of Heath-Robinson connection involving multiple adaptors connected to one another. They had brought this back, but it was a complete mystery even to the tech guys.

"So, unless you can come up with a cyber security specialist somewhere, we're fucked" was DC Priddis's concise opinion of the IT scenario. I thanked him for his succinct and accurate summary of the situation and returned to DS Holden to hear what he had managed to glean about the mysterious Mister Tom Jędrzejczyk.

The phrase that DC Priddis had used - cyber security specialist - had triggered something in my memory bank. But the pathways up there are a little cluttered, and what it had triggered and why part of my brain thought it was important to let me know it was important, was not exactly forthcoming, so I decided to postpone thinking about that for a while.

He confirmed that they had briefly looked inside the loft, which contained the usual rubbish with the only interesting item being a holdall with several thousand pounds in used twenties and fifties. I told him that disappointingly it was probably not suspicious because John admitted to having sold his car for cash recently.

Lastly, there had been no other items of football memorabilia found in the house – unless I wanted to include some old copies of the football club's newsletter and match day programmes. Like so much else in the investigation so far – it was generally disappointing.

DS Holden had been beavering away while I had been de-briefing DC Priddis and brought me an update on what he and the rest of the team had managed to find out.

He confirmed his earlier findings that there had been no admissions of a John Jackson to any local hospital in the period between four and seven months before today. But there had indeed been a Tom

Jedrzejczyk admitted some five months ago when an ambulance had been called by the police very late at night to the club that Mandy had told me about.

'Tom' had been an in-patient for a week until his injuries had been patched up, and he had been discharged and referred to outpatients for ongoing investigation and treatment. The hospital was unable (or possibly unwilling, DS Holden added) to give any more information.

Something about this did not ring completely true, but we had so many other avenues to investigate right now, that I let it slip for a while.

"Our Mister Jedrzejczyk is proving to be *very* interesting," DC Holden continued, stressing the word 'very'. "He is indeed resident where he stated and is sixty years old - but there was no record of his existence until about five years ago when he commenced working as a self-employed computer programmer," he continued.

"Now I may have an unusually high threshold for declaring something as *very* interesting", I replied, "but I wouldn't exactly see that as qualifying".

"Ah, but there is one piece of information that does make him very interesting. He has managed to fulfill this demanding employment for the past five years even though he died fifty years ago."

"Ah, now that is a little more interesting," I replied. "So, we assume that his existence was made up by John Jackson."

"Correct", he smiled.

"And is there a connection, may I venture to ask?"

"Yes, boss. Mister Jackson changed his name in 1988 – from John Jedrzejczyk. Tom is – or rather was – his older brother."

"So, John invents him – or rather reinvents him - for some reason five years ago. And then when he has a brush with the law one night at a disreputable establishment, he decides to use his brother's name instead of his own. Either because he was temporarily discombobulated by a bump on his head, or more likely it was so that his name is not besmirched in any way by association with a house of ill repute."

I paused, but DS Holden knew me well enough to know my mental hamster was still moving his wheel and so he waited for me to finish.

"You say Tom was a self-employed computer programmer. I wonder if Mister Borshell might know something about him. Maybe we should ask."

DS Holden smiled in agreement.

The following morning, we put exactly this question to Mister Borshell in the rent-a-posh-room-for-visitors section of his shared office.

"Look, John Jackson is my star performer. He's worked more hours, more productively, and longer for me than anyone else I've ever employed. The average programmer puts in thirty-five to forty hours a week. John often does eighty. And it's all good stuff. So, when he says he has a housemate who's also a programmer and he vouches for him, I'm happy to put some work his way," was how he answered it.

"Presumably you have never met the man."

"There are several programmers I employ that I've never met," he replied.

I thought that this was probably the first true statement we had had from him that morning.

"And you never suspected that this Tom Jedrzejczyk may be a tax dodge being used by your star employee?" I continued. At this point, Mr Borshell did something very smart. He kept his mouth shut and just shrugged his shoulders.

We got very little else from him. He promised to look up the dates of employment of this unusual freelance contractor and the amounts and dates he had been paid, and to send us the information. I was not particularly concerned with this level of detail but thought it might be useful to supply it to the Inland Revenue when asking them for information, which I expected to soon need to do.

We returned to the office and considered our next move. By the end of the afternoon, we discovered that there was no forensic evidence on any of the items taken during the search of John's house. There was also no forensic evidence on the scarf that had been found at the scene of Megan's murder. This seemed a little odd and I spoke to the forensics team to clarify it. They confirmed that there were no fragments of skin or hair on the scarf – which was indeed unusual. Anyone wearing a scarf for more than a few minutes would naturally shed some skin and they would expect to find it in their tests. But this scarf had been totally clean. Which looked like it had either been purchased by Megan or left there, unused, by one of her gentlemen callers. Another mystery to unravel.

DS Holden and I talked some more about the significance of this, our one piece of evidence in the case so far. We agreed that John, who seemed so organised, would not have left such an item behind him – and if he had done so, surely it would have had some trace of him on it. It would appear to be a very unusual gift for a gentleman caller to have brought for Megan, and once again if the caller that she had allegedly seen after John's visit had inadvertently left it behind, then there should be some trace of him on it.

The possibility that it had been deliberately left to point to John as a suspect seemed almost too strange to be true. But then again, 'too strange to be true' was an everyday occurrence in some murder investigations, including this one.

When we considered our situation with John Jackson, we had some evidence of tax evasion, but nothing concerning the murder we were investigating. The only evidence that might be in our hands was stored on the pieces of computer hardware in our office, hidden behind passwords and possibly other barriers.

Someone needed to perform the fools' errand of asking John to let us have the passwords for his computer. We all agreed that he was unlikely to do so – but the question had to be asked. In the unlikely event (as they say on all the best plane journeys) that he might be susceptible to a little female charm, I agreed to visit him alone.

-

He answered the door promptly when I rang the bell early the following morning.

"Come in," he said, "I'm on the phone but it won't take a second."

He dismissed the caller with a promise to call back in a few minutes and turned his attention to me.

"I've brought you a list of everything that was taken during the search," I said, handing him an envelope that contained the typed list. "I have to formally ask you if you could tell us the passwords for the laptop and the storage unit," I said in my best impersonation of a helpless female.

He went a roundabout way to refuse.

"The stuff on the laptop and the storage unit is the text and the notes for the book I'm writing. And I've already had my suspicions that someone has tried to get hold of it. If I let you have access to it, I'm worried that somebody somewhere in the police service will pass it on to someone else, and suddenly all my work is in vain, so I'm afraid that I'm going to have to say no."

It was a good excuse, as excuses go, and the only opening it left me was to try to find out who he suspected of trying to steal his precious work. I would try to appear interested to elicit more from him.

"What's the book about?" I asked.

"Oh, it's the standard stuff – a mad serial killer pursued by the righteous forces of law and order," he replied with a chuckle that had to be one of the most forced I've ever heard.

"And who do you think was trying to steal your work?"

"It was Denis. A guy on the online writing course I went on."

"Would that be Denis Fittaley?" I asked and John briefly looked puzzled before he presumably remembered that it was written on a piece of paper on his desktop. He nodded his head.

"I've tried to find out some more about him – but without any success, I have to admit."

He paused and I wondered if he was waiting for me to raise the issue of his use of a false name after his accident. I thought I would keep my powder dry and let him sweat on that for a while. I knew he'd done it and he knew I knew. Let him worry for a while.

"Well, as long as you understand that we will do all we can to read what is on those two devices, I guess we'll have to leave it there."

He could not disguise the relief he felt as I made my way to the door.

"I'll let you know if there's anything else we need to know," I replied and left.

I went home to a ready-to-cook meal-for-one and a half-empty bottle of Chablis that needed putting out of its misery. The phrase 'cyber security specialist' was still bouncing around in my head. With my hunger and thirst assuaged, I was returning my plate and glass to my cupboard when I remembered where I had heard it before. I dated a guy in that line of work a few years ago. But just remembering that I had dated him was not going to help a lot. Between finishing university and joining Her Majesty's constabulary I'd dated quite a few guys. More accurately, quite a lot of guys.

University had been a struggle for me. I had to work very hard to keep up – which I did. I wanted to join the Police Service, and for me, the only sensible way to do this was via the graduate entry scheme.

So, I had to stretch my little grey cells to their absolute limit to get a degree. And that was not the only challenge I imposed upon myself. I was also determined not to fall into the trap that so many of my friends fell victim to. I did not want the millstone of a huge chunk of student debt hanging around my neck for the rest of my life. And in the absence of rich relatives or a generous benefactor, I had to take the unpleasant alternative of working bloody hard. I waited tables several nights a week, smiled at the customers, refused the propositions, and pocketed the tips.

Between working hard to pay my way and working hard to get a degree there wasn't much time left for a social life, let alone any relationships. So, when my three-year stint was complete, I returned to the bosom of my family with the objective of paying my mum some rent for a while to thank her for the help she had been in getting me to and through university. And to have one hell of a year of fun before I went into the police. I did just that. I was still young enough to burn the candle at both ends, keep a clean record in my boring job, and date much of the eligible young male population of the county.

I did have some basic principles. If he was cute, and he asked nicely, I'd date him. But if he hadn't attempted to jump me by the end of the second date, then I'd dump him. If he did try to jump me, I might let him succeed, I might not. But if he didn't even try, then it was time for me to move on.

I never gave my phone number to any of them. If they interested me, I'd take their number – and write it with their name in my diary - but they never got my number.

And so now, somewhere in one of my diaries of the time, there was possibly the phone number and name of a guy who told me he was working in computer security, and one day aimed to be a cybersecurity specialist.

I remembered him because it was not the exciting job title that some men would make up, nor was it the boring job title that many had but would not confess to. It had to be real. And, if my memory was not letting me down, he was kinda cute too. I think I even made an exception for him and let him take me on a third date. But there was no sign of any action, so I dumped him. But what the hell was his name?

A fresh glass of wine - from a fresh bottle - helped me remember that it probably began with R. But Roy? Richard? Rick? Rupert? (Be serious, I did some crazy stuff, but I'd never go so far as dating a Rupert!) Nothing was coming to mind, but I had not given up hope. I just knew that my best hope was when I woke at three tomorrow morning to answer nature's call, it might be there.

And it was there at three the next morning. Robin, that was his name. Remembering this meant that inevitably a quick dash to the bathroom was not going to be the end of my activities at this ungodly hour. I had to get up, pull on jeans and a sweater, find my torch, and climb up into my loft. I knew I wouldn't be able to get back to sleep once I'd remembered his name. I had to find the diary with his number in it.

The box full of all the wonderful souvenirs I had kept from that period of my life was handily located in the far corner of the loft with several other highly useful items in the way. It was over an hour later when I had managed to move various objects, locate the right box, drag it across the loft, and carry it down to my kitchen table.

Once I had it on the table, I also had to resist the temptation of looking at all these magnificent mementoes – ticket stubs, birthday and valentines' cards, small cuddly toys, stupid cheap plastic things from fairgrounds, you get the picture – and concentrate on finding my diary. Once it was found I had to read through the pages of scrawled notes for the time, venue, and name of the dates - and the occasional phone number.

By five a.m. I was able to crawl back into bed, secure in the knowledge that I had located Robin's number. I was, of course, full of optimism that he had not changed his number in the last five years and would no doubt remember me after all this time. And that he had indeed become a cyber security specialist and would be delighted to help me crack my cyber security problem. Not a lot to ask for, surely?

I called him at nine the next morning. The phone rang and after a few strange clicks and other noises, I was connected to a metallic voicemail which informed me that the person I had called was not currently available and told me – yes it didn't ask me, it told me – to leave my name and number and a brief reason for the call. I obeyed.

"Hi Robin, this is Linda Evans. I'm hoping you'll remember me. We dated a few times a few years ago. Well, I'm now Detective Inspector Linda Evans and I need some help with a cyber security issue on an important case I'm working on. I'm hoping that you might be able to provide that assistance."

I added my mobile number and was left feeling slightly puzzled by the oddness of the voicemail message, but strangely reassured that this indicated that Robin had probably taken up a career in security.

This was confirmed when he returned my call late that afternoon. It was a few seconds before I realised that he had called me on the office number and not the mobile number I had left on the voicemail message. I asked him about this after we had said our hellos and had reminisced briefly about our short time together a few years back.

"I had to check you were who you said you were," he said. "We have to be careful."

"So, you did continue your career in cyber security?" I asked, even though his words and his actions had pretty much substantiated it already. He confirmed this was the case, and when I asked him whom he was working for he simply said "The government" in a way that didn't encourage me to ask which part of the government. I was reasonably sure it wasn't the Ministry of Agriculture, Fisheries, and Food.

"Tell me more about this cyber security problem that made you dig my phone number out. It must be pretty important because I don't expect you've kept me on speed dial all these years."

I gave him a summary of the case, ending with my strong suspicions that there was likely to be valuable material on the laptop and server and possibly some gold dust on the mysterious black box."

"I can probably help you with the first two – but probably can't help you with the black box," he replied. "Can you do one thing for me? Find the label on the laptop that has all the details of its make, model, and serial number, and leave me a message on my phone with as much information as you can see. I assume you have the thing in your possession?"

I told him we did and offered to send him a text message with the details.

"No, don't text me," he replied, "That'll take longer to get cleared than a voice message. Once I know what systems he is using, I'll need to lay my hands on it. And it'll have to be in my spare time. Is there a chance that if I came up to you on Friday evening, we could look at it?"

This was better than I'd hoped – both professionally and personally - and I rapidly said yes.

"OK. Look, I'm not exactly sure how long it'll take me to get up there on a Friday evening, so maybe we could meet up in the Black Lion? I'll aim to be there around seven if that's all right?"

Of course, I agreed

He had done his homework. He had found out which police force I was in, where I was working, and then the details of the local pub. Either he was incredibly efficient, or he was deliberately trying to impress me, but either reason was fine by me. I promised to be waiting there for him.

In the end, he got to the pub about quarter past seven and refused my offer of a drink. "Maybe we can have one when we've seen if I can get into this laptop of yours?" he suggested. I agreed, downed what was left of my spritzer – a compromise between the soft drink that common sense recommended I should be drinking and the glass of wine I was gasping for – and followed him out of the pub.

At the station, I showed him to the nicest of our interview rooms and went to fetch the laptop.

He opened it and inserted a USB stick he had brought with him. A few seconds later John Jackson's home screen was on display – his extra-secure password having been completely bypassed.

"How did you do that?" I asked – not necessarily expecting an answer.

"Well, when you log in normally, you are asked for and you enter a password. The computer goes to the place where it keeps the passwords and compares what you entered with what it has stored, and if they match it lets you in. Now, if you know where the computer keeps the passwords, you don't have to tell it the password. You can just tell it to use the one it's got stored."

"And you just happen to know where it stores them?"

"Let's just say over the years we've worked it out for most makes and models."

"And I guess you don't share the contents of that memory stick too freely," I replied.

"That would be an accurate assessment. But I will let you know the username and password for this box if you could pass me a good old-fashioned piece of paper and a pen," he answered. And he smiled, which was nice.

He wrote the details down and passed the paper to me. And I filed it safely in my back pocket. Between now and Monday morning I was going to have to spend a lot of time in front of this computer screen, armed with this vital piece of information. But not just now.

Robin showed no sign of wanting to rest on the laurels of his already helpful achievement. "Can we have a look at the black box you told me about? I think I know what it is, but I'd like to see it to make sure," he asked.

Under normal security procedures, I should not take any visitor into the area where we kept confiscated property – but I reckoned that I could justify this exception. Someone who can crack the password of just about any laptop must surely be a highly trustworthy individual, mustn't he? Either that or an extremely untrustworthy person, I thought.

When I showed him the black box and the strange amalgamation of connectors he nodded sagely and muttered a knowing "Aha."

Rather than say anything, I took the opportunity to look at him quizzically. It was the first time since he'd arrived that I'd had the chance, and I liked what I saw. I decided he was still quite cute, handsome even, and in a nicely more mature way than he had been when we had dated. I felt it was almost possible to detect the cogs of his mind whirring rapidly around as he examined the black box.

"These were quite popular once upon a time," he said.

I'd noticed this habit among technical people before. They tended to talk about any technical items that were more than five years old as if they were ancient Egyptian artefacts.

"It's approximately ten years old, which is why it has that old-fashioned connection on it. And I can see your guy has had to cobble something together to get it to connect to his laptop. It's very secure though. It came with software that automatically encrypted everything as it was written. Without knowing its unique key, I won't be able to get anything off that, I'm afraid," he said. "Have your guys been able to see anything?"

"They told me they couldn't see anything. Not even a list of files. Just a meaningless jumble of data is what I believe they said."

"I can possibly improve on that – can we connect it to my laptop?"

I probably violated several other security protocols by allowing this – but it was Friday evening so there was nobody around, and I was convinced that my strategy of getting hung for a sheep instead of a lamb was a good one.

He connected his laptop and spent a few minutes typing rapidly on his keyboard. I noticed how long his fingers were and how smoothly and flexibly he moved them. Luckily, he started to explain what he'd found before my mind ventured too far down a path wondering what else he might be able to do with those long lean supple fingers.

"As I said, it encrypts everything that is stored on it, using a unique 256-bit encryption key, which is saved in a small file. And your man could have stored that file almost anywhere. On his laptop or server, on a memory stick - anywhere. But the system has weaknesses as well as strengths. It would be considered way too slow and way too low in capacity to be used with files from modern systems, which tend to be much larger. And it uses the same key for every file it encrypts. So, once you can decode one file, you can decode them all. But all I can tell you is that there are exactly six files on the system. Five of them are small and one is a bit bigger. The biggest is about a Megabyte in size, the others much smaller. That's all I can say."

"Six? And there's no way you can tell me what type of files they are or anything about them?"

"Sorry, no."

"Great"

-

We went for a brief chat over a drink in the pub. I was pleased that Robin allowed me to pay for the round to say thanks. He was treating me as an equal. I hoped. I was also pleased to hear him order a pint – "Just one because I'm driving." I find it very hard to trust men who drink halves. And I made sure I understood what he'd told me about the black box.

"What you're saying is that if I can find out what one of the files is, then you'll be able to crack all of them, is that right?" I asked.

"It's a bit more complicated than that. If you knew exactly which one of the files you have the answer to, then I can crack them all. But if you only find one of them, unless you know which one it is on the box, it's no good. I don't see how you would know which one it was. You'd have to find multiple files. Then I should be able to unlock all of them."

That was the depressing part of our chat in the pub. The less depressing part was that as he was leaving, he gave me a very friendly hug and a little kiss on the cheek and said he hoped he would hear from me and that we could crack the case together.

I now had both professional and personal reasons for wanting to solve the case.

8. John Jackson's Blog (4)

Saturday, 14th October

One of the problems with writing any kind of diary is that once you've started it can be very difficult to stop. So, even though the police confiscated my laptop and server, they didn't take every computer. An advantage of being a bit of a magpie and never throwing anything away is that I can easily lay my hands on an alternative. They would have needed a small truck to contain all my techno rubbish – and an army of police to check all the old personal computers I have kept. I will probably end up donating them to a museum one day!

Anyway, I've found a serviceable old laptop so I can keep going. This post will be a reminder to me when I join the two blog files together to check for any formatting issues since I'm now using an old version of Word.

I'm not sure how I feel about the events of yesterday. I have been expecting a thorough questioning from the police, ever since I owned up to having spent some time with Megan (I had to delete the word 'Suzanne' and insert 'Megan' there – I find it hard to accept the change of name, but I guess that she will never again be known as Suzanne). And it was a thorough questioning they gave me.

I shouldn't have laughed when they told me about finding the gun. I know they didn't think it was funny, and it probably caused a bit of panic when they found it. It's just as well that the real one wasn't there. And thinking about that makes me worried again that it isn't there. But there's nothing I can do about that – it'll have to remain a mystery for the time being.

I'm sure that Megan had no interest in football. And I'm absolutely certain that she had no interest in the Bees. In all the time I've known her and all the many conversations we have had on all kinds of topics, she's never mentioned it. I must assume that the scarf was left there by another of her customers. I'm pretty sure it wasn't there when I saw her

– because I would have noticed and asked her about it. No, it had to belong to someone else. And that someone else must have visited her after I left. And when the police follow up on that lead, then I should no longer be the suspect that I am now.

The alternative is just too concerning to even contemplate. Could someone have left the scarf there deliberately to implicate me? I've never made a secret that I'm a big fan of the Bees – and I wear my colours to the game – and sometimes on other occasions too. In fact, in the last few months, I've noticed that I feel the cold a little more and so I've probably worn a black and yellow scarf quite a few times in public. So, if someone wanted to implicate me, that would be an obvious way. Thankfully I'm sure I haven't lost or misplaced any of my scarves, so there should be no trace of me on the one the police have.

I wouldn't even think about it, but for the fact that that gun disappeared from my cupboard. That bothers me a lot more. It is a sad fact of my life that nobody visits me. I think Stephen might have been here a couple of times when we felt the need to drink just a little longer than the restricted opening hours of the local pub. But I've never mentioned the gun to him. In fact, I've never mentioned it to anyone. The only place you could find out about it (unless the guy who sent it to me told you) is by reading this blog. I'm going to step up my data security. And then I'm going to think long and hard about asking Jim in Texas if he ever told anyone about my little purchase. It will only worry him to know it's gone missing, but if there's even a slim chance that he's told anyone I need to know.

And then there's that Denis guy. I'm cross that I deleted his emails because I want to find him and I now don't have anything to go on. I'll do some more online searches tonight; so far, I have found absolutely nothing about anyone with that name. And that worries me.

In my whole life, the only person I've ever had a row with was Billy Rodriguez. I've never heard from him since he left – and both Stephen and I are confident that his threats were pretty empty. But has he been waiting all this time? I know they say that revenge is a dish best served cold, but could he have planned all this? And waited this long? Maybe I should spend some time looking for him on the Internet too. Why not? I've got time, and I can't spend it on the book.

It was also a little worrying to me to see that policewoman as I was leaving. She's the one who kept visiting me in the hospital after the accident. I'm not sure why. I know that there was a police raid that took place on the night I went to the club. But they must have established that I was just an innocent customer. One who'd had a bit too much to drink – I've never been able to handle my drink, I'm afraid.

I thought they would follow up on that and find out about my tax arrangement using Tom's name. But that woman police detective didn't say anything when she came round last night, so perhaps they haven't found out yet. I'm sure they will, but I'll cross that bridge if and when I have to.

I should write down what happened that night – I know I haven't put it in the blog, and it is an important event since it's the reason for my early retirement, which in turn is the reason for the book, the blog, and everything else. So here goes.

The full story started about a month before the actual fall. I had been chosen to lead a programming team on an interesting project down in London. Apparently, a major British bookmaker was looking to develop its presence in the US market. Develop might be the wrong word, since the size of the existing online betting market in the USA, at least the legal part, was approximately zero. However there was some legislative process in play that would allow this activity to be legal in the USA for the first time, and the potential reward for the early entrants to the market was huge. Unusually, the legal process had moved more quickly than expected and this betting firm needed to move rapidly to present a workable (although not yet working) set of software to its US partners in record time.

They had assembled a small team of programmers and rented a set of apartments in London. We had to move into the apartments full-time, live in the allocated suites, and work in the communal workspace. The target was to have something complete in four weeks. We worked like …. (I can't use the either of words I was planning to use to complete that simile because they're bound to offend people). Let's just say we worked very hard.

I was there for two reasons. Firstly, as team leader – a role I was suited to as I was almost old enough to be the father of some of the team members – and secondly for my expertise in interface work. One of the key aspects of software for betting applications is that it often stitches together lots of bits of software to produce a fully working program.

I'll give you a simple example. A popular way of betting on football (proper football, not the American sort) is to try to predict the exact score of a game. There are about fifty different scores that can occur in any given game (0-0, 0-1, 2-1, etc.), and thus preparing odds for each of these possibilities for each game would be a massive task. So, what happens is that the Odds Setter just creates odds for the three possible results – home win, away win, and draw – and then the program refers to a table to extrapolate the odds to a set of odds for individual scores.

So, if the chance of a game finishing in a draw is, one in three, and the percentage of draws that are 2-2 is 25%, then the chance of a 2-2 draw for this game is one in twelve.

So, there are lots of interfaces needed between different sets of programming code (of different ages and sometimes written in different programming languages). Like the link between the input of the odds by the Odds Setter and the program that extrapolates all the individual results. And then there are all the usual interfaces to other resources – credit card verification, customer account records, company accounts, and many more etceteras.

We had to learn some of the unique aspects of American sports betting, and we had a guy seconded to us for this very purpose. He let us know that the range of possible scores is so vast that predicting exact game scores is not a bet that would be popular. The established practice is that the Odds Setter determines a 'spread'. If he believes that the Dallas Cowboys will beat the Miami Dolphins by nine points, then the spread for that game is nine. And all other odds are set from this baseline.

I cannot take American sports completely seriously though. Just looking at their team names makes you think you're not in the sporting world at all. It's as if the owners of the teams want to return to a children's play area populated by Warriors, Wizards, Titans, Vikings, Pirates, Cowboys, Chiefs, Braves, Buccaneers, Cavaliers, Kings, and Giants. Or else they aspire to own a menagerie populated by Timberwolves, Mavericks, Broncos, Bears, Hornets, Lions, Tigers, Jaguars, Panthers, Bears, and Cubs. Surrounded, no doubt by an aquarium full of Sharks, Dolphins, Marlins, and Rays. With an aviary of Eagles, Seahawks, Orioles, Penguins, and Cardinals (the bird, not the religious lot who elect the pope).

Anyway, we had to prepare a working system for the two main sports for betting interest – American Football and Basketball. As well as what

I would call normal bets like win/loss (apparently, they don't have draws in American sport) and margin of victory, we had to allow for a whole range of other bets. These bets were on things like the number of points scored by individual players (basketball), the number of yards gained or thrown (football), and subsets of this called running yards and passing yards. I learned a whole lot of jargon – understanding it well enough to complete the task, but much of it faded rapidly with time once the job was completed.

And it was completed on time. Which resulted in a very handsome completion bonus and a few bottles of champagne being opened (and drunk) on the last day. Most of the team lived in or close to London and determined that the party would move from the apartment block to a nearby bar and from there to a club. Citing my longer journey time – and the longer time that I have already spent on this planet – I made my excuses and left.

And now I realise that I'm doing that thing again. I'm being verbose because it delays the bit where I have to write down something I'd rather not reveal. I'll get to it as soon as I can.

I took a taxi to Saint Pancras Station and caught the next available train home. I had decided to invest the completion bonus as soon as possible in shares of the company for which we had been working since the news of their bid would be bound to break soon and the market would be sure to react positively. Unfortunately, I never got to make the expected financial killing because of the accident that happened later that evening.

When I arrived in Nottingham two hours later, I was not yet ready to call it a day, so I asked my taxi driver to take me to the club (the one close to the M1 motorway that I've mentioned previously) so that I could complete my night of celebration.

At this point, my memory of the events becomes a little hazy. I clearly remember arriving at the club, paying the driver, and giving him a generous tip. I went upstairs to the lounge which forms a waiting area. The club was busy, and I had to wait around for a while until a hostess was available. Then, when I was crossing the landing, I must have tripped and fell down the stairs.

The next thing I can clearly remember is waking up in a hospital bed. (I have vague memories of uniformed ambulance staff and possibly some police helping me into the ambulance and a blue-light journey, but not much more in between). Shortly after waking, a white-coated doctor informed me that I had broken my arm and a couple of ribs, dislocated my shoulder and cracked my skull.

I remained in the hospital for a few days. A pleasant middle-aged woman came to see me a couple of times. I had no idea who she was and assumed she was some version of a hospital visitor or general do-gooder until she told me she was a police officer who had been there when I had my fall. She asked me several times if I remembered what happened immediately before my fall and I had to admit that nothing was coming back to me. I even confessed that I expected the drinking I had done earlier in the day had played its part as I'm not much of a drinker. She seemed satisfied with my answers, and I can only presume that she was relieved that I wouldn't be suing the club or something.

But she was friendly enough and it was nice to have one visitor while I was trapped in my hospital bed. But of course, she'll have let them know that I used a fake name. I have no idea why I did that. I must have been a bit woozy from the drink and then the fall. I know I had a bang on the head, so if I have to justify it, then I'll blame that. My shoulder had been fixed by the time I woke up. My arm and my ribs healed – slowly and painfully, but they healed. Luckily it was my right arm, so it was not too much of a handicap.

Subsequent visits to the doctor, which now occur regularly, have confirmed that the headaches and the difficulty in concentrating that I now experience are the direct results of the blow to my head that night.

And I'm now worried that when that detective woman finds out about me using a fake name that night, it will become something else that she finds suspicious about me.

I don't think she likes me. That's sad because up until now I was quite a fan of hers. She seems so different from most women. Not just that she's confident and assertive. But she seems to be comfortable in her own skin. I like that. – but I think she's a very suspicious woman by nature. Upon reflection, I'm beginning to think that I don't find her that attractive, after all. A suspicious nature is not an appealing character trait.

The young bloke who's her sidekick seems alright, him being a Bees fan and everything, but I know I must watch what I say to her. I'll have to watch my p's and q's, that's for sure. No doubt they'll be back at me soon enough. I'm concerned that they'll be able to read my blog on the laptop. It's password-protected, but I'm guessing they'll eventually be able to crack that. I'm not sure what priority they'll give to a case involving the murder of a prostitute, but one day they are bound to read my blog and then I suppose there will be more questions.

And something else I've been meaning to do is look up the information about that killing down in Kent. Just imagine – I sold my car to a murderer. I can't even really remember what he looked like. The white hair and beard – and his height, that all stood out. But when it comes to describing what he looked like, I'd be no use at all. I'm just not good at that sort of stuff. Not very observant, I guess. I've even wondered if I'd recognise him if he dyed some colour into his hair and shaved his beard off. Probably not.

And I need to find out how long they're going to keep my stuff. I can carry on with my blog – in fact, I am carrying on with it, on the old laptop – slowly but surely. And I can store it under password protection on another server in the cloud. But I want to work some more on my book. I've got the essential details all written, but it needs some polish. I'm loathe to work on the online backup copy, so I'll just have to wait until this all blows over and I get my secure storage system returned.

9. What's On The Laptop?

Detective Inspector Linda Evans   Friday, October 13th

Once Robin had left, I knew that I had no choice but to get cracking on John's laptop. The little piece of paper in my back pocket with the passwords on it was metaphorically burning, and you know how painful a metaphorical burn on your bum can be. I had to go back into the office and start looking at the laptop.

Knowing I was likely to be there for a couple of hours, I found the most comfortable chair in the office – that is to say, one that was not actually uncomfortable to sit in. I opened the computer, logged on with the information on the piece of paper, and started to look around the contents of the PC.

The computer 'desktop' was empty – which was disappointing. You always hope that the person you're investigating is lazy and just leaves all their active files on the desktop (like I do). But John was better organised than this.

John's files had been grouped into folders, and these were listed alphabetically in two sections – business and personal. The list was almost identical to the one I had received from DC Priddis earlier, detailing the names of all the folders in John's filing cabinet.

There was a distinct lack of the kind of personal data I expected to find. No photos at all. But there were many files of music, grouped by artist. And a file which I thought was typical of the man – a spreadsheet containing details of over eight thousand tracks from more than four hundred albums. I guessed that if I looked around his office, I would find Bluetooth speakers that he used to listen to these tracks as he worked. I resisted the powerful human instinct of looking through his album collection – at least for the time being!

I was quickly drawn to a folder labelled Suzanne, remembering that this was Megan's working name. I wondered if it might have something important in it, but the file contained only the content of her website, which he'd admitted helping her to set up.

Methodically I opened each folder, scanned the list of files, and read one or two of them. But there was nothing out of the ordinary.

I'm not sure I knew what I was looking for, but it was just after midnight when I found it. A file named simply 'Blog'. A word file that was several hundred kilobytes in size. Once I opened it, I could see immediately that it was what I wanted, but I could see it was several thousand words in length, and as my eyes were already swimming with fatigue, I took the sensible decision to postpone the joy of reading it to the next day.

I was once again able to congratulate myself on what a good decision I had made buying a flat close to the office as I walked home and was able to settle into a good night's sleep without so much as a drop of alcoholic assistance. And I was back in front of my favourite laptop screen early the next morning, reading John's Blog.

The background information on John was interesting and would help us a little in our investigations. I had hoped to read more about Billy Gonzalez since he was the only person that we had found in John's background who had any potential as a suspect for framing John, but there was nothing.

It was the information about the elusive Denis, John's suspicions of someone planting evidence to implicate him, and most of all, the information about the 'waitress in a Greek restaurant in the Northwest of England' that concerned me most of all. Reading about his slightly spooky way of cyberstalking these women to put their details into a book about a deranged serial killer was a little unsettling, so I had to satisfy myself that there was a clear line drawn between fact and fiction – by myself, if not by my suspect.

I knew I had to immediately investigate this waitress and find out if by any chance there was any record of a victim fitting her description. I contacted CID in both Merseyside Police and Greater Manchester Police. The first call proved to be a waste of time, but the second made the hairs on the back of my neck stand on end.

The member of GMP who had drawn the short straw of minding the office on a Saturday afternoon told me that the waitress's name was Gerri Milburn and she had been murdered almost five months ago. I didn't ask for the full details – I knew that this information would be best sourced from the DCI that was handling the case and protocol dictated that the person asking for the information should be of equivalent rank. In other words, I had to call my boss on a Saturday afternoon and ask him to drag himself away from his family to work on the weekend. Not only that, I'd be asking him to get another DCI in another force to do the same. My chances of winning the Most Popular Employee of the Month award were looking slim.

I left a message on DCI Lancaster's phone and decided to treat myself to a pub lunch. This could be a long day. And I hadn't even dug into John's email system or social media history yet.

By the end of the afternoon, a disgruntled DCI Lancaster had spoken to an equally disgruntled DCI in GMP (don't we police love our acronyms) and we had enough details about Gerri to enable us to decide on our course of action. A motorbike would be on its way to us with a full copy of the case file as soon as the photocopier in Manchester had churned it out.

We now had three coincidences linking John to three separate murders. He was a customer of one victim, his car had been used by the killer of another victim, and now here were details of a third victim stored on his computer.

Us coppers don't like coincidences – two are bad enough, to have three was completely unacceptable. Conferring with DCI Lancaster, our immediate thought was that we would have to bring him in again. But our problem was the lack of any solid evidence. Even though we could theoretically link him to all three murders, we had nothing that could possibly be classified as a line of inquiry.

DCI Lancaster asked me if I thought that John was a flight risk and I told him that I was pretty sure that he wasn't. He knew we had him on our radar and had shown no signs of running. And there was no sign of any further evidence forthcoming on the Megan McCormick case.

So, our agreed tactic was to redouble our efforts to link John to either of the other two victims to give us some leverage. We had to hope that our input to GMP might give fresh impetus to the Gerri Milburn case and that progress might be made on the murder in Kent.

What I didn't say to DCI Lancaster was that I felt sure that there was vital information on the black box we had taken from John's house and that I would focus all my thoughts on cracking that part of the mystery. I certainly didn't tell him that I also wanted a reason to spend some more time with Robin – and that making progress on the black box contents was the only way I could think of making this happen.

DCI Lancaster returned to the bosom of his family, and I returned to the laptop. I re-read John's blog, hoping to find a clue, but nothing sprang to mind. And by the time I'd finished, it was dark outside, and my stomach was rumbling. Once home, I completed a healthy day's diet by heating a frozen pizza and washing it down with a couple of glasses of Chianti. I had just enough energy left to wash the dishes and return them to their proper places before collapsing into sleep.

The next day I read through the file on Gerri Milburn from GMP. It was not very large and there was almost nothing of assistance in it. It established the date of her death and the presence of a tall dark stranger in the restaurant where she worked some days immediately before. I noted that in common with Megan McCormick and the victim in Kent, no real leads were being followed. The crime seemed motiveless and there were no suspects.

Considering the three cases – in Kent, Nottingham, and Greater Manchester - there seemed nothing to connect the three victims – not even the method of killing.

I went for Sunday lunch in the Black Lion and tried to think.

The black box contained six files - according to Robin. One of them was larger and five were smaller. It was highly likely that the large file was John's book. If only I could identify what the other five were. The fact there were five of them was significant, I was sure. And the fact that John had felt it necessary to keep these files but had taken the trouble to hide them must surely be a clue.

He had been methodical in all his record-keeping. Everything that was on paper was in his filing system. What I had to find was something that he thought was important but was not there in his filing system. Neither in his paper system nor his digital files. Something of which there were five. Or something that had happened exactly five times.

Something was nagging at the back of my mind, and I hated it. Something had happened five times and we had heard it during our investigation. I called DS Holden – why should he be enjoying a weekend when I wasn't allowed to? Of course, he couldn't remember the significance of the number five either. I promised him a meal out – for him and his other half – if he could remember it and finished the phone call before polishing off a passable apple crumble.

To give DS Holden his due, he did take the time to call me later in the afternoon and even though he didn't realise it – he put himself in the frame for a free meal.

I had asked him to think about what might not have been in the filing system and during his Sunday evening call he had asked me if the files had had anything about John's brother in them.

I checked my memory and, more importantly, the list of files and contents that DC Priddis had recorded. There was both a paper file and a digital folder labelled 'Family'. The paper file held birth, death, and wedding certificates, for the immediate family members and a copy of his mother's will. The digital file had copies of correspondence relating to funeral arrangements and other matters relating to his mother's passing. There was nothing about Tom's employment and I turned my mind to this topic.

John was thorough in all his dealings. He had created a fictitious person to save himself tax. And he had made sure that this fictitious person had not done anything to fall foul of any of the authorities. Ralph Borshell had sent us the employment records.

John would have filed a tax return for Tom, wouldn't he? And Tom had been 'working' for five years. That was where I could remember hearing the number five. Yes – John would have kept Tom's tax returns, certainly. Just in case there had been some come-back from the authorities. But he would not have wanted these records to be too easily discovered since they were proof of his illegal activity.

Delight and frustration washed over me. I felt sure I was on to something, but there was nothing I could do about it immediately. I would have to wait until Monday when there was a possibility of contacting the tax authorities. I felt sure they would have sent a PDF of the tax return each year – and I was confident that this would be the document that John would have scanned and filed.

I called the Inland Revenue first thing on Monday morning. (Yes, I know they're now called HMRC, but they'll always be Inland Revenue in my mind) and was connected to a police liaison officer. I explained the situation and he confirmed that Tom Jędrzejczyk had indeed submitted tax returns for the previous five years and a pdf file had been emailed to the gentleman each year.

When I asked for a copy of these files, I was met with the standard set of security gobbledegook that HMRC's liaison officers must specialise in. He had to consider Mr Jędrzejczyk's right to privacy.

I respectfully prompted him with the information that Mr Jędrzejczyk had been dead for over forty years, and so was less than likely to be concerned about the safety of his personal information. I stopped short of asking why the tax office did not check that Tom had died so long before submitting his first tax return. After all, good old Frederick Forsyth exposed this method of obtaining a false identity in his novel in the 1970s. I decided this was not only unwise and unlikely to increase my chance of receiving cooperation, but also considered the accuracy of police records. Let he who is without sin cast the first stone and all that. Weren't many people on our records (and possibly in our prisons) using false names or identities? And based on recent events some members of our workforce probably were too!

HMRC promised that the files would be emailed to me later that morning.

While waiting I brought DS Holden up to date with the new information from John's blog. His instinct, honed after working with me for a couple of years, once again proved faultless. He didn't even ask me how I had cracked John's laptop. Finding out about the online writing course that John had attended, and the spectral Denis Fittaley were two actions that were added to the top of his to-do list. Although Denis did not have any obvious reasons to have a grudge against John – he had been given details about Gerri Milburn, and so we needed to find out who and where he was.

I thanked him for his inspired guess as to the significance of the number five and let him know that it might lead to getting more information about John. And the likelihood of me treating him and his other half to a meal out was increasing by the hour.

I had to back my hunch. If the five files from the tax office were the five small files on John's security box, I had to ask Robin to come back to attempt to decipher them. So, I left a message on his voicemail. Each time I called I was getting more accustomed to the clicks and whirrs as my message was recorded.

I also discussed possible next steps with DCI Lancaster. I informed him of what I thought were the crucial pieces of evidence I had gleaned from John's blog (whilst managing to avoid revealing how I had managed to get into it when our best IT brains had failed).

I believed that the key pieces of information were the gun that had been (allegedly) stolen from John's house with other items. Especially since the details would appear to match the type of gun used in the Kent murder. Then there was the connection between John and the waitress in Salford. And finally, the mysterious Denis – with whom John appeared to have shared information.

My boss wondered why I had not yet brought John in for further questioning. I told him that I had considered this as the obvious next step, but we were still lacking any serious evidence of a motive in the three murders, and any definite connection between John and the Kent murder. While I maintained a high level of suspicion, I also believed that if we brought him in now, he was highly likely to 'lawyer up' and, which would be worse, to completely clam up.

I wanted to question him again, of course – and to let him know that we had managed to read the content of his laptop (since he would work this out anyway as soon as I questioned him about the things I wanted to ask him). But I thought I was likely to get more out of him at this stage by keeping a softly softly approach – questioning him in the relaxed environment of his own home.

Having asked me once again if I was worried about John doing a runner – and being reassured in my confidence that he wouldn't – I was given the OK to delay bringing him in for the time being.

With DS Holden tied up with his search for writing courses and Fittaleys, I decided to go unaccompanied again to question John. If it was possible to build any rapport with the man (and I had my doubts as to whether that was possible), then I was probably the most likely one to do so.

He welcomed me politely into his house and reassured me that he would have no problems giving some more information if it could help catch Megan's killer. While John disappeared to the kitchen to make coffee, I looked around his living room and was once again struck by how neat, but somehow empty it felt. It was difficult to believe that someone had lived almost their whole life in this house, but yet made so little impression on it.

It was easy to see which was 'his' chair – slightly more worn and with the best angle to view the large TV, so that was where I sat. John passed me a mug and sat on the small sofa. The window was protected by a smart set of vertical blinds, which were only partially open, darkening the whole room.

"I was out a bit late last night, so sorry if I'm not at my best," he began.

His voice sounded a little hoarse and his eyes were supported by two large dark circles. I recalled him writing in his blog that he did not often drink much. 'Just as well, if that's the effect it has on you,' I thought - but said nothing.

"You believe that some property was stolen from this house while you were in hospital, I understand," I began. "Could you give me some more information about this?"

John's expression could have been a suppressed smile, a grimace, or almost anything – it was hard to tell under the dark shadows of the room and his stubble.

"I lost a set of sovereigns if that's what you're referring to," he replied.

"But that was not all you lost, was it?" I continued.

"I chose not to report the theft. I didn't believe it was in my best interests to do so."

He was obviously fencing. I couldn't ask him about the loss of an item that I would have difficulty proving had ever been in the house, and he knew that.

"Can you tell me anything about the sovereigns you lost?" was my next gambit. I thought it highly unlikely that he would tell me anything of any value since he knew that if we ever did find them, we would be one step closer to finding the other item that was stolen – and that was the one he didn't want us to find.

"Not much to tell you, I'm afraid. There were half a dozen of them. I bought them from a customer a few years ago because I thought they'd make a good investment."

"Any idea what year they were?" I continued.

"I only looked at them once – I think they were all very early twentieth century. That's about all I remember."

"Well, thanks for that. We'll see what we can do. Can you remember anything else about any other items that were stolen at the same time?"

"I think I'd prefer not to answer that."

Changing tack, I asked him about his brother. "John, we have evidence that you filed tax returns in the name of Tom Jędrzejczyk for several years. You are aware that this is against the law."

"I'm going to have to defer answering that question until I have legal representation," he replied.

"John, you know that I'm investigating a murder. I'm not going to spend any of my team's time on a tax avoidance issue for now – but we will return to it, you can be sure." I waited for him to say something, but he didn't.

"You seem to me like someone who knows a bit about the law, John. You've answered our questions when it suited you, and you've exercised your right not to answer those that you choose not to. And you have refused to give us a sample for DNA identity purposes, as you also have every right to. But let me ask you this – are you aware that the offence of perverting the cause of justice carries the possibility of a sentence of life imprisonment? Now maybe you could think again about any other item that might have gone missing at the same time as the sovereigns."

John thought for a moment before replying.

"I guess you've read my blog," he paused, waiting for me to acknowledge this, but when he received no response he continued, choosing his words with obvious great care, "So you know that the replica gun you took away was, as close as I could tell, identical to another, which is now missing."

This was as good as I was going to get, so I changed direction again.

"When we searched your house, we found a piece of paper on your desk with the name Denis Fittaley written on it. What can you tell us about this man, and why you kept a note of his name?"

"I suspected he might have been trying to steal some of the stuff I'd written, so I cut off all correspondence with him – and I was trying to find out anything I could about him."

"And did you find anything?"

"As you saw, there was nothing else written on the paper. I couldn't find a thing about him."

"And what can you tell me about Gerri Millburn?" I asked, hoping to catch him off guard.

"Gerri Millburn? Not sure I know anyone by that name…."

"She was a waitress in a Greek Restaurant near Manchester."

"Oh, Gerri. I'm sorry – I didn't know her last name. She was one of the women whose details I got from the internet to include in my book," John paused and then, seeming to realise something, "You said she *was* a waitress…"

"Yes, she was murdered." I watched for a reaction and just about got one. It seemed a little delayed, but I put that down to his hungover state.

"Did you ever visit the restaurant?"

"I got her details from the Internet – she was always posting stuff, so it fitted in well with the story in my book. Then Denis said I would need more detail about her to describe her to my readers, so I visited the restaurant where she worked to have a look at her. That's all." Then, after a brief pause, "Murdered? Shit"

"John you've mentioned this book you're writing a few times now, but we have not been able to find any sign of it anywhere. Why is that?"

"If you've read my blog, you'll know I was worried that the people I signed up with for the writing course were operating some kind of a con. So, I put the files where nobody could access them."

"And would you care to share the book with us? It might prove of assistance in our inquiry."

"I'll have to get some advice on that. You understand, don't you?" he asked in what was probably the worst attempt to gain my sympathy that I've ever had the misfortune to witness.

"John, I understand your concern about the security of your book. But I believe you also understand refusing to disclose information that could assist our inquiry might result in a charge of perverting the course of justice. Shall we just leave it there?"

It seemed that the interview had reached a natural conclusion, so I thanked him for the coffee as he showed me out.

"I hope your hangover improves," I said.

Another slight hesitation preceded him saying "Oh, yes, thanks," and closing the door.

Driving back to the station I asked myself some questions – metaphorically, that is. I haven't quite reached the stage of openly talking to myself yet – but if this inquiry goes on much longer, it's probably on the cards.

Had I got any new information from the interview? Other than the fact that he couldn't trace Denis despite his obvious IT skills – which didn't bode well for our search – and confirmation of the type of gun that had gone missing, I was not much further forward.

I've never totally bought into the theory of 'female intuition'. In my opinion, it's just that women tend to be more observant than men are. But whatever dose of this mystical ability that I do have is leading me more and more to believe that there's something not right about John.

Hopefully, I'll be confirming this soon – by getting access to John's book. With the assistance of Robin when he gets around to returning my call.

10. Secret Sources

Detective Inspector Linda Evans Tuesday, October 17th

I had no reason to expect that Robin would return my call within twenty-four hours. Nonetheless, I was very disappointed when he didn't. Thankfully there was still plenty to keep me busy. DS Holden had discovered the company that provided John's online writing course. They confirmed that he had dropped out after a couple of sessions and had made no attempt to rejoin the same course when it was run again (which he was fully entitled to do). The company was a bona fide organisation with plenty of positive references from past pupils, which made John's suspicions seem completely groundless.

They had no record of a Denis Fittaley associated with their company in any way neither as an employee or contractor nor as a participant in this or any other course. They admitted that it might be possible for someone to hack into their system in some way and gain attendance for free – but they had never known it to happen. And as a provider of online material whose income depended on data security, they took thorough precautions to prevent unauthorised access. It was always possible that someone had breached this security, but it was very unlikely. They promised to contact us if they had any suspicions of any such activity in the future.

Which left us nowhere to go on that line of inquiry.

I was in daily contact with my opposite numbers in both Kent and Greater Manchester Police forces – exchanging routine information on the progress of inquiries. But the amount of progress being made by the combined efforts of our three forces could accurately be described as the square root of bugger all.

Hence, I placed a second call to Robin on Wednesday evening, leaving a polite but obvious reminder, "Not sure if you got my earlier message, so I'm leaving another. Hope you can find five minutes to call me back – there's some news to share with you. Thanks."

When he eventually called me back on Friday morning, I needed a metaphorical bandage to repair the wounds caused by biting my tongue. He apologised – profusely and totally unnecessarily. He was just finishing a short holiday – which he had told me about and I had completely forgotten he was taking. He was in Scotland doing something archaeological at a remote location and he'd had to climb halfway up a mountain to get a signal. (I'm sure it was more of a molehill than a mountain but didn't make the comment).

All of which meant that he wouldn't be back home until Friday night. But (whether from guilt at delaying the return call, or in joyful anticipation of seeing me again, I don't know) he promised to drive up to Nottingham first thing on Saturday. I promised to buy him a sandwich for lunch – and passed on the opportunity to crack a joke about something a foot long.

-

He either left home quite early or drove too fast – from what little I knew about him I strongly suspected the former – and arrived at Nottingham Police Station by mid-morning. We had only had the brief windswept phone call, so I had quite a bit to update him on. However, for now, I concentrated on the computer files.

"I'm pretty sure that the five files are five PDFs of tax returns", I told him. "John needed to keep them – just in case there was ever any comeback from the authorities – but he would have wanted to hide them too. And we have been unable to find them anywhere else in his paper or digital files, so there's every chance that this is them."

"Let's hope so", he replied. Not the most positive comment I'd ever heard, but then I had to remember that he had just left a flat full of a week's dirty washing and driven a couple of hundred miles – so a smidgeon of grumpiness was forgivable.

I passed him the memory stick containing the files, and he opened John's laptop.

Thankfully Robin possessed a quality not seen in many men (in my experience). He could multi-task, and so was able to explain things to me as he simultaneously set his fingers whirring across the keyboard.

"The secret is to find the offset," was how he started his explanation as he glanced in my direction. He correctly guessed that I was not entirely on the same page as him.

"It's like those code-breaker devices we used to have as kids. You know, the ones you make from two circular pieces of card clipped together.

I had to work on the look I was about to give him when he next raised his gaze from the screen. The look had to convey a complex message – one which said "No, I didn't make codebreaker devices out of two circular bits of card when I was a kid – and I am not the oddly behaved one in this conversation."

I must have managed to convey my message successfully to some extent, because, having received the look, he started again. "When I was a kid, I had some friends, well, one in particular, who shared my fascination with codes and codebreaking. So, we made these devices… "

"Don't tell me – you made them out of two circular bits of card…" I joined in with the chorus and got a small smile from him.

"Yes. One piece of card had the letters of the alphabet and a few other symbols written around the edge, and the other had two holes punched on its edge to line up with the letters on the first disc. One of the holes had a blue line around it so whatever was in the blue window was encoded to whatever showed through the other hole. Later, we moved on to having multiple holes – each with a different colour around its edge and we would send messages – code red or code green. Get it?"

I was on the same page as him. Not quite as enthralled as I maybe should have been, so I just said, "Got it."

"Well, the difference between the hole that has the message and the hole that shows the code could be called the offset." Of course, it's a lot more complicated than the code wheels – but the principle is the same. What I've got to do is compare one of your files with all five of the small files on the black box and work out what the offset is in each case. Then I have to do the same for a second one of the files on your stick. Hopefully, when I compare the two sets of offsets, one pair will be identical. If that happens, then we can assign that offset to all the files on the black box and decode them."

Quite a speech when you consider he'd appeared to hit half a million keystrokes with complete accuracy whilst giving it. I'd even understood it, I think. Enough to know that he had said "Hopefully … one will be identical". I didn't dare ask what our next step would be if none were identical.

I was also able to accurately assess the contribution I was likely to make to this process.

"Can I get you anything to eat or drink?" I asked.

"Oh yes, he sighed. I didn't have anything in the flat for breakfast so a Greggs and a large orange juice would be wonderful."

I passed up a second opportunity to do the foot-long gag and, having received detailed specifications for his sandwich that confirmed that this was not Robin's first Gregg-sponsored rodeo, went to get brunch for both of us.

When I returned, Robin was scrolling through something on his phone while casting an occasional eye over the characters cascading down the screen of John's laptop.

"I have to set it to go through one file at a time, unfortunately – one down, lots more to go…"

I passed him his brunch and he set about it with a terrific impression of someone just leaving a hunger strike.

The laptop continued to show lines of random text, white characters on a black background, scrolling down the screen. I was not sure whether watching this, or Robin devouring his sandwich was the more interesting. Then the computer stopped. Robin put down his sandwich, typed a couple of lines on the keyboard, and updated me.

"Two down, still lots to go."

And that's how we progressed for the next couple of hours. Both of us using our phones to update email, read social media, and fill time. We both kept half an eye on the laptop screen and whenever it stopped spewing text, Robin would give it a new line of instruction, and off it would go.

After the fifth, he turned to me and said "If you are praying or invoking any other form of external influence, now's the time to start. I've run the first of your files against the five on the disk and got five different offsets. Now I've started running the second of your files. We've got to hope that it produces an identical match to one of those we've already got. Then I can run that offset against the bigger file and you'll have what you want."

I had to ask. "What if it doesn't produce a match from any of the five?"

"Well, I will run all five of your files through, just in case. But based on what you've told me, I would think there's very little chance that we will get anything useful."

"Great, thanks," was all I could think of as a reply.

There is some unwritten but logical law that when you are looking for something it is always in the last place you look. (It's totally logical because once you've found what you're looking for, you don't look anywhere else.) By an extension to that law, the match that Robin was seeking, and for which I was hoping (and, I must admit it, praying), happened on the fifth run-through of the second file.

"There it is," he said with a calmness that I couldn't match and that I was sure he was faking.

He entered a couple more lines of code and sat back. More data crawled across the screen, slower than before but no more understandable.

"What's happening now?" I asked, barely able to contain my frustration.

"It's decoding the biggest document and writing the result onto your memory stick," he replied. It'll take longer than the previous ones." He looked at his watch and did a quick piece of mental arithmetic. "About twenty minutes, I'd guess.

I had to go and get another cup of coffee and visit the ladies' room just to fill the time. Robin had sensibly declined my offer of a cup of police coffee and forced me to further boost the profits of the local coffee shop.

He was standing, watching the screen when I returned. I put my latte on the desk next to his black Americano with an extra shot and then went to stand next to him.

A few minutes later, the scrolling stopped, and Robin leaned forward and pressed a few more keys.

"Would you like to press the final key?" he asked. I looked at him carefully to check that I was not being humoured but could detect no telltale signs.

"Just hit the enter key and you'll be able to say you did the final decode," he continued.

The screen display returned to what I would describe as normality, a Windows interface showing a list of files, one of which was titled "TheBook.pdf".

"Go ahead," Robin said – indicating the mouse on the mousepad next to the laptop. I clicked and the screen displayed a PDF document – the title page of a book, in large print.

"The Book" by John Jackson.

"You did it!" I said, louder than I'd planned, and put my arms around Robin, to give him what I had intended (I think) to be a congratulatory hug. But it turned into something more. Something much more.

I'm not the sort of person who claims to hold any records – the biggest long jump in high school or the highest set of scores on a police intake course, that sort of thing. But I believe I might hold the record for the longest and most passionate kiss to ever take place in the interview room of Nottingham Police Station. (Actually, I'm the joint holder of the record, as I'm sure you've worked out.)

If anyone lays claim to beating our record, I'd like to see it. On second thoughts, considering that it's a police interview room, and knowing the usual clientele it serves, if someone has beaten our record, I actually do not want to see it!

These were some of the crazy thoughts going through my mind as a natural reaction to displace the much more serious thoughts I really should start thinking.

"So now what do we do?" Robin said as we separated. I was pleased to see he appeared as surprised and confused as I felt.

I took a moment to answer, realising we were holding hands as we faced each other.

As I maintained silence for a few more seconds, Robin obviously felt the need to fill the space.

"I guess you'll want to have a look at this document, won't you?" he said, with something of an air of disappointment.

I looked at the memory stick, protruding from the laptop and the five words on the screen. The possible solution to several crimes was within my reach. Playing for a few seconds I looked at my watch and realised we had moved from Saturday afternoon to evening. There was nothing that would change if there were a few hours of delay.

"I reckon I've got an issue with a computer file that's been around for a few weeks", I said, pausing and pointing at the computer screen, "and I've got another issue with a computer expert that's been around for a few years," I continued, looking up into his eyes. "And I reckon it's the second one of these that I would like to tackle first."

I believe we now hold both gold and silver medal positions in the contest for the longest kiss in interview room A. Having completed it, I pulled the memory stick out and put it in my pocket. Robin switched off the computer.

"Would you like to see where I live? It's only five minutes' walk from here." I asked.

"I'd love to."

Once again, I congratulated myself on what a good decision it had been to live close to the office and reckoned that this was going to be one of the more enjoyable journeys between the two places, certainly the one that was filled with the most anticipation.

We talked as we walked back to my place, but I cannot for the life of me remember what either of us said. And there was very little talk in the hour or two after we got there. Any concerns I might have had that Robin's only passions concerned cryptography or archaeology were thoroughly dispensed with. He was thorough in all that he did.

-

It was dark when I woke, and there was very little sign of life from my bedmate. I got up, put on my dressing gown, and retrieved the memory stick from the pocket of my jeans (when I found where they had been discarded somewhere between the front door and the bedroom). I filled a glass of water from the tap, gulped it down, refilled it, and took it through to the lounge where my laptop was waiting for me on the coffee table. I switched it on, plugged in the memory stick, and double clicked on the file. The PDF reader told me it was page number 1 of 119, which I thought was way too low a number for the file to be a full book. I began to read.

"The Book"
by
John Jackson

1   Diagnosis and Decision
2   Nelly
3   Gerri
4   Emily
5   Carol
6   Macie
7   Megan
8   Detection and Reward
9   A Major Puzzle
10 Confession

.1 - DIAGNOSIS AND DECISION

FRIDAY, 28TH APRIL

The diagnosis was brutal. Brutal and unexpected. What should have been a routine blood test and a routine scan following up on an earlier injury, turned out to be life-changing – and not in a good way.

He had received a request to attend an appointment with a consultant whose name he did not recognise from the list of medical people he had already seen. And the letter encouraged him to bring someone with him if he wished.

Until recently, Bruno's experience with the whole world of professional medicine was close to zero – he had been healthy and accident-free for his whole life. So, he neither received nor decoded any of the warning signals present in his letter and was totally unprepared for the dreadful news that he was about to receive.

When the specialist saw that his patient was unaccompanied, he made a point of saying that he had hoped Bruno would bring his partner or a close friend with him, and Bruno replied that sadly he currently didn't have a partner and would think it really odd to bring a friend with him to a doctor's appointment. So, he spoke very carefully and told Bruno that he had important news, and sometimes it was useful to have someone with you to make sure that all the news was taken in.

Bruno's background and lifetime experience made him automatically consider technological solutions to a problem and so he asked if he might record the session, which the consultant readily agreed to.

He took out his smart phone, opened the Voice Memos app, and clicked the red Record button.

It was a good job that he did record the meeting. When you receive news that you have a life-limiting disease – especially when that news comes completely out of the blue, your ability to remember and process information becomes severely limited. So, Bruno replayed the recording a couple of times later that day as he tried to take in the full weight of what he had been told. Even then, he only really grasped some of the details. But enough for him to get the full impact and realise that he had to make plans. But hearing the message twice was enough – he decided that whatever the detail was that he missed, he would do without. Any more replays would start to be maudlin.

What he understood from the consultant's explanation was that cancer normally first presents itself as an attack on one part of a patient's body: the lungs, the prostate, the bowel, or whatever. The medical profession assists a patient in fighting off this cancer using drugs and/or radiotherapy, monitoring its success through frequent check-ups after the treatment is completed.

Sometimes, at the end of a course of treatment, the cancer is cured, and no trace is found in the patient. On other occasions the cancer is not removed or re-appears in the same part of the body and further treatment takes place. Alternatively, the cancer spreads and re-appears in a different part of the patient's body, and sometimes reappears in multiple parts of the body. When the cancer is present in multiple parts of the body, as it had presented itself in John's case, it was highly unlikely that anything could be done to stop it. That was how Bruno understood what he had recorded.

In a very small number of cases, the cancer makes its first appearance in multiple parts of the body. And in these cases, there is probably nothing that can be done to defeat it. Thankfully, such cases are extremely rare, and often when this happens to a patient, investigation shows that this is a genetic trait.

This was, in simplistic terms, what had happened as far as Bruno was able to understand. Based on the information that he had provided about his mother, the consultant thought that it was highly likely that this had been what had happened to her, and the genetic trait had been passed to Bruno from his mother.

The only good news was that Bruno did not have any siblings whom he might need to alert to the problem, and he had not passed this defective gene on to any children. This latter fact helped prevent Bruno from doing what everyone does to some degree or other, spending time and energy becoming depressed about the eternal question – Why Me? He could take consolation in the fact that he had neither inflicted this curse on any other human being – and his early demise would not cause emotional or financial hardship on anyone else. It was scant consolation.

He asked for a prognosis, and this was one of the few moments of the meeting that he took in completely. He was told that he had been diagnosed very much sooner than most patients. Before even any symptoms had shown, and only because of the routine tests he had been undergoing after his accident. Much more common was that the diagnosis would be made much later in the progression of the disease when the patient was noticing one or more symptoms.

The upshot was that he had still got about six months to live. It was highly likely that he would not notice any deterioration in his health for at least four months, but then deterioration would be rapid.

Replaying the recording on his phone, Bruno came to terms with it over the next few days and slowly turned his mind to how he would spend the four or five months he effectively had left.

He was financially secure, and, within reason, could do whatever he wanted. He certainly would not waste any of his time working, and so would quit his job immediately. He thought about the classic 'bucket list'. He had never prepared one, and strangely now could not come up with many ideas to place on it. There were a few places he had seen in his life that he might like to see again – and some that he hadn't, which might warrant a visit. But he didn't want to make this too long a list – as it might become more depressing to continually be thinking "How beautiful this place is – and how sad it is that I can never see it again."

His thoughts turned to whether there was anything he could do to leave a legacy. And this was when his fascination – some might say obsession – with puzzles began to surface. His mind turned to the idea of buried treasure.

Bruno had always been interested in puzzles, even as a child. His first real involvement with a major puzzle came in 1979. He had seen a TV programme about a man named Kit Williams who had buried a piece of treasure – a jewelled hare – and then published a book called Masquerade which was full of clues to tell the reader how to find it. Bruno had nagged his parents to buy him the book for his birthday and they had eventually conceded. Even though the book had been a big disappointment to Bruno – the clues were far too difficult even for a very bright ten-year-old to decipher - it was the start of a fascination for Bruno that lasted his whole life.

He began by borrowing books from the library on puzzles and riddles. He found books in boot sales and second-hand bookshops and devoured their contents. And then, as he began his career in computing and the internet spread, he joined online groups that shared puzzles. First, it was via online chatrooms and message boards before the World Wide Web opened it up.

It had become an obsession and the online puzzle-solving community was the place where he had more friends than anywhere else. Even though some might dismiss online friends as not being real, they were the people with whom Bruno had held many a conversation online over the years. There were new puzzles posted by group members from time to time, as well as frequent notices when well-known puzzles reappeared. If a TV program or magazine article brought up a well-known puzzle from the past, such as the Voynich Manuscript, (an illustrated codex hand-written in a unique writing system from the fifteenth century that elicited interest from time to time), then activity would resume on the site. Or when a well-known puzzle featured in the media with a wrong answer, the online community would join in a mocking chorus.

Probably the most well-known was the story of the man who looked at a picture on the wall and recited "Brothers and sisters have I none, but that man's father is my father's son". From time to time, this would reappear and the wrong answer, "It's a picture of himself" would be given as the correct one. "Here we go again" would be the theme for the online puzzle community as one of them told the group that he had either simply corrected the error or had a long discussion with the perpetrators before getting it put right. (The correct answer could be easily discovered by realising that for a person with no brothers the phrase 'my father's son' was synonymous with 'me'. Substituting this in the original puzzle meant that he had actually said "That man's father is me' and so the correct answer – it is a picture of his son – would be produced.

The group had seen an uptick in membership activity a few years previously when one of the most famous (and difficult) puzzles of modern times was published in book form.

The Book was "Cain's Jawbone" and the author's name was listed as Torquemada. The title referred to the bible's reference to the world's first known murder weapon and its author was probably the most famous crossword setter of all time. The book was billed as the world's most fiendishly difficult literary puzzle, a claim that was suitably as extreme as the puzzle. The book comprised one hundred pages in random order, which had first to be sorted into the correct sequence to solve six murders. There was only a paltry £250 prize offered, but the complexity of the puzzle set some of the best puzzlers to work and the dialogue on the website was intense. Years later there would be speculation within the group as to whether this story of six murders inspired Bruno in any way.

Bruno's longevity within the group, his experience, intellect, and his lack of significant other interests led to him being the moderator of the group and something of a celebrity within it.

He thought more and more about how he could leave a final puzzle for the group to solve. Hopefully, one that would last longer than him and preserve his place in posterity. He realised he could leave a significant prize – even if he burned up his bank balance between now and his death. His home was mortgage-free and worth a six-figure sum. Adding this to his private pension meant that his estate would be worth at least £250,000. Surely a prize of over a quarter of a million pounds would get some traction.

He decided that the puzzle would not be publicised until he was gone – he didn't want to spend any of his precious time dealing with questions beforehand. But what puzzle could he set that would be interesting enough – even newsworthy enough? Gradually an idea began to form. The puzzle would need to be straightforward so that its design could be understood. But it also would need to have a complexity that challenged potential solvers. And it needed to be important.

His mind turned to those puzzles that lasted years and years. There were several that had been deliberately staged (like Kit Williams and his jewelled hare). None lasted too long because they were either too easy and solved too quickly or too difficult and then needed helpful hints to come from the originator. He would not be able to do this. And he didn't want the trouble of pre-programming hints to be released after a fixed period of time if a solution had not been found in the meantime. He knew how to do it - he just couldn't be bothered.

More and more his thoughts drifted to one long-lasting puzzle that was real but had not been deliberately staged. The identity of Jack the Ripper. And gradually an idea formed. What if the puzzle was related to actual deaths? Maybe his conscience should have closed off this avenue much earlier, but it didn't. The more he thought about it, possibly in the light of his recently received huge slice of bad luck, the more he forgot about some of the checks and balances of good and evil that should have ruled out this idea immediately.

His thoughts focussed increasingly on how the puzzle could be set, rather than whether it should be done. If the puzzle was essentially a simple one – but the pieces in the game were real human victims it would surely be compelling, wouldn't it?

He thought of a simple word puzzle that might link together multiple names. He might have been put off by the difficulties of finding victims who fitted a pre-set pattern, but he was a geek. The internet and the vast quantity of information available on various forms of social media would provide him with all the details of as many victims as he could ever need. And if he spread the victims across the country he would not be easily traced by the police. Several different police forces would be involved and until his puzzle was announced there would be very little chance of them being connected.

He would set up an announcement of the puzzle to take place on the last day of the calendar month. He would postpone this every month while he was still alive so that when he died the announcement would come out within thirty days. Then all he needed to do was to make an arrangement that would provide the puzzle winner with a proof document that could be presented to his solicitor to claim the inheritance.

And so, the idea coalesced in its horrible way. He would use a well-known puzzle framework. To complete it he would need to find six different girls' names that would fit the pattern. Then he would find women, one with each of the chosen names, and murder them. And having crossed the huge moral gulf with such ease, he now focussed solely on the practicalities of making it happen.

He would leave a clue at each murder so that it was possible for the crimes to be linked. And he would use different methods so that the linking would not be too easy. The solution to the puzzle and the solution to the crimes would be two different issues. Maybe someone would do both – but if they only linked all the crimes to him, they would not get to claim the prize. And maybe the prize could be worth much more than just the value of the house he was leaving. Whoever solved the puzzle would be able to write a book about it. And Kit Williams' original Masquerade book sold hundreds of thousands of copies. So, he could realistically state that solving his puzzle could be worth well over a quarter of a million. That would get some attention, wouldn't it?

Methods? He would need three or four different methods. He could use some methods a couple of times, even if this ran the risk of the murders being connected by the investigating police. But there would need to be at least three different methods to make it more difficult to trace all six.

He was confident that his strength would enable him to use strangulation. And maybe a heavy implement, wielded with his strength would be another way of quickly accomplishing his objective on other occasions. He briefly considered poisoning – he knew that there were powerful poisons, such as ricin, that could theoretically be homemade from recipes readily available on the internet but rejected that as it might be both time-consuming and would always carry an element of hit-and-miss about it when it came to administering the dose.

He rejected the thought of using drowning – he had read that it was a particularly unpleasant way to die, and he had no intention of inflicting unnecessary suffering on anyone. He would investigate a theory he had long held about how easy it would be to get hold of a firearm as it might be necessary to have a method that could be executed when he could not get close enough to his target to use other methods. A firearm, strangulation, and blunt force trauma - that should be enough.

He had already decided that the internet would be his way of finding his victims, which might well necessitate some contact to be made. So, he set up two false accounts – one male and one female – using methods of connectivity he had used in his work. These two personae would be almost impossible to trace back to him.

Their names came from an employee list from one of his customers that he found in his filing cabinet. Their Twitter handles came from his fertile imagination.

There was Richard Horsenell, who he decided worked in the financial sector and was located somewhere in the West of England – the exact location would only need to be specified if it helped his cause later. He would go by the handle of 'Inn Cider Trader'. And then there would be a woman working and living in London. She was Harriet Hale. Her handle would be 'So Shall Work Her' – which might lead people to conclude what she did for a living. At present, these were just outlines. Their detail would be filled in as events unfolded.

What would be the clues that he would leave at the crime scenes? This came to him intertwined with the idea of his alias.

He had been watching a nature programme on TV a few nights previously. Apparently, there were incidences of poisonous animals throughout the world that were all coloured black and yellow. It was as if nature had adopted this colour combination as a universal danger sign. There were snakes, lizards, other reptiles, insects, and arachnids that were completely unrelated and separated by thousands of miles and huge oceans. All were poisonous and all coloured black and yellow. And even more fascinating were some of the 'copycats'. Animals that were innocuous but had adopted the same colours to fool other animals into thinking they were dangerous.

He decided that he would be 'The Stinger' and would leave something black and yellow at every crime scene. Hopefully, the police would pick up on this, and his name – and his fame - would spread. If not, maybe some amateur sleuth would uncover it in his search for the reward that would be announced on the internet when he had finished, and he would become posthumously famous.

Having laboured for so long over the decision, once it was made, Bruno found it easy to start planning its implementation.

He needed to find six girls' first names that would fit the pattern and form the answer to his puzzle. The pattern would then create the key that would unlock the reward.

He downloaded a list of the top one thousand girls' names from the internet. The puzzle needed the names to be five letters long, so he quickly pared the list to two hundred and twenty-eight names of this length. It took him half an hour to write a simple program to find six names that could be combined to fit the pattern. He felt sure that there would be multiple possibilities, but, having run the program, he discovered that it produced almost a hundred possible answers – but many would be totally unsuitable.

There were less than six months to find these women and deal with them, so the task needed to be achievable. The first set of six names contained Ettie, Elana, and Elara – these names were, he believed, relatively unusual and it would take him far too long to find suitable subjects from that list. The next set included Ffion, Amely, Raine, and Honey. Again, completely impractical.

He returned to the list of names and removed the ones he thought were likely to prove too difficult to find. There may well be plenty of babies and small children with some of these exotic names, but he would need to find adult women. Maybe one unusual name in the list would be OK, but no more.

Re-running his program against the reduced list of a hundred and twenty-two names produced a handful of possible groups. Looking through them, he decided which one he would use. There was only one relatively unusual name in the list, and two of the names were in very common usage. As a bonus, there was one name that he already identified as a potential target. She was very old, and her death would not be suspicious. Her murder would be easily accomplished, and it would give him a head start by completing the first link in the puzzle quickly.

She was local, which was a distinct disadvantage since it might alert the police to his presence. He would prefer to put distance between himself and his victims but was reasonably sure that he could make her death look like it had resulted from natural causes. If this was not how it was presumed, and an investigation was held – he was still confident he could get away with it. And it did not matter that one of the six murder victims was local – the rest would be scattered all over the country. Even if they were linked by the police – which he thought was distinctly unlikely, there would be nothing to pinpoint his location.

These would be the six women who would be the victims of the six murders that one intelligent person would connect. Eventually. And that person would then be able to solve the puzzle and collect the reward – which was enough money to be life-changing. And if they had connected the names and solved the puzzle, they would deserve the reward.

It was getting late, but Bruno was on a roll and was not yet ready to stop.

He now needed to find the women. He set about Twitter with renewed vigour. He initiated searches from his account, as well as the two additional accounts with fake names that he had purposefully set up. He was searching for five of the names – one he didn't need to look for was Nelly. He already knew her, and it would be all right for one of the women to be known to him. None of the others would be – yet.

He would follow the accounts of these women with the names he had chosen, interact with them, find out about them and, he was sure, ultimately be able to locate them. One of each name on his list. Carol, Emily, Gerri, Macie, Megan and Nelly. They would become famous in a way – unwillingly and unfortunately so.

And if a moment of worry about what he was doing passed across his mind, he dismissed it. These people were, after all, not that important. Their lives were so empty that they could squander a significant portion of their time interacting with strangers on social media. They would not be missed.

.

.2 - NELLY

FRIDAY, 19TH MAY

She was christened Eleanor Dixon. Maybe her mother chose the name Eleanor, which many considered to be too posh for a miner's daughter, because she harboured aspirations for a better life for her. A better life than she had experienced herself – a life lived completely within the borders of the small town where she would no doubt die and be buried. But Eleanor was too grand a name for a little girl at that time and in that place, so by the time she went to school it had already been shortened to Nelly, and it was by this name that she had been known for more than eighty years since.

She had been friendly with Bruno's mum ever since they had attended school together. And when Nelly was widowed, it was Bruno's mother who made sure Nelly was alright in the small but important number of ways in which she could. Which included sending Bruno around to Nelly's house whenever there was a bit of DIY needed doing, or something heavy needed moving. After his mother's death, Bruno felt he was doing something for his mum whenever he popped around to Nelly's house to check on her or help her in some practical way as her age increased and her strength diminished. He was her handyman, gardener, financial adviser, secretary and so much more.

Over the years, he had often seen her and frequently spoken to her while he was out on one of his runs or picking up groceries at the local shop. But now she was housebound, he was one of the few people who visited her with any regularity. The other visitors were almost all professional carers attending according to a timetable each day to get her out of bed, feed, wash and dress her, and then return her to her bed at the end of the day.

It was not much of a life, and Bruno felt he would, in many ways, be showing kindness by bringing it to an end before nature had completed its downward path for her. It was bad enough the way she was now when she still had most of her marbles. It would only get worse as her physical and mental state deteriorated; he knew. And once he had decided to do what he was going to do – he knew he had to proceed as soon as possible. If Nelly continued to live and deteriorate it would not be good for her. If she deteriorated too quickly and died naturally, he would either need to find another woman of the same name to fill the gap in his puzzle, or else rethink the whole damn thing. And he was working to a deadline that was not likely to be extended.

The largest gap between carers' visits was the afternoon – between the lunchtime feed and the evening light snack, wash, and return to bed. So that was when he visited, picking up the key from the key safe by the front door, entering the house, and calling her name out loud.

He was as familiar with the layout of her house as he was with his own, and so stopped en route to the lounge to visit the front room, which had been converted to a bedroom for Nelly many years ago when she could no longer manage the stairs. He picked up a pillow from the bed and entered the back room - where Nelly was in her usual place, slumped in her electrically operated chair which he had helped her to buy and to install.

He remembered the unbelievable amount of time it had taken to explain it to her and show her how to operate the simple controls to tilt the chair forward and back. That was in the past when she was able to get in and out of it unaided and was able to show some interest in the TV which was positioned in front of the chair. Nowadays she was placed into the chair by the morning carer, and the TV just provided noise and colour to her life. She was not able to follow anything that it showed.

He spoke to her but received no reply. She was asleep as usual. But this time he didn't gently shake her and speak loudly to get her to recognise him. Instead, he took the large plastic bag from his pocket – one of those bags that charities frequently left by his door with a notice for him to fill it with spare clothing and leave for them to collect in support of refugees from some godforsaken part of the planet. It was the thinnest form of plastic he had ever known – and a washed-out pink in colour. It made him think, ridiculously, of an elephant's condom. But he had brought it along because he had seen on one of the recent TV crime shows that if someone died of suffocation, the autopsy could detect fibres in their lungs. He did not want there to be any suspicion that her death was from anything other than natural causes.

He placed the pillow inside the bag and placed it over Nelly's face. She choked a little, struggled a little, and then expired. He held it there for a long two minutes just to make sure. Then he simply rearranged Nelly into a resting pose, replaced the plastic bag in his pocket and returned the pillow to its place on the bed in the front room.

There was just one more chore to be completed before he left. In the top drawer of Nelly's dressing table upstairs in what had been her bedroom in better times, there was her jewellery box. He opened it and searched for a brooch which he knew was there. It was made up of a large piece of amber, surrounded by black stones. It had once been a favourite of Nelly's, and he had remembered her telling him that it had been a present from her late husband. But to Bruno, it was the first vital clue for his proposed puzzle. Having found it, he returned to the downstairs back room and pinned the brooch onto Nelly's dress. He had to hope that its presence would be noted by whoever found her.

It was the sign – hopefully to be recognised by a detective at some time in the future. A black and yellow item at the scene of a death, showing that 'The Stinger' had struck for the first time.

He closed the front door, replaced the key in the key safe, and began to walk back home. He would dispose of the plastic bag in his own rubbish bin – it would be collected the next day and he was sure there was no chance of it being traced to him.

As he walked, he took the opportunity to examine his feelings. He felt very little. A job well done. A mercy killing possibly. He certainly felt no guilt at what he had done. He knew that Nelly had no joy in her life. And he had saved the council, or whoever paid for it, the cost and the drain on scarce resources that were used to prop up Nelly's life. But far more importantly, he had started his task. The first piece in his puzzle had been put in place. He was now certain that he had all the necessary skills to complete his quest and was ready to take the next steps.

Later that evening, after his customary meal-for-one, he treated himself to a glass of port. It was the only alcohol he kept in his house – in fact, it was the only alcoholic drink he had ever really enjoyed. He naturally had the occasional pint of beer – there were just times when you would draw unwelcome attention to yourself if you did not join in with the guys and have a beer. But he didn't enjoy it. He'd tried stronger liquor and found it harsh and unpleasant to drink. Even wine always seemed to have a sour taste, unless it was light, white, and fizzy, and that was, of course, seen as a woman's drink. But port was pleasant to taste, warming and gentle. A wineglass of it at the end of a trying day – which today certainly qualified as – was most welcome. He downed it, cleared away the glass, and went to bed, enjoying an undisturbed night's sleep.

-

Nelly's death did not make the news. Bruno heard about it in the local shop a few days later, and read the small obituary in the local paper, no doubt composed by a guilty daughter who had rarely visited her mother in the last years of her life. Bruno was not invited to the funeral and did not attend. He was already starting to look for the next piece in the puzzle. The next victim for The Stinger.

.3 - GERRI

TUESDAY, 20TH JUNE

Gerri was not one of those people that hate Mondays. She quite liked them. The restaurant was usually quieter than the other nights of the week, so she got the chance to chat with customers if she felt like it. And if she didn't feel like it, then she could have a quiet glass of wine with the chef or just appreciate the chance to work at a slower pace and recover - if it had been a hectic weekend.

Tonight, it was quiet. Only a couple of tables were in use, and none of the customers seemed keen on having much of a conversation with her.

Her mind drifted back to the previous Monday when she'd had a long chat with a new customer who had asked her about her tattoo. Her pride and joy. A serpent – the tail just visible on the back of her hand, the scaly body coiling all the way up her arm, the head cleverly fashioned into a three-dimensional image on her shoulder with the – what were they called? – tendrils, yes, that was it, the tendrils being just visible on the side and back of her neck. She had had it done in three sessions a couple of years ago as a present to herself. A congratulatory present for reaching her target weight.

It was good not to be fat anymore. She'd let herself go a bit during the last throes of her marriage, and in the down period shortly afterwards. It wasn't a particularly bad break-up. Just one of those things. Two people who had got together a bit too young and after ten years and two kids had found that they didn't have much in common and didn't want to be tied to each other any longer. But for a long time, neither of them had the nerve to do anything about it.

Eventually, her husband had been offered a new job which would mean moving house – which she had no wish to do. They'd talked briefly about making a new start, and then both agreed that the new start they wanted did not involve the other party. And so, he got a new job and a new address, she got custody of the children and a new, single life.

But that was all in the past. Initially, she had been quite down, but she'd kept her job and was able to pay the rent, give the kids and herself a reasonable life and all in all felt quite good about herself.

She had even had a bit of room for some sympathy for the poor guy who had admired her tattoo. A bit too old for her, but not bad looking and certainly fit. Apparently, he really wanted a tattoo but was allergic to it. When he'd first decided to get a tattoo, he had reacted badly to the ink and had to have antihistamines and everything. But she had enjoyed a healthy flirtation with him as he expressed every interest in seeing the tattoo which was mostly hidden by the long-sleeved blouse she had to wear as her waitress outfit. He'd also flattered her – she wasn't sure if it was deliberate or accidental, by asking if she was named after a Spice Girl.

"No, pet, I'm much too old for that", she smiled as she answered. "But thanks for the compliment. All I can say is that we both decided that Gerri was a lot better thing to be called than Geraldine – only I put two r's in mine."

"Good decision", he'd replied, "I always thought Geraldine sounded like some lotion that you rubbed on an embarrassing rash!"

This time she laughed out loud. "I've never heard that before but I'm sure I'll use it". she replied over her shoulder as she disappeared to the kitchen.

Her laugh was awful. A high-pitched, squeaky cackle.

It never occurred to her that it was strange that he should know about her tattoo when so little of it was visible.

Of course, her customer knew all about her tattoo and so much more about her from following her extensive posts on social media. She had become a frequent visitor to and poster on social media when she had split with her husband. It had helped her during the dark times, and she had now built quite a circle of followers and the daily interaction with them filled at least an hour of her day, every day.

She posted about everything: her tattoo, her kids, her job, her weight loss – posting every milestone no matter how big or, more frequently, how small. Reading her history of activity here Bruno had built a thorough picture of her in his mind, and he was surprised how accurately his imagined version of her was matched by the reality. It was so easy to slip into a friendly conversation with her, knowing so much about her.

But, from Gerri's perspective, her conversation with the tall dark stranger (as she was already christening him for her next social media post) was only the most minor of flirtations. She knew she was attractive to men, but she was not seriously looking right now because things were going so well with her new boyfriend. They had taken things slowly – both bearing mental scars from previous relationships, but it was looking good. And she was pretty sure that he'd be moving in with her soon. Now that her daughter was away at college there was certainly enough room. And an extra wage coming in could improve their lifestyle significantly.

The attention the stranger showed her made her pleased and proud once again that she had managed to keep her weight down. The exercise of climbing the stairs between the kitchen and the restaurant five nights a week – plus lunchtimes on Saturday and Sunday – helped make sure of that. And then there was plenty of exercise with her boyfriend most nights – she smiled and blushed slightly as she thought about it. She'd quit the comfort eating – and the comfort drinking. And the twenty-minute walk to and from work rounded out the exercise regime.

Later, about halfway along her walk home in the quiet of the late night, her minor reverie was brought to a halt as a tall man stepped out in front of her. The "Oh" that escaped her lips was more surprise than shock once she quickly recognised him as the customer that she had been chatting to a couple of weeks ago (and was thinking about earlier that same evening.)

There was a second, more muffled "Oh" as he surprised her with how quickly he could move for such a big man. The tie in his gloved hand was quickly wound around her neck and pulled with considerable force. She resisted and struggled briefly and noiselessly. In less than two minutes she was lying dead on the dark pavement.

Bruno made sure her body was in a straight line along the pavement and left the tie around her neck. Black and yellow stripes. Purchased from a large department store some two weeks ago.

He walked a few yards in the dark to his car and drove home. He thought of how pleased the people in the restaurant must be that they would never have to hear that awful laugh ever again and how easy it had all been. There were now two down with four to go.

.4 - EMILY

MONDAY, 17TH JULY

They say that pride comes before a fall. That was not entirely true in Emily's case – but it was a contributory factor, that's for sure. She was so proud of her new little car. And it was going to make it so much easier to visit her dad now he was in the care home.

She'd kept in touch with him after her parents split up – her mum knew she still went to see him and was happy if it was good for both her ex-husband and her daughter to see each other. She wasn't sure how much good it was for him. From what she had heard, his grip on reality was slipping day by day. But if it kept her daughter happy then it was a good thing for her to see him occasionally.

When Emily Moss moved away from home to start her course at Swansea University, she found it difficult to fit in visits to both parents – it was bad enough tackling the complex journey from Swansea back to Swindon by public transport, and no university student wants to have too many interruptions to their social life.

She had quickly fallen in love with Wales and tried to learn all she could about its history and traditions. She took classes in the Welsh language, and when she graduated found a nice job in the tourist department in Swansea. She stepped up her weekly language classes as they now had real practical value. Some of the people she dealt with reacted very favourably when she spoke a few words in Welsh. She aimed to get good enough to be able to do some translation work later.

She posted proudly on social media as she achieved each step on the way. "Today I handled a phone call from a local totally in Welsh language," she tweeted. "They obviously knew I was very new, but they were so kind and helped me a lot".

Then "I did a whole PowerPoint presentation in Welsh in the office today. Getting better all the time!"

Even though the salary was not the best, she could afford a small car so that the journey home would be more manageable, more convenient, and more frequent. There was not currently a partner in her life – she was still at the stage of thinking 'Why have just one man when you can have them all?' but she was sure that one would come along sometime and was not yet in any hurry to make it happen.

Of course, she did not know she was on Bruno's database. She was a regular contributor to social media – keeping in touch with her friends from her hometown – some of whom still lived there and others who had dispersed to the four corners of the UK in pursuit of further education. So, when he searched for women with the name Emily, she showed up and became a record on his database.

Bruno was pleased. There was no need to prompt her - which he had found necessary with some of his other target accounts. No, Emily was happy to converse far and wide with her friends and tell them all about her life.

Bruno knew her original hometown was Swindon, and that she had settled in Swansea. He knew that she had thoroughly enjoyed the nightlife of the city, and visited one or more of the bars, restaurants, and clubs of Wind Street at least once a week.

He read about her sadness as her father was admitted to a care home when his dementia reached the state that he could not look after himself any longer. He noted it on her record. All information could be useful, so her record was updated accordingly.

Harriet, Bruno's female account (So Shall Work Her) on Twitter, engaged in conversations with Emily about the terrible sadness of having a parent with dementia, inventing a similar situation for herself and her own father. In this way, he was able to gather information about Emily's father – noting that he had worked almost all his life in the local car factory and that he was now unable to recognise anyone other than Emily either in photos or in real life.

When Emily proudly posted a photo of her new car, Bruno was, at last, able to get the vital information he had previously lacked.

The database of UK car registrations is, coincidentally housed in Swansea at the Driver and Vehicle Licensing Agency. Once upon a time it was a somewhat obscure system, accessed relatively infrequently by police forces and councils in the UK. But the advance of technology, allowed the government to open up access to the database and profit from it.

Access was granted to insurance companies and then to providers of car parking services and operators of transport systems such as chargeable tunnels and bridges. And the spread of number plate recognition technology meant that access was far more frequent.

Bruno had worked on a couple of these systems over the years and had kept the details of the DVLA login he had been provided. It never ceased to surprise him how often he was granted 'temporary' access to an organisation's database and that authorisation continued to function long after his project had been completed.

He was pleased to see that this one still functioned, and keying in the registration number of Emily's car, which was so clearly visible on the photo she had posted, gave him her address, which is what he wanted. He also noted her date of birth. He had no plan to use it, but all information was always noted. He never knew when it might be useful.

Now he knew her address, he could more easily make contact with her. Real, physical contact, not just the ephemeral online contact that he had had for months.

He needed a plan that would make use of this vital piece of information. Any thoughts of making social contact seemed unlikely. There was such a gap in their ages that he would not dare enter the kind of clubs she frequented. He would stick out like a sore thumb, and she would have absolutely no interest in talking to him.

When she posted that she was planning to visit her dad the next Sunday, he knew his opportunity had arrived. He could not imagine that she was an early riser, so he could travel down to Swansea in the morning, find her address, locate her car, and wait for her to set off. Having looked at where she lived on Streetview, it was obvious that her flat would not have any parking space and her car would be parked on-street nearby. It was simply a matter of turning up early enough, finding it, and then waiting and watching. And that was exactly what he did.

She emerged from her flat around ten thirty, by which time he had found himself a parking space with a clear view of her car. She unlocked the car and placed a bag containing gifts for her parents on the passenger seat before setting off. He followed her as she drove across town, parking in a side street when she stopped for petrol at a cheap station close to the main university buildings. When she set off he pulled out behind her and followed her onto the M4, around the speed-restricted section that bypassed Port Talbot.

He saw the sign in both English and Welsh that told him the speed restrictions were imposed to improve air quality. This made him laugh to himself at the ridiculous nature of this imposition when the whole area was dominated by the UK's largest steelworks and was permanently shrouded in mist from the fumes billowing out the giant chimney.

He did not need to stay immediately behind Emily's car the whole time since he knew where she was going. He kept a few cars between her and him just in case she noticed him but pulled within sight of her before each service station just in case she stopped for any reason. But she didn't. He followed her through the seemingly permanent traffic delays around Newport and the roadworks where the M4, M5, and M32 motorways intersected, all the way to exit number 15 and then to Ashgrove Nursing Home on the outskirts of Swindon.

Bruno drove on when he saw her pull into the nursing home's car park. The building had once, no doubt, been a large family home, probably built for one of the many Victorian Railway barons who had made this area their home a hundred and fifty years ago. It had been converted and extended by the addition of an ugly plain block building and was now a home specialising in the care of the elderly with dementia or special needs.

Having driven past the home, a little further along the road he saw what he expected; the houses petered out after about a mile, and the open countryside began. He looked for a property that would be suitable for his plans and soon saw a small row of cottages – once no doubt somewhat isolated, but now within yards of a housing estate that had almost swallowed them up. He noted their address details and, returning to the car park of the nursing home, he parked well away from Emily's car before putting this new information into the notes section of his phone. He then looked up the postcode of the address and added that.

He checked his watch. About an hour had passed since Emily had entered, and it was now time for him to join her and her father.

Bruno was not looking like his normal self. Before setting out, he had put some white grease paint on his hair, so it was now mostly grey-white. He had not shaved for a couple of days and had applied a little pale makeup to his skin and stubble. For a younger man, dark stubble can be mysterious, attractive, and even sexy. For a man, over fifty grey stubble does nothing to improve looks, it simply ages him.

He'd also used a make-up pencil to ink in some of the wrinkles on his face and forehead. The YouTube video on how to use makeup to appear older had been very useful. When he looked in the mirror it was a seventy-year-old man that looked back, not a fifty-five-year-old one.

He placed a small stone inside his shoe, took the walking stick out of the boot of his car, limped up to the front door, and rang the bell. When a carer opened the door to him, he asked if it was OK to visit his old workmate, George Moss.

"Yes, of course. George is in the lounge now," she said, pointing to the right where a large room was filled with large upright chairs containing old people of both sexes. Some alone, a few with visitors at their sides. "His daughter's with him now, but I'm sure he'd like to see you. Just sign in here," she said, indicating to the visitors' book on the nearby table. She walked away and left him. He entered the name Stanley Williams and the address he had just memorised from his notes, one of the row of cottages at the edge of the housing estate.

He had no idea what George looked like – all these old men looked the same, anyway - but he knew Emily very well from all her posted photos, so he had no problem in picking her out. She had done what all good daughters do when they visit their aged dad in a care home – dressed in bright colours so that even if it didn't cheer him up, at least he could see her clearly.

He walked up to the pair of them.

"Hello, George. Remember me? It's Stan" he said.

George looked vaguely at him.

"His memory's not so good these days," Emily said, getting up from her chair and shaking his hand. "I'm his daughter, Emily. Have you visited him before?"

"No, I just found out from another old workmate that George was in here, and since I only live a mile away, I thought I'd pop down and see him. We used to work together you know."

"At the car factory?" she asked. A pretty stupid question of course, since her dad had worked there and nowhere else for the previous twenty years.

"That's right," he said and turned towards George. "We must have made a fair few cars in our day, mustn't we George?"

George gave the welcoming vague smile he gave to all of his carers and his few visitors.

George for once joined the conversation, "She's Emily. She's my daughter," he proudly stated.

"I'm so pleased that someone comes to see him. I've got some mates who never see any of their family and it's so sad," Bruno-Stanley continued.

Emily smiled at him, liking the implied praise he had just given her. The time visiting her father always dragged. He just about recognised her, and on each visit, they went over the same few memories he still kept, and she searched for something in her own life that would be of interest to him. With the arrival of this friend of her father, she saw the chance to make her excuses and leave.

"I'll leave you two together to talk about old times then, she said. She put her coat on and kissed her father. "I'll see you again in a few weeks. Goodbye, Dad."

George said goodbye and turned towards Bruno. Their conversation was brief. Bruno stayed about fifteen minutes, talking inanely about the cars that were once made in the big Honda plant nearby. Once Bruno was confident that Emily would have departed, he said goodbye to George and drove home. Stage one of his plan had gone perfectly. He now had to wait for Emily to post advance details of another visit.

A few weeks later he noted that one of her messages to a friend contained the information that she would not be at the club on Saturday as she planned to get an early start the next day to visit both her parents.

This time, Bruno did not follow her. He planned his journey to reach Swindon mid-morning. He parked his car close to the property which he had noted on his previous visit and had made his imaginary Swindon home address. He once again wore his Stanley disguise, and once again put the stone in his shoe and used his walking stick to appear the correct age. By the time he had walked the mile to the care home, his limp did not need exaggerating. Stepping on a small pebble every step of the way meant that his foot really did hurt.

He made the briefest of visits to George, making sure to enter his false address details in the visitors' book, and then took a seat on the bench outside the home and waited for Emily to arrive. Half an hour passed before he saw her car pull into the car park. He stood up and walked back past the entrance, which meant he would pass close to her car. She recognised him and walked towards him, noting his limp. She asked if he had been to visit George. 'She does have a wonderful knack for asking obvious questions,' he thought to himself.

"Yes," he said, if I visit him early enough it gives me a chance to get home by lunchtime. My neighbour is really good to me and cooks me a lovely Sunday lunch," he smiled. He was hoping that she would notice his bad limp and offer him a lift before he needed to awkwardly ask for one. Sure enough, she did not disappoint.

Having established that he was planning to walk back to his house a mile or so away, she said "You seem to be limping badly today, can I give you a lift home?"

"Yes, we've had a lot of rain this week – it always plays up in wet weather," he replied, pointing to his 'bad' leg. "If it's not too much trouble, I'd be very grateful."

They got into her car, and she asked him how to get to his house.

"Just turn left out of the car park and carry on for about a mile, then turn right," he answered.

When they pulled up outside 'his house' she asked if he needed any help getting out of the car.

"No, I'll manage. I'm a bit slow, but I'll get there," he said, feigning difficulties with the car door handle.

Bruno was not only large and strong but was also left-handed. So, when made a fist with his left hand and swung it in an arc towards Emily's jaw, it hit her with great speed and power. Taken completely by surprise, she was knocked out and slumped back in her seat. From his coat pocket, Bruno removed a meter length of rope (part of a car-towing kit available from every branch of Halfords and thus totally untraceable). He looped it around Emily's neck, and pulled hard for a minute or more, depriving her of life and making sure that poor old George would not be seeing any more visitors today.

He leaned across, switched off the engine, and then removed one more item from his pocket 'I hope this is not too obvious a clue,' he thought, laughing inwardly at his joke as he dropped a screwdriver on Emily's lap. In black capital letters on the yellow handle was the word 'Stanley'.

He got out of her car, took the stone out of his shoe, limped to his car, removed his coat, hat, and gloves, and drove off. Only a seventy-year-old man would have needed to wear gloves on a warm day like today. Or a man who did not want to leave any fingerprints.

Two hours later he was back at his house. His make-up was removed, and a bobble hat replaced the old-man flat cap he had worn in Swindon. That was now in a bin-liner with the coat, the walking stick, and every other piece of paraphernalia associated with his disguise. He would dispose of that the following day.

Not yet ready for sleep, he turned on the television and began flicking through the channels. One of the nature channels was showing a documentary on a new species of killer hornet that was invading the south of England, killing large numbers of rival species in its wake.

Bruno settled down with a glass of port to enjoy it.

INTERMISSION

Detective Inspector Linda Evans   Early hours, Sunday, October 22nd

I had to take a break. Sitting motionless for so long was producing aches where I didn't want or need them so I got up from the chair, swigged the last drops of water from the glass, stretched my arms, and moved my head up and down and from side to side. I drew circles in the air with my nose. Three clockwise and three anticlockwise to relieve the pain which was beginning to spread from my neck to my shoulders.

'What I could do with is a nice massage.' I mused to myself but stopped this train of thought before it led to actions that might delay me reading the rest of the book. For the last hour I'd barely moved a muscle, save to take a few sips of water and to press the 'Page Down' key several times with the index finger of my right hand.

I've read John's book this far and have been almost spellbound and, at the same time, thoroughly horrified. The cold, unfeeling nature of the man has come as a shock even to me with my years of finely honed police cynicism.

I've realised that far from reading something that could even begin to be thought of as a serious attempt at a first novel, what I've read is a straightforward catalogue of crimes. The page size has been set at eight inches by five inches for a small page-size novel, but he hasn't even bothered to change from the default Calibri font or to set the paragraph spacing properly.

Coupling the information that I've gathered from the first half of the book with what I already knew, it seems obvious that John Jackson is a serial killer. He has invented this alias of Bruno for some weird reason that I cannot begin to understand. And the book was just a self-aggrandising series of admissions of his evil deeds.

I wondered whether he was overcome with guilt at what he had done and had decided to hide it all behind this false front of a novel. But I quickly closed down this train of thought.

'Your job is to catch 'em and bring 'em to trial,' I told myself. 'Leave the psychoanalysis to the professionals!'

The chapter about Gerri contained enough detail to form a complete confession to the murder of the unfortunate waitress in Salford. I have to assume that the murder of Emily in Swindon will tie in with the one that had been mentioned by DS Khan at the meeting a few days ago. The details will be no doubt confirmed by a phone call to Wiltshire police tomorrow.

The murder of Nelly is something I will have to check up on. It should be easy to find out if an Eleanor Dunn died around May this year. He will presumably be charged with her murder, but that will not be my decision. Thankfully such matters of whether the upset it would cause to surviving relatives and the amount of paperwork it would generate was worth the trouble are above my paygrade. I will leave that for DCI Lancaster or maybe even his boss to decide.

There are still three more grizzly sets of details I have to read through. One of which will no doubt be the young woman in Kent, and one of which will be my case – the murder of Megan McCormick. And there will be one more to surprise some other police force which is no doubt currently collectively scratching its head over an unsolved murder of a woman on their territory. At least I'll be bringing someone some good news that will clear an unresolved matter from his task list and improve crime detection figures in his patch.

I'm still hoping that I'll read something that will change the conclusions I've drawn so far. Maybe something about the elusive Mister Rodriguez or the mysterious Denis. But I somehow doubt it. They will probably turn out to be part of his tissue of lies.

Thankfully, the style of prose (if it could be called that) that John used is direct and largely unadorned, so it won't take too long to complete my reading task. I suppose I should be grateful for this small mercy.

I've also begun to understand what a trail of lies and deception John has been feeding us. Not so much in his interviews, but in the contents of his blog. So many red herrings and downright falsehoods. So many contradictions between his blog and his book! The whole thing will have to be unravelled so that the morsels of truth can be extracted from the morass of lies in which they had been sprinkled.

Could the contents of 'The Book' be trusted though? Was John genuinely suffering from a terminal illness? His health has seemed to deteriorate slightly from when we first met – but a man who had written so many lies could well have invented this too. It will be easy enough to verify. For now, I'll suspend judgement. Even if he was suffering from that dreadful disease, it might at best go some way towards explaining his motivation. It could never ever justify his actions.

As I've read the contradictions and lies, it's made me begin to doubt almost everything about the case. I even for a moment wondered if this

'Book' was even real. I have only got Robin's word that this is an actual decryption of the file on John's strange black box. I don't seriously think that Robin has made it up – but I will get him to decrypt those other files and produce five tax returns for me, just to settle my nerves!

There was a phrase my father sometimes used to describe interviewing an unpleasant suspect. "Talking to him is like hand washing a hankie," he'd say. Thinking of how much time I will probably have to spend with John to unpick the story, this seems like an excellent description of what my next few days could turn out to be.

I tiptoed to the bedroom door and opened it to verify that Robin was OK. He was sound asleep, and I had to resist the temptation of discarding my dressing gown and snuggling in next to him. 'I'll make time for that as a reward for finishing the book,' I told myself.
For now, though, I must simply plough on, finish 'The Book', and then (hopefully after a little more sleep) begin the process of arresting, charging, and prosecuting John Jackson. Maybe the final chapters of his book will contain something that will help explain the dreadful deeds he has done and the reasons behind them, but I doubt it.
I fetched another large glass of water and picked up reading where I had left off.

.5 - CAROL

MONDAY, 31ST JULY

Social media was an important part of Carol's life. Something that provided friendly conversation and was free to use was a godsend to someone whose social life was minimised by circumstances.

If you had asked the younger Carol if she would end up like this - a single parent in her early thirties, gaining most of her social interaction at the keyboard of a computer - she would probably have either laughed in derision or cried.

Carol had been a bit of a wild child. She had, in the opinion of her parents, squandered her musical talents by playing rock music. In truth, the group she played in was not all that good. But they toured the country, living the rock lifestyle. She had even enacted the romantic stereotype and eloped with Johnny, the lead guitarist. They married at the age of nineteen.

Three years later the group had disbanded, Johnny's whereabouts were unknown, and she was a single mum to two children, born almost exactly a year apart.

Her parents, she was pleased to discover, gave her wonderful support in her hour of need. With no time wasted on 'I-told-you-so's', they helped her get a place to live and provided free childcare so that she could get a real job and start to fend for herself. She now made 'proper' use of her musical talents and had a couple of part-time positions in local state schools teaching music for half a day per week. She also secured a more profitable one-day-per-week teaching gig at a local private school. There were a couple of pupils who came to her once a week for piano tuition in her small, terraced house. And she provided paid-for accompaniment for several pupils sitting their music exams and played for two local choirs – one for love (a women's choir with an emphasis on helping troubled women) and one for money (a proper local choir).

Financially she was able to keep her head above water, pay her mortgage (which she had gained after her parents had given her the deposit), and to console herself that things could be a whole lot worse.

She didn't blame Johnny for leaving. She realised that they were both too young and too stupid when they got together, and now she was paying most of the price for their recklessness. No, she didn't blame him for leaving, but she did blame him for poisoning her memories. He was an important part of every memory of those wonderful carefree times, and she couldn't enjoy those memories as much as she wanted to - precisely because he was present in all of them.

It was as if he was some old-time movie star who had done something really bad and now his films could not be shown on TV. And any episode of a show where he had made a guest appearance could not be shown either. But these were not TV re-runs. These were her memories - and they were all poisoned by his shadow. But she wanted to re-run them because they had been such fun times. And so, she cursed him for the way he had stolen her chance to reminisce.

The psychological wounds were healing, and she was beginning to socialise again – albeit with no budget to actually do anything or to go anywhere. But she had hope. And she was still young enough and good-looking enough to justify her hope. No longer the stunning good looks she had possessed and squandered. But still good-looking, she thought. And the frequent admiring glances from men of her age (and even the occasional one from younger men too) justified her optimism.

'Let's just hope I find someone before I move from being good-looking to being fine-looking, or, even worse *handsome,*' she thought.

Hence social media was important to her. Conversation with fellow mums and teachers; music-related stuff; general chit-chat; and the occasional flirtatious conversation. She even had a running joke with some of her followers about the possibility of renting a boyfriend rather than taking one on full-time. All of this was possible without impacting her non-existent budget for a social life.

She was an extremely frequent contributor to social media. Being a single mum with a precarious method of earning a living, it was not too dangerous a presumption that this provided a valuable and cheaper alternative to real social life, as well as a source of adult conversation that might have been difficult for her to achieve in any other way.

She was cautious and sensible. Most of her interaction was with other women – experience had made her cautious about the members of the male gender. And she had a dry and self-deprecating sense of humour that many of her followers enjoyed.

Her caution did not extend to keeping her identity obscure – she posted photos of herself quite frequently. Her appearance was pleasant, warm, and natural - and her smile seemed to exude friendliness. But she never showed any photos of her children and kept her location details vague enough – naming only the region where she lived – a small town in the North Midlands. But she made one small error. A selfie, taken and posted on her walk into town one day showed, in the far background, a large green road sign for a nearby traffic intersection. And that was enough for anyone with some image-enhancing software, a wish to find out, and a small amount of spare time, to identify exactly where the photograph was taken.

She didn't realise that among her regular correspondents were two of Bruno's aliases.

Her posts were frequent enough and gave Bruno sufficient information that he did not need to engage with her too often. If he needed to, he used his Harriet alias to increase the chance of her replying, but he was building a sufficient picture of her anyway. Once he had worked out the name of the town she lived in, what he was waiting for was a break that would give him the chance to find out precisely where she lived. And eventually, the break came, as he knew it would.

Bruno could not afford to have any feelings for the strangers that he had chosen to be the pieces in his puzzle. But if he was ever going to like one of them, then it would have been Carol. Her posts made it very clear that she had had a very bad time during the later stages of her marriage, and she was very careful about any dialogue with men. Bruno thought of her as toughened but neither brittle nor bitter. And there was a sweet centre to her, he felt sure.

One Sunday afternoon, Carol Prentice posted a picture of herself. Nothing unusual about that. But this one was a picture of her sitting in a railway carriage with the caption 'On my way to join the Messiah from Scratch at the Albert Hall. Deeply Excited.' It was the break Bruno had been hoping for. He re-checked his records to confirm the town where she lived and worked out that it would take him just over an hour to drive there from his home.

It was not a surprise that she had posted about the event. It was one of the most important social events on her calendar. Not difficult when there were so few, but it was still important, nonetheless. The chance to travel to London and enjoy not only the wonderful music but also to share the company of so many like-minded people and the elation of creating what was always a joyous experience for participants and audience alike. No wonder it brought her a girlish sense of excitement.

He googled the Messiah event and found that it was taking place in London's Albert Hall and was scheduled to start at 7:30 p.m. There was no finishing time listed, but he reckoned that if it finished at 10 p.m., she would be catching a train at around eleven and arriving at the railway station in her hometown at around midnight. Giving himself plenty of time, he set off from home at 10 p.m. and on arrival was able to find a very convenient place to park his car – one that gave him a clear view of the entrance to the station. He was sure that having looked at the extensive library of photos of Carol that he now had, including one which showed what she was wearing tonight, he would be able to recognise her easily. He was sure that there would not be too many passengers arriving on the midnight train - and he was proved right.

But his guess at how she would proceed from the station was wrong. He expected her to take a taxi at this late hour, but, still full of the excitement of the evening and fuelled and warmed by a couple of large gin and tonics, she felt confident enough to walk the short distance home.

She set off quickly and confidently out of the station forecourt and down the street. He had to rapidly get out of his car, donning a coat against the cool night air, to follow her on foot. The reason for her not taking a taxi was soon obvious. The walk from the station to her house took only ten minutes. Bruno was pleased not only because he was unaccustomed to walking for much more than this distance but also because he was beginning to worry that she might notice him following her.

But she didn't. He watched her open the front door of her house and enter. Hidden in shadow, he waited for a few minutes until, as he had expected, her front door opened, and a woman emerged. She said goodnight to Carol and then made her way to a house three doors further down the street. The babysitter had finished her night's work.

Bruno walked back to his car and drove to a secluded location close to Carol's home. The house was in the middle of a terrace, and a walk around the corner showed him that the houses all backed onto an alley. He made sure he knew which was her house and walked down the alley until he was immediately behind it. There was enough moonlight to allow him to see a large wooden gate at the end of her small back garden. He checked the latch and it opened easily. He did not need to enter the garden – he could see that the back of the house was, like the front, largely unchanged since its construction about eighty years ago. He could see the original back door which was half glazed and therefore – conveniently for him but not for her - easy to break through. He quietly closed the garden gate, made his way back to his car, and drove home. He now began his final period of waiting - for the social media post he knew would come one day from Carol that would be his final signal.

He had only to wait for the next half-term to read the post he had been anticipating. 'Much as I love my children,' she posted, 'I can't tell you how much I'm looking forward to a week alone when they spend half term with their grandparents.' To Bruno this meant only one thing – she would be alone at night. Her frequent posts bemoaning the lack of a man in her life made him confident that there would be nobody else in the house.

He checked several online sources of information before finalising his plans. There was nothing scheduled in her town that would affect him, and the fullest moon and best weather were both set to occur on Wednesday.

He left his home late Wednesday night, arriving at his destination in the early hours of Thursday morning. He had read somewhere that 2 a.m. was the lowest point in the body's natural cycle. The time when most people were likely to be deepest asleep, and those that remained awake would be at their least attentive. He parked his car close, but not too close, to Carol's house. He was dressed in black from head to foot, the pockets of his long black coat carrying the only things he thought he would need: a small torch, a plastic apron, a balaclava, a glass cutter, a crowbar, and part of a child's toy.

A few months earlier he had seen someone posting an amusing family incident on her Facebook page. To entertain their small child, her husband had taken a rattle with a suction cap – presumably intended to be fixed to a wall or the side of a cot - and had applied it to his forehead. As he moved his head, the toy rattled, and the child laughed. But what was more amusing, and her main reason for the post was that he had subsequently found it very difficult to remove the toy from his head and he had been left with a vivid red circle in the middle of his forehead for the rest of the day. An item with suction like that was what Bruno needed, and so he had bought a similar toy – keeping the suction cap and discarding the rest of it.

He reached the alley behind Carol's house just before two a.m. The garden gate opened easily, and a few strides brought him to the back door. He applied the suction cap to the pane of glass on the back door, drew around it with the glass cutter, and pulled the circle of glass out. He put his arm through the hole, felt around, and as expected, found the key in place in the lock. A quick turn and he was inside. No need for the crowbar. Yet.

He paused to listen for any unexpected sounds of late-night activity, but there were none. He donned the balaclava, removed the plastic apron from his pocket, and put it on – ensuring that as much of him was covered as possible. Using his small torch for guidance, he found his way up the stairs and to the front bedroom where Carol lay fast asleep. He removed the crowbar from his coat pocket and, with three swift blows to the back of her head, despatched her from this world to the next.

Having manoeuvred her so that she was lying in a straight line across the bed, he removed the balaclava and the apron, which had caught the bulk of the blood splatter, rolled them up, and returned them to his pocket. He would dispose of them, and every item of clothing he was wearing, as soon as possible.

He left the crowbar on the bed before silently retracing his path through the back door, out the back gate, and thence to his car.

The reason for leaving the crowbar at the scene was that it had been slightly modified. Originally a plain black iron tool, Bruno had changed its appearance by sticking several loops of yellow tape around it at intervals so that it now appeared to be black and yellow striped.

'The Stinger has struck again,' Bruno thought to himself as he drove home. He had to concentrate hard. He was feeling extremely tired and knew that this was not solely due to the lateness of the hour and the mental strain of what he had done. He was beginning to notice a reduction in his levels of energy and knew it had to be caused by his illness.

As the journey progressed, he began to relax and even felt a little light-headed. As he relaxed, he stupidly began to sing to himself as he drove. The song that came into his head was an old number from the Beatles "Abbey Road" album, inappropriate in its lightness, but nearly perfect in its content.

"Bang, bang, Maxwell's silver hammer came down upon her head", he sang with little tunefulness but increasing lustiness.

"Bang, bang, Maxwell's silver hammer made sure that she was dead."

Later that night he removed every trace of Carol from his database – the Carol who had become his latest victim and all the others that were in there, as alternatives, just in case. There were now only two names in the database.

The following day he took two bags of rubbish to his local recycling centre – one of which contained all the clothes he had worn the previous night. He then spent the rest of the day on social media, working on the two remaining targets. Time pressure was beginning to build, and he knew he had to complete his task as soon as possible. And he had not yet got enough information on any Macies or Megans.

.6 - MACIE

TUESDAY, 3RD OCTOBER

September 11th is an auspicious day in more ways than one. The anniversary of the world's worst-ever terrorist atrocity makes it a significant day for everyone. Bruno often wondered if the date of the attack on the World Trade Center was planned so that the number by which it was forever to be known, was the same as the USA's emergency telephone number. He thought it unlikely because to plan such an occurrence you would have to possess two pieces of knowledge. First, the Americans always refer to dates 'backwards' in the eyes of the rest of the Western world – so September 11th is not 11/9 but 9/11. And second, you would need to know that the number for emergency assistance in the USA – equivalent to the UK's 999, Australia's 000 or mainland Europe's 112 – is 911. He thought it unlikely that too many people involved in the planning of the atrocity would possess both these pieces of information – but it was just one of those things that puzzled and fascinated him.

This particular 9/11 was also a significant day for Bruno because Macie, after creating hundreds, possibly thousands of posts that he had been forced to read, finally posted some information about her planned whereabouts on a specific future date. One that was far enough in advance for him to make a detailed plan for her demise and yet not too far that it lay beyond the likely enforced closing date for his plans.

He had started to grow concerned that with so little time until nature imposed its harsh deadline upon him and his task, he would have to take some risks. He knew so much about Macie – and in the absence of any hint as to where she might be on a specific date, even at an approximate time, he was worried that he might need to follow her physically as well as electronically. Trying to find space and time when a young woman is alone in the centre of a busy, twenty-four-hour-a-day city such as London would be difficult and highly risky. Risks he would only be willing to take if it was essential for the completion of his mission. But now that was thankfully not going to be necessary.

-

Coming from a good catholic background she had been baptised in her full name of Ezmiralda Kristina Levenaj, but unless you saw her passport, birth certificate, or payslip you would never know those to be her full names.

The name Ezmiralda was too much of a mouthful for a young child, and so whenever she was asked "What's your name?" or asked to identify herself in a photo, she would reply "Macie". Her parents, who were just about the only people in the world who still called her Ezmiralda, were always aware that it was likely to be shortened. They hated the thought of her becoming Ezzie, and so accepted her being called 'Macie' - and the name stuck.

Right from the start, Macie (@agirlnamedmacie), with her huge internet following, had been the chattiest of all Bruno's targets. He had decided to stop searching for anyone else with the same name, feeling quite sure that in the end she would provide him with enough information to make his connection. But that would involve the sifting of a few grains of wheat from a very large quantity of chaff.

He estimated that Macie was in her mid-twenties. She was very left-wing in her politics and voluble on many topics. She often seemed to be violently for or violently against almost everything. But her violence was purely vocal, not physical. Her ethnicity was somewhere in the East Mediterranean region, Bruno guessed. She would espouse any cause relating to Turkey, Greece, or the Balkans, as well as many relating to Eastern Europe. But she never let it slip where exactly she originated. Such photos that he had seen of her showed her to be dark-skinned and short of stature– as well as quite attractive. He was also reasonably sure that Macie was either an anglicization or a shortening of her birth name – but since it was the name by which she was known it was a perfect fit for his selection rules.

Initially, he had started a dialogue with her via his own social media account, but this was terminated when he corrected some of the mistakes she had made when ranting about the development of socialism in Eastern Europe. His background had led to him being well informed about this topic, from anecdotes and brief tales told by his East European father, which had prompted him to read quite extensively on the subject in later life. But Macie did not take well to his corrections and immediately blocked his account. Bruno was mildly irritated and took heed to be much more careful in his future interactions – which were all made much more sympathetically via his false account for Richard Horsenell in the West Country.

Macie worked as a web designer for a charity in central London. Bruno wondered whether this meant that she was not very good at web design and could only get a job with a charity that would never pay top dollar for the job. Or was she good at her job but with a social conscience strong enough to make her accept lower pay in return for the good feeling that resulted from knowing that the organisation for which she worked was doing good?

When he looked at the web pages of the charity, he concluded that the answer was somewhere in the middle of his two assumptions.

She lived in a flat in Pimlico – an area which Bruno had some familiarity with.

Many areas of London have a strong identity with which they are easily associated by anyone who lives or works in the capital. But Pimlico is not one of those areas. Whereas everyone knows that Mayfair and Kensington are posh; Tower Hamlets has a lot of low-income and immigrant residents; Canary Wharf is the new financial centre, full of yuppies, and so on, nobody has a stereotypical opinion about Pimlico. Most people might even have difficulty locating it in its correct position, between Victoria and the River Thames in the southwest quarter of central London.

It is an area of some faded elegance and has a mixture of mostly residential properties inhabited by a broad spectrum of economic groups. The higher income bracket owns some of the grander houses, others rent the flats into which the less grand houses have been split.

Bruno's knowledge of the area resulted from a project at the UK Passport Office relatively early in his career. They had insisted he work in their offices, which lay on the northern edge of Pimlico, for the four-week duration of the job and had booked him into a nearby budget hotel with which they had a contract. Early in his career, Bruno did not have the funds to visit any of the places of entertainment nearby and had spent most evenings walking around the area, and most mornings running around it. So, he knew about the lovely old houses, the interesting churches, and the attractive gardens. And the not-so-attractive flats in the wrong areas.

Bruno felt that Pimlico ideally suited Macie's personality as he perceived it through the lens of social media. He could imagine a conversation with her at a dinner party, or more likely at a trendy, crowded, and noisy wine bar.

"Where do you live?"

"Pimlico. Do you know the area at all?"

If you answered, "No, I don't" then she would say something like "Oh I have a flat just off the Belgrave Road" because the word 'Belgrave' would associate her with Belgravia, a much more affluent area of the capital.

But if you said "Yes, I lived there for a brief while a few years ago" then her reply would be more accurate but still vague. Something like, "I've got a flat just off St. George's Road in South Pimlico."

He was reasonably sure that Macie lived in one of the flats at the wrong end of Lupus Street, close to Pimlico Hardware and the local Greggs. Thinking of that location reinforced some of his prejudices about the area. Who names a street after a disease? Lupus Street. What's next, he wondered – Cholera Close or Dysentery Drive?

In her many social media posts, there was never one which clearly showed her flat. He knew where she worked, where she socialized and even where she shopped, but not where she lived. Not that it would have helped him much – the area was too crowded and too busy at just about every hour of the day and night. He needed to find an opportunity when she was going to spend some time in a less crowded place. And in due course, the opportunity arrived – completely out of the blue.

Macie announced to the world that she was going to walk the Kent Coast Path. It was unclear exactly why she had chosen to do this – and her announcement was quickly qualified to state that she would initially be walking only the first stage of the path. The entire path ran to several hundred miles and would be a long-term project, but she would commence it by walking the stage from Woolwich to Grain in three weeks' time.

This was exactly the opportunity Bruno had been waiting for. He read her posts and, via a conversation with her using Richard's account, verified that she would be walking it alone. After her exchange with Richard, she even took the opportunity to create a post informing everyone that it was vital for her mental health that she complete the task alone and she did not want any company on the walk.

Bruno researched as much as he could about the path – and invested time and money going to a bookshop in Nottingham to acquire relevant books and an Ordnance Survey map (he didn't dare buy them online as this could eventually show up on his search history and would be a detection risk).

Using Richard's account, he offered some advice and, in the dialogue, established that she would be breaking the walk into four stages. She would start in Woolwich on Tuesday morning and stop overnight at cheap hotels in Dartford, Gravesend, and Cliffe before completing the final stage on Friday, walking from Cliffe to Grain, where a friend would meet her and drive home. It was on this final stage, which he could tell from the map was the most deserted part of the journey, that Bruno planned for her to meet her end.

The deserted nature of the area held an obvious advantage as it should be easily possible to find an opportunity to be alone with her – but it also posed a difficulty. He would need to get quick access to the area and make a quick departure, and that was going to be difficult. There were a few roads that would enable him to leave his car within a few minutes' walk of a part of the path. But this would mean that if he had to leave his car for hours

– being unsure of exactly what time Macie would arrive at a given location – he would run the risk of the car being noticed and identified.

He toyed with several ideas – false numberplates or a stolen car were obvious possibilities, but he had no skills in stealing a car, and buying any 'dodgy' car or commissioning false plates would leave too much of a chance of him being identified. Even if his plan was successful, and there was always the chance that the plan would have to be abandoned, he still had one more woman to find to complete his task and he would hate for things to go wrong when he was so close to completion.

Finally, he came up with a plan that would not only give him some protection if his car was spotted but would also lay a false trail pointing to a potential perpetrator of the crime. He was proud of the idea as it came together.

He had noticed, by following the online editions of the local papers in the areas where his previous killings had taken place, that the police had not linked any of his previous crimes together. Now, he planned to give their investigations a little shove in this direction. Otherwise, he was in danger of completing his task without them ever connecting the crimes. His hopes of fame as the mysterious Stinger who left a black and yellow item at the scene of each of his crimes would be permanently dashed.

He planned to sell his car to a person who did not exist and then use the car quite openly as transport to and from the area he had identified for the killing to take place. As he thought more about it, he decided to develop this person from his Richard Horsenell identity. After all. Richard had recently been corresponding with Macie, and this would further strengthen him as a suspect. Although this would 'burn' the Inn Cider Trader social media account, he was happy to do this. With only one more woman needed to complete his puzzle, he might not need a third male persona any longer – and if he did, he could always create some new accounts.

He began implementing the plan immediately. He took his car to a nearby cleaning service and paid for a thorough job. He cleared out a load of rubbish from his garage so that once the car had been 'sold' he could hide it from view. And he made sure that there were plenty of provisions in his house – his plan necessitated him staying undercover until closer to his date with Macie. Enough time for him to grow a beard.

So, Bruno placed his car up for sale on a well-known online car sales site and set up a false email correspondence between himself and Richard – eventually leading to the car being 'sold' a week later. Bruno even completed the government paperwork to transfer the registration to the fictitious Swindon address he had come up with for Richard. He chose Swindon as being close enough to the West Country to fit in with Richard's established fictitious identity which included his employment at a financial institution in the west of England. It also linked the location to the prior demise of Emily while visiting her father's care home. Surely, he thought, the police would connect the two crimes if there was a geographic link – even if there was nothing else connecting the victims, the methods, or anything else.

-

On the week of her planned walk, Macie set off on Tuesday morning, (Monday had been completely taken up with preparation, which had been impossible to fit into her crowded weekend social schedule). She took the 436 bus from Pimlico to Woolwich. It was slower and less convenient than using the train, but it was two pounds cheaper and so was much more in line with her socialist principles.

Each night she posted highlights of her day, what she had seen on her walk, the meals she'd had, and all the other exciting stuff so typical of the medium. By Wednesday night she had reached Gravesend and settled into her cheap but cosy hotel, eating her evening meal in a nearby Indian restaurant before taking her weary body to bed for a good night's sleep ready to set off early on Thursday morning.

Bruno had set off even earlier on the same day. He had hidden his car in his garage for two weeks – having cleaned out the space for it to be parked there for the first time in years – and did not want any of his neighbours to witness his departure. He also did not want them to notice that he had not only become bearded but both the beard and his straggly hair were now completely white (courtesy of a tube of grease paint applied the previous evening). He donned his driving gloves which he knew he would have to wear for every minute he was in the car.

His initial destination was Swindon and he had packed various items that were needed for his elaborate plan. The first was a small Faraday cage in which to place his mobile phone as it must not show any trace of his journey until it suited him to do so. His early departure was also necessary since he intended to take the scenic route to his destination. You could never tell which roads might have Automatic Number Plate Recognition Systems active on them – but he was reasonably sure that roads like the A6002 through Stapleford and the B6540 through Castle Donington would be free from such surveillance.

Upon reaching Swindon, he parked in one of the main city centre car parks for an hour. He visited a phone shop in the city and bought a new smartphone, paying cash and making sure that the phone became immediately live on the network. He needed to have a phone with him the next day – just in case something did not go as planned. The new phone not only fulfilled this need but would also play a vital part in his plan to misdirect the inevitable future investigation.

He then moved the car to a nearby street where he parked on a double-yellow line while enjoying brunch in a nearby café. The parking ticket which he inevitably incurred, together with the record of his city centre parking session and phone shop purchase were valuable points that he knew would be picked up by the police in their investigation. Richard Horsenell had certainly spent the day in central Swindon. His new mobile phone did not join the other one in the Faraday cage – it was placed in the glovebox of the car.

He then drove to a small town called Taplow and parked on a side street close to the station. The location had been chosen as an easy drive from Swindon and on the western edge of London with fast access via the new high-speed Elizabeth Line to central London. It would also lay a false trail for the police when they started to trace Richard Horsenell's movements. His brand-new phone stayed in the car overnight, making it look like Richard was staying in the area. After all, why else would he have parked his car on a side street here?

After parking his car Bruno walked the short distance to the station and took the first available train from Taplow. His arrival at Taplow station coincided with the rush hour return of commuters, which he was pleased to note would make it harder for him to be picked up on the station's CCTV. After a couple of changes on the underground, he reached his hotel close to Euston Station in central London an hour later. His own telephone left its Faraday cage when he exited the tube station closest to his hotel and, after checking in, he went for an evening meal in a nearby Italian restaurant before settling down for an early night.

He had a small piece of luck when checking in to the hotel. An American married couple was ahead of him at check-in and, as they asked question after question of the hotel receptionist, they seemed oblivious that a queue was building up behind them. When they finally departed to their room, accompanied by a heavily laden porter, the receptionist rushed through the next few guests and did not pay any attention to any of them, including Bruno. He would use this to his benefit later, if possible.

He left the hotel in the very early hours of Friday morning, retracing his train journey to Taplow before collecting his car and driving around the M25 motorway to the south of London. He stopped once on his journey to refuel the car (and its driver) at a motorway service station en route to his next destination - the tiny village of All Hallows on the estuary of the River Thames – close to one of the most remote parts of the Kent coastal path.

He reached All Hallows just before ten in the morning as he had planned and turned the car around at the end of the small village as the road came to a dead end. As he parked the car, pointing in the right direction for a smooth getaway he realised he would have to compromise. Parking closer to the caravan park which lay between the end of the road and the Thames estuary would make his car more visible to more people. But the further away he parked, the greater the distance he would have to walk on his way both to and from his planned meeting with Macie. He compromised and parked about a hundred yards from the holiday village entrance.

He got out of the car and swapped his driving gloves for a pair of latex gloves. He swung his pack onto his back, locked the car, and, with his hands wedged firmly into his pockets, headed towards the footpath that he knew ran for about a quarter of a mile through the holiday camp to the waterside, where it intersected with the coastal park.

His backpack could not have been lighter. It was crammed full of two pillows and had a hole, about five centimetres in diameter cut into the pack on its inner side. A cardboard tube had been taped through the hole – a fraction of it showing proud of the backpack and the remainder forming a small tunnel through the stuffing, pointing outwards. The tube was just wide enough to contain the barrel of the handgun that he now held, ready to fire, in the left-hand pocket of his kagoule. The side pockets of the backpack contained a pair of binoculars and a small pack of wet-wipes.

He walked briskly down the path, past the small cabin where security staff manned the barrier barring entrance to the park. There was a solitary vehicle leaving the park, its details being checked by the guard. He noticed the strange speed limit sign on the road going through the park. Nine and three-quarter miles per hour. He could only assume that its novelty caught the attention of holidaymakers and reminded them that at any moment the path of their vehicle could intersect with that of a ball-chasing child or dog. The only other alternative was some connection to Harry Potter, whom he remembered had some connection with a train on platform nine and three-quarters - but he thought that connection was highly unlikely.

He continued along the path, past the fishing lake where he saw the only person who seemed to be outside on this blustery day. A park employee busily strimming the long grass between the lake and the first row of chalets, several hundred of which comprised the park's accommodation. At this time of the year, the tourist season was coming to an end and the park would no doubt be winding down, with few guests present, and the off-season maintenance tasks being started.

Five minutes later he was at the water's edge and turned right along the coastal path. This stretch of the path was raised about ten feet above the level of the water and was gravelled wide enough for two people to walk abreast. Bruno walked about five hundred yards along the path as it curved slightly to the left until it reached a small headland. From here he had a great view.

He could see the path in a wide sweeping arc of about a thousand yards in length. In front of him, the Thames estuary was broad, but the heavily built-up Essex coast was clearly visible on the other side of it. A large ship had just come into view on his left, sailing out to the English Channel, heavily laden with containers that it had no doubt acquired in the port of Tilbury, just out of sight to his left. Behind him, a few cattle were grazing on what he assumed would be marshy land. Beyond, he could see the large oil storage tanks for which the Grain peninsula was best known. Except for the lone strimmer user, not a soul stirred among the ranks of holiday cabins that completed his panorama.

Above it all was a truly big sky. Autumn seemed to have arrived as he surveyed the sweeping vista of clouds of every shade of grey. Beneath some of them in the far distance, he could see the mist which meant rain was falling somewhere to the south and west of him.

He briefly considered what the impact of a heavy shower would be. It might make it more difficult to see Macie when she approached from the west. And there would be an increased possibility of leaving footprints. Not that they would matter – his shoes would be consigned to landfill, accompanied by every other item he was wearing, before they could ever be traced.

'Thank goodness this is all coming to an end,' he thought to himself, 'Otherwise I'd run out of clothes soon!'

But he could do nothing to influence whether the rain would come or not, so he stopped worrying about it.

Bruno scrambled down the ten-foot bank to the tiny strip of sand at the water's edge, sat down, and began his wait. If his calculations were correct, Macie had about twelve miles to complete before she reached this part of the path, two miles before the end of the path at Grain where her friend would be waiting in vain. He expected to see her in the next hour or so.

It was more like an hour and a quarter when he saw a black dot appear round the headland on his left and make its way slowly along the path in his direction. He took out his binoculars and checked – it was almost certainly Macie, and there was still not another person in sight in any direction as far as he could see. He was not concerned that she would be able to see him. He would appear to be a lone backpacker, stopped for a rest on his weary way.

When she was about two hundred yards away from him, he got up from the sand, brushed himself down and grabbed his backpack. He slowly clambered up the bank and began walking towards her. His pack was not properly mounted on his back, it hung off his left shoulder, with his left arm looped through it, and his left hand firmly in his pocket.

He walked towards her and when he was about ten yards away, said a cheery "Good Morning" which a tired young woman barely answered. He then stopped somewhat theatrically and said, "Aren't you Macie?" which caused her to stop.

"How the hell…" she began but did not get to complete the question. In a move he had practised scores, maybe hundreds of times, he swung his backpack in front of him, pushed the gun barrel into the tube, pointed it at Macie's midriff and pulled the trigger.

There was a bang, and his makeshift silencer seemed to have done its job because even at this close range it did not sound unnaturally loud. But he couldn't be sure because he was somewhat distracted by a couple of events that happened at the same instant.

First, there was the recoil from the gun, which was more severe than he had anticipated. His experience with guns was limited to a day's corporate clay pigeon shoot when he remembered that the shotgun hit his shoulder pretty hard when it was fired. He had not expected to have been so affected by the recoil from a handgun and he stumbled backwards, concentrating hard on not losing his footing and falling down the bank.

The second surprise was the effect that a large calibre handgun fired at close range had on its victim. He had worried when planning this killing that he might only wound her and that a second shot would be necessary – which would cause him difficulties and possibly alert people nearby.

But he need not have worried. The bullet had hit her right in the middle of her torso, where it had punched a surprisingly large hole. Her hand clutched ineffectively at the hole and her face showed a look of pained surprise. A lot of blood had sprayed out in all directions. And she now lay on the path, alive, he knew, but not for long, he was sure.

He had things to do. He dropped his blood-splattered backpack and took a brief run along the path before hurling the gun as far as he could towards the water. The ten-foot-high bank, the many times he had practised the manouevre, and his recent concentration on building upper-body strength in his workouts, all combined to enable him to propel the gun some fifty yards into the estuary. It was very unlikely to be found, he was sure.

He returned to Macie who he was reasonably sure had stopped breathing. He moved her body so that it lay across the path. Her position would make no difference to her, but this could be a vital clue for the puzzle he was creating and the followers he hoped would try to solve it. He made sure that the binoculars were in his pocket, and then took the wet-wipes and cleaned the front of his kagoule and his face. He pocketed the wipes, checked the scene one last time, and began walking back along the path. He left his backpack – black with the yellow logo of some construction or engineering company where he had once been part of a project team that had each been given a pack with various other corporate-sponsored items. Everyone knows that computer programmers love backpacks, don't they? But nobody ever imagined how this one would be used, he thought. The Stinger had struck again.

As he passed the check-in station at the entry to the park, there was a small queue of vehicles awaiting the security guard – a couple of holidaymakers' cars and two small vans. Their occupants would see him - and they might remember him. But that was inevitable. Five minutes later he was back in his car, the latex gloves replaced by driving gloves and the last stage of his day's journey in front of him.

When he reached Ebbsfleet Railway Station about thirty minutes later, he parked the car at the edge of the large car park. The last car in the last row. It was not going to be seen by too many people and it was not separated from the rest of the cars in any suspicious way. Now he packed everything from the car into a small holdall, made sure the car was empty, and walked to the station. Fifteen minutes later he was on a train to London Saint Pancras Station.

Once he reached Saint Pancras, he did not immediately take the short walk to his hotel but descended the escalator to the London Underground Station, taking the detour for two reasons. The inevitable cameras on the station platforms and concourse would lose sight of him in the throng headed for the Tube, and a brief ride on an underground train would enable him to secrete Richard Horsenell's new mobile phone down the side of one of the train's seats. It didn't matter if the finder handed it into the lost property office or decided to dispose of it more profitably – it would throw the police off the scent when they traced it.

After ridding himself of the phone, he decided that his return journey would end at the station before the one closest to his hotel – he did not want to run the risk of being seen at the railway terminus so soon.

After the brief walk back to his hotel, he went as quickly as possible through the lobby and up to his room. He sat on his bed and started to think about how well his day had gone and to plan the rest of his visit to the big city. But such was the strain that he had placed on himself that day it was not surprising that minutes later he was fast asleep, still wearing his jacket and shoes.

He awoke in shock – the level of distress being higher than the normal level of shock experienced when waking from an unplanned nap. He had incurred a risk by falling asleep in his clothes. Lying on the bed without first removing his clothes meant that there could be evidence transferred from those clothes to the bedcover – which would not be changed before the next guest. There could be traces of the murder scene and the victim on the bedspread, which might well be forensically examined if the police traced his movements. He needed to mitigate this risk.

He stripped, putting all his clothes into a black plastic sack and placed the sack into his suitcase. He thought about his trace evidence problem while taking a long shower to remove the notoriously difficult grease paint from his hair. He also had to have a long and slightly painful wet shave. And he had to allow plenty of time for the tell-tale grease-painted bristles to wash away down the plug hole.

Cleaned and refreshed, he had come up with a plan. He took a small bottle of red wine from the minibar and tipped it across the bedcover. He then removed the bedcover and placed it in the bath, covering it in warm water. He knew it would now have to be changed before the next guest.

He wrote a small note of apology to the cleaning staff, explaining that he had put the bedcover immediately into warm water in the hope of soaking off the red wine stain. He left the note on the bedside table with a five-pound note.

That evening he took the opportunity to capitalise on the events that occurred during his original check-in. Noticing that the young woman who had checked him in was on duty again, he went up to her and said, "I'd like to say how well I thought you handled the situation with those two Americans last night."

"Oh, were you held up? I'm so sorry."

"No need to apologise. You kept them very happy and then moved swiftly to deal with the rest of us. I'll make sure to mention it when I do a review of my stay, Angela," he said, reading the name on her 'How Can I Help You' badge.

There was the slightest trace of a blush on young Angela's face as he continued the conversation. In response to his next question, she happily recommended a nearby Greek restaurant and genuinely hoped he would enjoy the meal. He was confident that she would remember if asked, that it was him – clean-shaven and dark-haired – that she had checked in the night before.

A three-course meal, with a carafe of wine and a generous glass of ouzo with the compliments of the restaurant's proprietor, ensured that Bruno slept well that night and renewed his energy for a day of sightseeing and supporting his football team on Saturday.

He had enjoyed his meal in the Greek restaurant so much that after a few post-match drinks with his fellow Bees supporters after their game, he made a repeat visit and enjoyed another large glass of Greek hospitality with the proprietor on Saturday night.

On his Sunday train journey from London to Nottingham, taken after a late and leisurely breakfast, he thought about the one task he still had to complete. One more name to fill in his matrix. Surprisingly it had proved to be the most difficult slot in the puzzle to fill. When he had first made his list of six target names, he had thought that Megan would be one of the easiest to complete. It was a popular name, especially amongst younger women, he thought.

He had found many Megans, whittling his list down to half a dozen potentials, and then targeting them with messages from his three different personae to elicit the details he needed to locate them. But for some strange reason, he had not been able to make any progress with any of them. Time was now running out, so he would have to redouble his efforts to make contact with one very unlucky lady.

He would begin soon. But first, he needed to complete the clean-up from his most recent assignment, dispose of any items that might link him to her, and write up the chapter in his book. And maybe take a little time to unwind from the tension he justifiably felt. Then he would go to work with a will!

.7 - MEGAN

SATURDAY, 7TH OCTOBER

Megan would probably now be a successful hairdresser if it hadn't been for what happened one Saturday night out with her friends.

She had completed her college course and started work at a popular hairdresser nearby. And life was pretty good. She didn't have the student debt that some of her friends who had done 'better' courses had. She was able to afford a very small flat of her own – a real necessity since she found herself consistently arguing with the man who had moved in with her mother when her father left. And she was starting to build up a client base at the local salon.

She couldn't even remember the circumstances that led up to her being alone at the bar with Izzie at that point in the night when it was time to go home. Izzie was only on the edge of her normal friendship group. Presumably, some of Megan's friends had not been there that evening – illness, holiday absence, or whatever – and some had left early with existing or newly-found boyfriends. And so, she was alone with Izzie, who was alright, but by consensus was considered a little odd and a little wild. And Izzie was in conversation with two guys.

As Megan cast her eyes in their direction, she could immediately tell that the body language was not normal. Were these two guys that Izzie already knew, or were they strangers who were on the pull? It was impossible to tell, and she had not yet been invited to join them to even up the numbers. Then Izzie came over to her and took her arm.

"You and me need to powder our noses, now!" she said with some insistency and steered them towards the ladies' toilets.

Once inside, Izzie came straight to the point, "The taller one wants to go with you. I'm going with his mate. Are you interested? There'd be fifty quid in it for you."

Megan was taken aback by the directness of her approach, and by the sudden discovery, and the explanation for much of Izzie's oddness and wildness. Her fringe friend was admitting that she went with guys – had sex with them presumably – for money.

"But I don't even know him," was her first line of defence.

"Look," Izzie countered, "If he came into your salon, you'd wash his hair for him, wouldn't you?"

"Of course," said Meg.

"Well, you'll just be rubbing a different part of his body and getting paid a whole lot more," Izzie answered with a dirty laugh.

Megan had, of course, looked over the two men when they were talking to Izzie. They weren't bad-looking. A bit older than she would normally consider, but OK. More than OK in fact. Clean, sober, and well-dressed, certainly.

Izzie was very persuasive. Megan had probably had at least one drink too many, and she was in a situation where there was still too much month left at the end of her pay. Fifty quid seemed very appealing. And, as she talked, Izzie made it sound more and more like a dare. And Megan had always accepted a dare. After a few minutes of Izzie explaining that she did this from time to time when she needed the cash, and when the guys looked OK, Megan gave in and agreed to do it.

"Make sure he uses one of these," Izzie said, pushing a pack of three condoms into Megan's hand. Adding, with a hard smile, "And make sure he gives you the money before you take your knickers off."

-

Any bookmaker will tell you that the worst thing that can happen to a first-time gambler is that he or she wins. When this happens, the punter is certain to bet again. And that first vital step that can lead to becoming hooked and unable to stop has been taken.

Something similar happened to Megan the first time she took money for sex. Considering the number of things that could have gone wrong, she got lucky. Clive, the guy she accompanied that night, was quite good-looking. More importantly, he was clean, kind, considerate, and relatively undemanding.

In the taxi on the way home the following morning, Megan thought to herself, 'That wasn't too bad. I've had worse nights where I've chosen my companion for the night. And I didn't have even the consolation of the three twenty-pound notes (Clive had given her a little extra) that are in my purse right now.'

And it was these thoughts that she expressed when Izzie asked how she had got on. Izzie did not have Megan's phone number, so it was a whole week before she got to quiz her. She extracted as much detail as possible from Megan about what had happened after they parted company the previous Saturday. And she made sure that they exchanged mobile numbers. She was certain that this would not be the last 'double date' she would have with Megan.

"You didn't stay the whole night, did you?" she asked after hearing Megan's story – or at least as much of it as a still somewhat shy Megan was willing to tell. "I never do that. They only expect another one for free the next morning," she lectured Megan Then, seeing Megan's reaction, she continued, "Oh no, you didn't, did you? I'm telling you – as soon as the deed is done, give 'em a kiss and cuddle, let them settle down to sleep after their exertions, and then it's clothes back on and a taxi home!"

Megan had, of course, spent almost all the sixty pounds within a week – the taxi home, shopping, and a little treat for herself had seen to that. (This was a few years ago when you could do all that for sixty quid.) So, she stayed in the club with Izzie, her newfound friend, and waited until the rest of the girls had gone, and then repeated the process of the previous week – this time taking Izzie's advice and leaving her partner before daybreak. She also did as Izzie told her and slipped a fiver to one of the club doormen before they left the club.

"That way they'll bring us customers, instead of throwing us out," was the simple explanation she got from Izzy when she asked why.

Earning more in one night (and only part of one night she thought to herself) than she did in a whole day on her feet in the salon was very appealing. And it caused her to entirely rethink her priorities. Izzie was not in the club the following week, and this gave her further pause for thought. She rapidly reached a decision. She might be cut out for this line of work – she found it very easy to dissociate herself from her actions, convincing herself that she was acting a role. But she didn't want the life, the moving between two worlds, and the resulting reputation that Izzie had. If she was going to do it – or at least give it a try, she would do it properly.

On the internet, she found a local Escort Agency's recruitment advertisement and went to chat with Marnie who ran the agency. Marnie was experienced in the work she now arranged and supervised - and was skilled at it. Megan joined the agency the next day, choosing the working name of Suzanne. She thought the name was just exotic enough to be interesting but plain enough that it might just be her real name. She did not attempt an exotic personality – she decided she would be just a 'girl next door' who was just a little more glamorous than the run-of-the-mill, and just a little bit naughtier. She spent the next year learning the ropes and receiving plenty of advice and guidance from her new boss and her more experienced workmates before she set out on her own.

She moved from her flat to a two-bedroomed house (one bedroom for herself, and a second for work – with its wardrobes where she kept a completely different set of clothes to the ones she wore when not working) and quickly built up a clientele for her new profession. She also employed an accountant and declared (almost) all her income. A couple of customers a day at a hundred pounds an hour (with extra charges for any additional services) and she was soon earning over forty thousand a year. And her clothes, cosmetics, and anything else she could purchase from Boots the chemist were all tax-deductible.

She was irked that she had to rent the house – she earned more than enough to pay a mortgage, but getting one, was a different story. 'Never mind,' she thought, 'at this rate, I'll be able to buy a house for cash in a few years!'

-

Bruno was attracted to her when he saw that her website included a little puzzle. Something stupid like "If you add the number of pairs of panties in my top drawer to my bust size in inches, what is the answer? I'll give you the answer next Friday (the thirteenth) and that will be a lucky day for someone because whoever emails me the closest number to the right answer will get an extra fifteen minutes of my time for free!"

A perfect match – he thought. A woman who regards sex as a transactional event - and has a liking for puzzles. And she obviously has a brain, he thought. A simple puzzle that everyone can have a go at, and one that focuses their minds on her panties and the size of her boobs. Clever!

On his first visit, Bruno asked if she would like him to prepare a few puzzles for her to use. Of course, she said yes, and the next time he visited he showed her a simple Sudoku-type puzzle and a message that she could put on her website to accompany it.

It was along the lines of "Hey guys, I've got a great new puzzle for you. It's like Sudoku but instead of the numbers 1 to 9, it uses the letters C, E, I, K, L, O, P, R, and V. The rules are still the same – the same letter cannot appear twice in the same row or column, or the same three-by-three box. If you fill out the puzzle, the first row will show you something I really do. And the last line will show you something I promise to give you when you get here."

A nine-by-nine grid with some of the letters already completed accompanied the message.

Line one, when completed, read LOVEPRICK and the last line read PRICKLOVE.

She liked the puzzle a lot and promised that he too could have fifteen extra minutes for free. Subsequently, he prepared a puzzle for her on every visit. One was a logic puzzle. The type of puzzle that usually goes along the lines of 'The first four houses on our road are numbered 1, 3, 5, and 7. The men who live there are called Andy, Bruce, Chris, and Dave and their occupations are Electrician, Fireman, Gardener, and Handyman. Chris lives between number 1 and the Fireman. The Handyman is not called Dave…. and so on.'

He created a similar puzzle for her listing four fictitious callers, their names, how they liked her to dress, and what their particular preferences were. It went something like "On Thursday I had to put on my nurse's outfit and be prepared to get on my knees. John is not the man who likes me to wear black underwear", and so on.

On another visit, he prepared a puzzle that purported to be an email she had sent to her boyfriend, and the reader had to decipher a secret message. It wasn't all that secret because in sequence buried within the purported email were the words Sierra, Papa, Alpha, November, Kilo, Mike, and Echo. She told Bruno that her readers had particularly liked that puzzle, and several had asked if they could do what she had asked her fictitious boyfriend to do. She charged them each an extra twenty quid and was very grateful to Bruno on his next visit.

She was looking forward to a relaxing weekend when Bruno visited one Friday afternoon. He had always called himself Jack, but she was sure this was not his real name. She noticed that most of her customers had short, ordinary names like Jack, Bob or Jim and was sure that very few used their real names. Jack had been coming to see her for years and was relatively undemanding. He liked to tie her up, and after several visits, she had allowed him to do this – and now she didn't even bother to tape the knife behind the bedhead (just in case she needed to cut herself free) as she had done at the start.

Bruno liked her and had often thought of letting her know his real name – but she continued to call him Jack as this was the name he'd given when they'd first met – so he stuck with it.

As their session came to an end, he was enjoying the sight of her lying face down on the bed with her wrists secured to the two corners of the bed head and got a strange additional buzz from the fact that she remained in this state even after he had got up and begun to dress. She knew he liked it and stayed this way even while they talked of the mundane things of their separate lives as they were wont to do. They had known each other for a long time, after all.

So, he was brought up short when he heard her say, in the middle of some rambling story "...I said to myself, Megan, you've never taken this in your life, so why should you start now?"

He let her finish the story before asking her to confirm her revelation. "So, your real name is Megan, not Suzanne?"

Megan realised she had let her guard down a little but wasn't too worried. Surely, he must know that women in her line of work did not use their real names either. And when she had let other customers know this little bit of information (which she had done very rarely in the past) they had normally felt a little privileged by being made aware. But Jack acted very strangely when she confirmed it.

Of course, he did. Bruno had begun to get a little worried over his inability to complete his task by finding a Megan to complete his set of six. None of the ones he was following on social media was providing the break that would make it possible for him to connect in the way he wanted to connect. Time was rapidly running out and his task was in danger of failing. And now here was one – a real live Megan – in front of him. And in a uniquely vulnerable position.

Bruno had long since ceased to worry about the rights and wrongs of what he was doing. He had never really worried about it at any time. These were not the considerations running through his mind. His first worry was the possibility of being caught.

He had already heard her say that she was going to spend a quiet weekend at home. She had no customers booked to visit and was going to do some cooking – which he knew was a hobby she enjoyed.

If she were to be killed, it would probably be days before she was discovered. And in her line of work, there would be many suspects. And, even if he was to be a suspect, he knew that his original six-month timespan had almost expired. He was prepared to risk being caught, now that the task was complete.

He baulked briefly at the thought of her being someone he had known – possibly could even be called a friend. But that was pushing it a little. He sometimes thought of her as a friend – and sometimes wondered whether they could have become closer if they had met in a non-commercial way. But that was just idle fantasy. The line between a relationship built on affection and one built on commercial transactions was very seldom crossed, and then even more rarely produced a successful outcome.

He also briefly considered the risk. He had already killed Nelly locally – but her death had been accepted as due to natural causes with minimal police involvement. He dismissed his concerns as quickly as they arose.

His next concern was the method that he could employ. If he were to simply strangle her, the police might link her death to the two others he had killed in this way. There was also a chance that hitting her with a heavy object might lead to a link between her and Carol. He would have to think of something else. Quickly. When he remembered her talking about how she would be enjoying one of her favourite pastimes over the weekend - cooking - the answer came to him immediately. A serious cook like her must have some sharp knives in her kitchen.

"Where are you going?" she called to him as he left the bedroom, clad only in his boxer shorts.

"I won't be a minute," he replied and headed downstairs to the kitchen where he quickly found what he was looking for – a knife block with a set of black-handled knives of varying sizes. Choosing one of the smaller ones, he touched the blade and confirmed it was razor-sharp. He took hold of it carefully and returned to the bedroom.

"Now what are you up to?" were Megan's last words as he joined her on the bed and squatted over her in a position very similar to the one that he had occupied a few minutes earlier, only this time his legs were outside her thighs, not between, and were helping him to pin her down.

"I'm sorry," he said as he grabbed her hair with his right hand and pulled her head back while pulling the knife's blade across her throat. She made a horrible gurgling noise which he hardly noticed – he was so taken aback by the flow of blood. He had heard the phrase 'arterial spurt' used more than once on the CSI programmes he liked so much on TV. But he was still unprepared for the sudden gush. Blood splashed back from the bed onto him and spread rapidly across the sheets, pooling briefly before beginning to sink in. She died in less than a minute.

Now he knew he had to take additional care. His DNA would certainly be easily found in the room, even on the bed, by police forensics. That was inevitable and he would not deny having been in the room. But he needed to make sure as far as possible that there was no evidence of him being in the room after the blood began flowing.

He moved carefully away from her and put his feet directly into his shoes. Leaving shoe prints was not a problem – the shoes would be in a landfill before anyone had a chance to look at them – but he must not leave actual footprints or handprints. And he still had tasks to complete.

He moved carefully towards the bedhead and cut the ties from her wrists. He needed to move her body so that it was lying across the bed. She must be found crosswise like Carol and Macie had been, as these would be vital clues for the eventual puzzle solvers. But this was going to be difficult.

He returned to the kitchen and found two other items – a pair of rubber gloves and a plastic carrier bag. He put the gloves on before moving the body – they were, of course, far too small but he did his best. The gloves and the ties he had taken from her wrists were then placed in the carrier bag.

Next, he knew he had to make sure that there was no blood visible on him as he might well be seen by witnesses on his way home. He decided to go the full hog and took a quick shower, using these few moments of relative calm to go through as much as he could in his mind. He towelled himself dry, adding the towel to the contents of the carrier bag. Returning to the room he was hit by the earthy, metallic smell of fresh blood. Thankfully the weather would remain cool for the next few days so there was no likelihood of any worse smells developing and alerting the neighbours for the next few days.

In the hall, he was about to put on his jacket when he felt something in the pocket and briefly wondered what it was. He had carried a burner phone with him to London the previous week but had thankfully never needed to use it. So, when he had disposed of the clothes he'd worn, he had transferred the phone to another jacket pocket. He had an inspired idea of how it could help him now.

He dialled Megan's number and then went over to her phone, and using a tissue to pick it up, answered the call. He let the connection last for about two minutes before terminating it. He would, of course, be disposing of his burner phone with everything else later – but he now had a red herring to complicate the police investigation. They would look for the owner of this phone as almost certainly the last person to speak to Megan, and, who knows, maybe the last person to see her alive.

Once he was dressed, he looked around the room for a final time to make sure there was nothing that he had forgotten. Only then did he realise that there was no clue to The Stinger. What could he do to correct this? Thankfully the answer was literally in his hands.

When he had left home a couple of hours ago, he had felt a slight chill in the air. (He'd noticed that recently he had felt the cold more than ever before – was this a symptom of his illness, he wondered). He had begun to wear a scarf whenever he went out. He had never needed one in his life before, so had bought one on the spur of the moment in the local department store. He didn't realise it was in the colours of the local football team – it was there in the shop at the time, and he needed it. After he bought it, he noticed that other people were wearing similar scarves and it had made him more comfortably anonymous wearing it.

So, he could leave this as the vital black and yellow item – he would have to suffer the cold on the way home. It would incentivise him to walk more quickly. But the scarf would be a dangerous signpost to him – it might well have some blood spatter on it, and certainly would have plenty of his DNA. So, he decided to wash it. He took the rubber gloves out of the bag, washed the blood off them, and then donned them to wash his scarf, using shower gel in the bathroom sink. He wrung it out as best he could and trusted that the house would be warm enough to dry it before it was discovered.

He draped it over the chair by the bed. He thought briefly about retrieving the money he had paid her an hour earlier, but then quickly came to his senses. He did not need the money, and the cash being in her purse might even help him establish his innocence. He had paid his money, had a good time, and left.

Casting a final eye around the room, he felt sure he had dealt with everything and left the house, carrying a plastic carrier bag, and shouting his goodbye to Suzanne on the doorstep (just in case there were any listeners or witnesses).

An hour later he was back home. Except for his jacket, which had not seen the inside of Megan's bedroom, he bundled every stitch of clothing he had been wearing into a binbag. He added his shoes for good measure, tied the bag securely and put it outside his back door, ready for disposal at the tip the following morning, first thing.

He also showered again, just to be sure. Adrenaline was still coursing through him as he tried unsuccessfully to keep it under control. He knew that this had been the riskiest of all his six – but it was the last. His time was rapidly running out – but he had done it. He had completed his six puzzle pieces. Now he had to complete the online puzzle. Then he could update his book, encrypt it on his system, and upload it to the remote server.

He was ready for the final stage of his journey.

.8 - DETECTION AND REWARD

SUNDAY, 8ᵀᴴ OCTOBER

So, we have reached the final chapter of the book. But this one is different from the other chapters. Firstly, I'm switching from writing in the third person to writing in the first person. I'm tempted to write this as if it is written by Bruno and refer to John as 'him' instead of 'me'. I'll resist that temptation – it might just make things too complicated.

The other thing that is different about this chapter is that I can only write part of it. You, the reader, will have to write most of it because only you know how you detected the solution and how you are going to claim the reward.

But first things first. You've now got the list of the victims and enough information to find them all. You can notify the relevant police departments, and so on. Whatever you need to do.

While I was writing this book, I remembered something about some politician once being accused of writing the longest suicide note ever. I couldn't remember the details, so I Googled it. Apparently, the accusation was made by Labour MP Gerald Kaufman who famously described his party's 1983 general election manifesto as the longest suicide note in history. Well, in that case, 'The Book' is possibly the longest confession ever written.

I assume you have worked out who the killer is by now. There is no Bruno. He is no more real than Dick Horsenell (Inn Cider Trader) or Harriet Hale (So Shall Work Her). For the avoidance of doubt, Bruno is John Jackson. Or, to steal a phrase from a much better (and more successful) writer than me, you might say that he is John's 'Dark Half'.

When did you work it out? Right at the start? Did you have suspicions all along? Did any of my misdirections throw you off the scent? Or did you only realise when you got to the chapter on Macie or even the one on Megan? It doesn't matter. I'm gone now. I'd love to know who you are, how you got here, how long it took you, how long it's been since I left and so much more. Who knows? Maybe I am somewhere where I can find this out, or even watch you as you metaphorically turn the pages of my grand opus. I guess I probably won't be, but we can hope, can't we?

If you are expecting me to give some grand justification for what I've done or some great apology for it, you are going to be disappointed. I tried to lay out my decision-making process at the start of "The Book" and that's all you're getting.

The only time that I became uneasy about the whole thing was with Megan. Up until then, I had dissociated Bruno and myself, but that was where we collided. And it caused me some difficulties. I found I was lying to myself. And I was quite disturbed when the police showed me the scarf from Megan's room because I was suddenly reminded that Bruno and I were one and the same, whereas I'd strived so hard to keep us apart. But the moment passed, and even if I did show a reaction to the coppers when they told me about the scarf, they didn't say or do anything, so I guess I got away with it.

Anyway, what matters is how you got to where you are now. I can envisage two possible paths that led you to read this book because there are only two places where it is stored. Possibility number one is that you cracked the case, identified the victims, solved the puzzle, and then went to the website where the reward is detailed. Well done – you have the necessary information to contact Crapnell Waters Solicitors to claim the reward. You have all the time you want to do that, by the way. There's no time limit.

If you are a member of the police, you will have to come to some decision about claiming the reward money. Tread very carefully because it may be deemed that the reward falls foul of Standing Orders and/or Police Conduct Regulations or whatever. Someone may decide that you cannot keep the money. So, I made sure that there would be no time limit. And if you've read the reward announcement you will know that the web page is automatically deactivated once you've done the necessary. But if you're not a copper – go for it!

I've decided to include a short form confession too – I've always been in favour of minimising paperwork - so you can forward just that page to the police if you want, instead of having to give them the whole book. That way you are free to convert this work into your book and you will not have to worry about the details leaking out via the police.

And then there's the consideration of what the reward is worth. Because in addition to the money that you will get from my estate via the solicitors, there's the matter of the book (or should I say "The Book"). There must be a lucrative publishing deal ready and waiting for this story. Maybe you can write it yourself, maybe you can hire a ghostwriter, or just sell the rights. Film and TV rights should be possible too. It's all up to you.

I know that there's not enough content in the eight chapters I've written to make it a full book. There are less than thirty thousand words, so you will have to add at least another forty thousand to make a proper book out of it. But if you add in the stuff from my blog, plus whatever information you can glean from the Police, and throw in your own story, I'm sure it will be enough.

And the book deal must be worth more than enough to double the amount of money I've left you, I'm sure. You will have to decide whether to include the stuff from my blog verbatim – or whether to rewrite your version of it. And you'll have to work out which pieces are true, and which are not.

I always suspected that the police would get hold of the blog, and get past the low-level security protecting it, sooner or later. So, it does contain some misdirection (I believe the late great Alfred Hitchcock used to call them MacGuffins), some half-truths, and some downright lies.

There was no break-in, no sovereigns, and there is no Denis Fittaley. He's a ruse drawn up because as soon as I suspected that my blog might be opened and read by the police, I decided to have some fun with them.

Denis Fittaley is an anagram of False Identity and, apart from those already named above, he is the only other non-existent person in the story. Everyone else is real. Including Billy Rodriguez. I have heard absolutely nothing from him since reading his letter to Stephen and myself all those years ago. I thought it was highly likely that he had disappeared and would not be found by the police, so I tried to hint strongly at him as a potential suspect. If the police had found him, well I guess I would have crossed that bridge when I came to it.

Returning to the subject of the reward, you'll no doubt decide how to spend the money – maybe you'll ease your conscience by giving some to the families of the victims. I don't know or care. That's about all I have to say.

Lastly, if you know you are the first person to read this, I'd be grateful if you could deliver an apology to my friend, Stephen Crapnell. He is, or rather was, the only friend I ever had, and I seriously misled him when asking him for advice. I led him to believe that I was asking him for advice about a theoretical situation in a book I was writing. Although that was, in some ways, true, in other ways it was not. As a result, he has been left with the task of implementing a strangely worded will whose beneficiary is un-named but will prove their bona fides by presenting a document at some time in the future. Sorry to leave you with this, Stephen.

But before concluding, I must also consider possibility number two. The alternative path you may have followed to get here. Maybe you were able to crack the encryption and read the book from the security device on which I stored it in my house. I thought that would prove very difficult, but I know there's no such thing as an unbreakable code, so I must consider the possibility that you achieved it. In which case, well done. And if that is the case, then you're going to need to crack the actual puzzle. You've got the names, now you need to read the Puzzle Announcement – I've included it as an appendix to the Book to make it easier for you. Solve the puzzle and the reward will be yours.

Good Luck!

John Jackson, Sunday, 8th October

.9 A MAJOR PUZZLE
WITH A REWARD WORTH OVER £250,000 TO THE SOLVER

CREATED OCTOBER 8TH, 2023.

The moderator of this website is pleased to announce a puzzle, with a reward that is worth at least £250,000 to the solver.

The puzzle is new and unique.

In the six months immediately preceding the date of creation of this page, there have been multiple unsolved murders of women in the United Kingdom.

This puzzle relates specifically to five of these murders. They occurred across the UK and several different methods were used by the killer.

All five of the victims were killed by the same man, acting alone. He left a clue – a specific item - at each murder scene. The clue links the crimes.

The five victims all had a first name containing exactly five letters.

A sixth victim of the killer was wrongly classified as having died of natural causes. Her name, also five letters long, was Nelly. This is important to note as you will need to add her name to the other five to solve the puzzle. It is also important to note that Nelly was the name she was known by; it was not listed as one of her names on her birth certificate.

This is the same for some of the other women – the name they were known by is the one you need to find. One of the women was known by two different names, but only one of them was five letters long.

To solve the puzzle, you will need to assemble all six names in a well-known pattern.

Form these names into the right pattern and you will see a twenty-one-letter string. Just add .com to that string of letters to create a URL and then open the resulting website. It will give you full instructions on how to claim a significant reward. In addition, it will also reveal the identity of the killer.

The twenty-one-letter string begins with the letter M, the second letter is A, and the final letter is Y.

To find the correct pattern, what you will have to do with some of the names is the same thing that the killer did with some of the bodies. But the names that will require this action are not the same as the ones referred to in the previous sentence.

.10 CONFESSION

I, John Jackson of Layton Avenue, Mansfield, Nottinghamshire, do hereby confess that I committed the following murders:

A woman, known as Nelly Dunne, at her home in Station Road, Mansfield, Nottinghamshire in May 2023

A woman named Gerri, a waitress, in a street in Salford, near Manchester in June 2023

A woman named Emily, in her car, parked in a street in Swindon, Wiltshire in July 2023

A woman named Carol, a music teacher in her home somewhere in the West Midlands in July 2023. (I am sorry, but I'm a little tired as I write this, and the name of the town escapes my memory.)

A woman, known as Macie, close to the village of All Hallows on the Kent Coast path in September 2023

A woman named Megan, who worked as a prostitute under the name of Suzanne, in her home in Mansfield, Nottingham in October 2023

I committed all these crimes alone, with no other person assisting me and with no other person knowing anything about the crimes either before or after their commission.

John Jackson, Sunday, 8th October

12. I've Read the Book - Now I'll Throw It At Him

Detective Inspector Linda Evans Morning, Sunday, October 22nd

It's difficult to explain my feelings when I finished reading the book. An utter revulsion was certainly one of them. This dreadful human being thought it acceptable to turn six women into pieces in a puzzle. But alongside the revulsion, there was also a sense of relief. We would shortly be able to arrest and charge him. And we could have every confidence that he would soon be tried, found guilty, and imprisoned. And that no more people would be made to suffer.

I knew that he had stated in the book that he was 'only' going to murder six people – and that he had very limited time left to live. But knowing that he had lied about so many other things, I was unsure whether this part of his story should be trusted.

Perhaps there should be some feelings of pride about the work that Robin and I had done to discover this information so quickly – but that wasn't there now. Nor was there any excitement, or any real interest in completing the last part of the quest by solving his stupid puzzle. No doubt that needed to be done to complete the case, but it was not a priority.

And, thinking of completing the case – there was now a considerable workload for me. John would have to be arrested and charged – and the case against him compiled. Even though he had written a full confession, every i would have to be dotted and every t crossed - so that some smart-arse lawyer was not able to get him off the hook for any part of his crimes.

And there would be police politics to tackle too. His crimes cut right across police boundaries, and everything would need to be processed without noses being put out of joint. Thankfully I could leave that to others – that level of infighting was thankfully way above my pay grade.

But top of my list of feelings was an awful ache across my neck and shoulders from sitting in an unhealthy reading position for the last two hours.

I turned as I heard movement behind me, and saw Robin, clad only in boxer shorts and a T-shirt, walking towards me. He kissed me gently before asking "You've finished the book, I assume? Only you were so engrossed that I didn't want to interrupt before."

"Yes, I've finished. And the interruption is very welcome. I'm aching from sitting too still," I said, rotating my neck and shoulders to indicate the source of the problem.

Robin began a gentle massage of the area - which was most welcome.

"Can you tell me anything about what's in the book?" he asked. He'd been more than happy to progress on a 'need-to-know' basis throughout our strange, brief relationship. It suited both of us. But I felt the need to let him know a little about the scope of what I now knew. It would help explain why I might not be able to give him as much of my time as I would like to in the immediate future.

"He confesses to killing six women. Over the last six months or so, having chosen most of them from social media. Apparently, their names fit together in some form of puzzle, which is going to be published on the internet. And he claims that he has got a terminal illness."

"Wow," was the immediate monosyllabic response. Then "Are the murders all on your patch?"

"No – two of them are – one is the one we're already investigating and the other was an old lady whose death had been put down to natural causes. The rest are all over the country."

"I guess you're going to have a lot of work to do then."

"' Fraid so," I replied, "but not right now." The massage was having an effect above and beyond just easing my stiff shoulders. I had no idea what time it was. We had gone to bed quite early the previous evening – but sleep had come much later.

Glancing at the living room clock, I learned that it was about six a.m. I didn't need to be a police officer for the next couple of hours.

-

Around eight-thirty, fortified by a breakfast that Robin prepared while I showered and dressed, I took pen and paper and made a list of tasks that needed completing within the day – even though it was Sunday.

"I guess you'll not have much time for me today?" Robin asked, slightly plaintively.

"There are a few things I'll need to do today – but I should be finished by mid-afternoon – if you can hang around until then?" I asked, hoping that he would guess my eagerness for a yes in response.

"You know I've always wanted to look around Nottingham for a day. Maybe learn something about Robin Hood," he replied with a smile.

"And this Maid Marian will be all yours when she returns from her castle," I replied.

After a brief kiss, I returned to my piece of paper. My task list appeared complete (for now – no doubt I'd think of other things later), and I was out the door. Once in the office I called DS Holden and told him the good news that I had enough evidence to arrest John Jackson and the bad news that there were enough things that needed doing immediately to ruin any plans he had for his Sunday.

While waiting for him to arrive, I arranged for a couple of uniformed officers to accompany us to make the arrest. I did not expect any trouble – but thought it would be sensible to have company, just in case. I also wanted John to have the full experience of riding handcuffed in the back of a patrol car.

I also called DCI Lancaster and informed him that we were about to make an arrest and that there were some developments in the case that meant I needed a meeting with him first thing tomorrow. He promised to clear space in his diary – and I took it as a compliment that he did not feel the need to ask me to justify my request for a meeting. Either that or he wants to keep the interruption to his weekend caused by my call to a minimum. Having assured him that there was no need for him to suffer any further interruption to his weekend, I hung up.

-

Half an hour later, DS Holden and I were waiting on John Jackson's doorstep, worried that there had been no response to our knocking.

We decided to check with the neighbours to see if they had any idea of John's whereabouts, His was the type of neighbourhood where someone would be sure to have an idea of where he was.

At the first door, we were informed, "There was an ambulance there yesterday," in the tones that are uniquely reserved for the delivery of important, confidential information. "Not a normal one, either. A posh one, more American than British it looked."

I remembered the line from John's blog 'A referral letter from an appropriate specialist and a small donation was enough to guarantee admittance' and I immediately knew where the American ambulance had come from and where our next destination would have to be. The local hospice. It seemed that the story of terminal illness in John's book may well be true after all, and I remembered that he was quite unwell when we last met. His story of having a bad hangover must have been a cover.

The duty manager at the hospice confirmed that John Jackson had indeed been admitted the previous day, and reluctantly agreed to escort me to the private room where John was accommodated. I agreed to go alone, DS Holden would wait in reception and the uniformed officers would remain outside the building for the time being.

John was sitting upright in bed. The room was not hospital-like at all. It was much more like a private bedroom that just happened to have some medical equipment placed by the bed – including an oxygen supply and a drip that were both connected to John. He had visibly shrivelled since our last meeting and was using the oxygen mask intermittently to assist his breathing. He acknowledged my presence with little more than a grunt.

"I've read the book, John," I said slowly – judging this to be the easiest way of telling him that I knew everything. He closed his eyes briefly and nodded. Taking as deep a breath as he could, he asked in a rasping voice, "And the puzzle?"

"Haven't solved it yet," I answered, adding quickly "But I will soon, I'm sure."

He did his best to smile, but I didn't spend too long wondering if he was pleased that I hadn't yet solved the puzzle or amused that I thought I soon would. Either way, he was probably confusing me with someone who gave a shit.

"John Jackson, I need to do this formally. You are now under arrest in connection with the murder of Megan McCormick and other offences." I read him his statutory rights, even though he was now dozing.

Leaving the room, I explained to the duty manager that John was facing some very serious charges, and although it was obvious that he would not be leaving the facility, he was officially under arrest. We would need to station a police officer outside the door of his room. I was not concerned about his ability to get out, but, knowing that news of his arrest would soon spread, it was more to ensure that nobody entered. And having someone permanently on-site would guarantee that we would know immediately if there was a significant change in John's condition. Which was a fine euphemism – there was only going to be one significant change in his condition. To quote the bad old joke, he would soon be in a grave condition.

DS Holden and I returned to the station, and I did my best to tell him what little I had not told him on our two journeys earlier in the day. Back at the station, I set him to the task of closing down the inquiry. I had to call the duty offices of Greater Manchester Police and Kent Police. Having interfaced – even briefly – with them on the murder cases on their respective patches, I felt duty-bound to let them know that good news would be coming their way very soon, but the exact details could only be revealed after I had spoken with senior management. I also nudged Kent Police to give good news to their contacts in Wiltshire. I also obtained details of a murdered music teacher from West Midlands

Police and informed them that as a result of an arrest we had made, they would also shortly be receiving an update on an unsolved murder on their patch.

I arranged for the guard outside John's hospice room to be maintained twenty-four hours a day for the foreseeable future. Then, having obtained the missing information about the two victims that were unknown to us – the one in West Midlands and the local one wrongly attributed as a natural death, I typed up the charge sheet and spent another hour or so making sure I was thoroughly prepared for my meeting with DCI Lancaster tomorrow.

With just over half an hour's work still to do I called Robin's mobile and left a message. I made a mental note that if our relationship was going to last, I needed to get added to his contact list so that my calls would go directly through to him.

When we had done all that needed to be done, I told DS Holden to go home and rescue what was left of his weekend.

I walked slowly back to my flat as a wave of weariness began to engulf me. Not only had I missed two meals in the last twenty-four hours, but I was suffering a few aches and pains on account of recent excessive use of some bits of my body that hadn't been put to work for a long time. Too long a time.

My phone rang as Robin returned my call. He had returned to the flat and used the spare key I'd given him, and we agreed that a takeaway meal would be the ideal plan for our early evening. Even though we didn't need to work up an appetite we did complete some enjoyable light exercise together before calling the meal delivery service.

"I'm going to need to go soon," he said as we finished the last of the rice and the bottle of white wine that Robin had thoughtfully bought and put in the fridge in the afternoon. "I've got a two-hour drive and a week's worth of washing to do – and a lot of catching up to do tomorrow."

We agreed that we would plan to spend next weekend together, and Robin suggested I might like to get acquainted with the lovely town of Cheltenham, which I agreed to. I reminded him to put me on his phone's contact list so we could speak without a half-hour cooling-off period every time I called him.

You're not cooling off about me already, are you?" he asked, and I assured him I was not. He obviously needed to check this out, as he removed most of my clothing once again.

13. A Web Address to Die For

Detective Inspector Linda Evans Evening, Sunday, October 22nd

Lying next to Robin, my mind somewhat fleetingly began to return to the puzzle. Robin was going through one of his sexual self-doubting phases. Men have them occasionally – at least the good ones do. And even they don't usually have them as often as they should.

"You really do enjoy it, don't you?" he asked.

"No, I'm just a fucking good actor. Or should I say a good actor, fucking?" I replied, smacking him with a pillow.

"It's just that I enjoy you so much I have to check from time to time," he meandered on.

"Look," I said, wanting to dispel these welcome momentary doubts. "Have you ever had one of those itches deep down in your ear and scratched it by pushing your little finger as far in as you could?"

"Yes," he replied with some understandable hesitation.

"Well, afterwards which felt better – the ear or the finger?"

For half a second, he thought about answering and then realised what my question actually meant. A playful slap with a pillow was my reward.

His playful mood continued. "We've tried it this way", he said, snuggling up to me, and then did a hundred-and-eighty-degree turn and rested his head on my thighs. Turning my head to the right my eyes were in line with a pair of bent knees.

"And this way," he continued, (as if I could forget it).

Then another ninety-degree turn, his belly across my lower midriff and his head hanging over the edge of the bed.

"Is there a way we could do it like this?" he asked, "Sideways?" laughing.

Whatever response he expected to receive to his question, he could not have expected the result it produced.

I sat bolt upright. His stupid comment had connected with the part of my brain that wasn't thinking about sex but was on its way back to tackling the puzzle Bruno had set.

"Sideways! That's it. Sideways." I slid out from underneath him, jumped out of bed, and crossed the bedroom to collect my dressing gown from the hook behind the door. I didn't have to look at Robin – I knew he'd be registering shock, but there was a case to solve.

My thoughts raced as I crossed the living room.

Sideways. Megan's killer took the time and trouble to turn her body through ninety degrees, significantly increasing his risk of getting caught by spending more time at the scene and risking leaving clues to his identity by moving a blood-soaked body. And none of us had been able to understand why he had done it.

And Kent Police were likewise baffled as to why Macie's body had been moved by her killer so that she was lying across the path. And it was in 'The Book' too. He'd moved the piano teacher's body to lie across the bed. Three of the six victims had been laid sideways.

This was the reason – all for his silly puzzle. To solve it, I was going to have to overcome some pretty strong feelings that were welling up in me. For some reason, I was even more sickened by his arrogance and the disregard he had shown for his victims. He had messed with their bodies just to set a riddle.

But I switched off those feelings for the time being. If Robin and I could put our minds to it, there was every chance we could solve the mystery in the next few minutes.

I moved into the lounge, gathered some sheets of paper from my desk drawer, and wrote all the names on a clean sheet – in alphabetic order, in capital letters, and well-spaced - to see if anything jumped out at me.

C	A	R	O	L
E	M	I	L	Y
G	E	R	R	I
M	A	C	I	E
M	E	G	A	N
N	E	L	L	Y

The puzzle announcement talked of a word beginning with M, and I was working on the hypothesis that some of the names would need to be written in one direction and some other names written in a direction ninety degrees different.

Two names began with the letter M, so I wrote them at right angles to each other, starting with the name of the woman who had started all this for me.

    M   E   G   A   N
    A
    C
    I
    E

With Robin now looking over my shoulder and confirming my every step, I now looked at the other four names. And there it was, staring at me. I had names beginning with C, E, G, and N. It was like one of those word puzzles that people play online.

I entered Carol and Emily's names into their obvious places in the grid.

    M   E   G   A   N
    A
    C   A   R   O   L
    I
    E   M   I   L   Y

There were now two obvious places for the remaining names to be entered and so the grid was completed:

    M   E   G   A   N
    A   E   E
    C   A   R   O   L
    I   R   L
    E   M   I   L   Y

And looking at it as an array of letters, there were twenty-one of them: MEGANAEECAROLIRLEMILY.

"I think I've got it!" I wanted to shout out – but couldn't until I was sure, so it came out as a hesitant whisper. I don't know what Robin said in reply – I was so focussed on solving this puzzle and nailing this bastard that I was thinking only of what needed to be done.

I pulled my dressing gown around me and crossed to my computer, clutching the sheet of paper in my hand.

My hand was shaking as I entered www.meganaeecarolirlemily.com into the browser.

Robin was a few steps behind me. He could have still been in the bedroom and would have heard me yell "Fuck!" as a message came up in large letters on the screen.

OH, YOU ARE SO NEARLY THERE!

BUT YOU DIDN'T READ THE INSTRUCTIONS QUITE CAREFULLY ENOUGH

GO BACK AND READ THEM AGAIN AND I'M SURE YOU'LL HAVE THE ANSWER

(AND THE REWARD)

VERY SOON INDEED.

I reopened the page with the reward announcement on it and read it again. The key phrase was "The string begins with the letter M, the second letter is A, and it ends with Y." The word I'd entered began ME, not MA. I took a few breaths while Robin filled the gap with the obvious comment, "You just need to turn it through ninety degrees." He took my piece of paper and rewrote the pattern:

M	A	C	I	E
E		A		M
G	E	R	R	I
A		O		L
N	E	L	L	Y

"Now the word is there", he said. And it was:

MACIEEAMGERRIAOLNELLY.

I entered www.macieeamgerriaolnelly.com and struck gold. The message appeared instantly on the screen:

CONGRATULATIONS!

YOU HAVE SOLVED THE PUZZLE

It was in plain text. Silently I thanked John for sparing us the sight of rockets bursting or balloons ascending. Considering the subject that we were dealing with – the murder of six innocent women - at least he had shown some restraint.

There was some text and some boxes for data entry on the screen.

> You are now entitled to claim the entire estate of the late John Jackson. At the head of the screen, you will see four PDF files that can be downloaded when you click on the icons.
>
> The first file is a copy of the blog that I have been writing for the last six months.
>
> The second file is a complete set of instructions that you need to take to Crapnell and Waters solicitors in Mansfield to claim my estate, which is held in trust by the solicitors. I suggest you first contact them by telephone, making it clear that you intend to lay claim to my estate. At the time of creating this puzzle in the year 2023, your initial contact there should be the senior partner, Stephen Crapnell – but that may have changed by the time you read this.
>
> The third file is titled "The Book" and is a complete background to the deaths of the six people whose names formed the puzzle you have just solved. It is written in the form of a novel – but the details of the killings within it are accurate. In the event of there being any discrepancy

between the contents of 'The Book' and my blog, you should accept 'The Book' as the true version.

Knowing it was likely that the blog would possibly be read in advance of my death, I found it necessary to be economical with the truth within it, and even to include a few misdirections.

The fourth document is a simple confession, acknowledging that I, and I alone, committed the six murders. You may find that this document is easier to use for some purposes than the full text of the book.

It is important now you have solved the puzzle, that nobody else reaches this page and tries to claim the reward. To prevent that from happening, you need to enter your name, home address, and email address in the boxes below and then close this page.

This will ensure that the four files are emailed to you – just in case there is any problem with the download. Your name and your home address will be merged into the document to be presented to the solicitors making clear that you are to be the beneficiary of my estate.

Once you have completed these instructions this page will be permanently closed. You can test this by re-entering the 21-letter word into your browser and verifying that the page displays a "BAD LUCK SOMEONE HAS ALREADY SOLVED THE PUZZLE" message.

Congratulations once again.

-

Once again, I faced difficulty in expressing the range of emotions that swept over me. Elation and the satisfaction that comes from solving a tricky puzzle – they were both there, for sure. But so were sadness and disgust that what this monster had thought of as merely a word game, had ended the lives of six women. And there was a growing feeling of tiredness and a little despair that the career I had chosen led me to deal with situations and people as low as this. I didn't even give a thought to the reward I'd just earned the right to claim.

"Well done. Now you'll have to enter your details into the boxes," Robin said.

"But I'm sure I'm not allowed to collect the reward. There's bound to be something in Standing Orders or Police Regulations or something to prevent that. And I'm not sure it's right for me to have it, anyway."

"Doesn't matter. You've got to enter something in those boxes to make sure the puzzle is wiped off the internet, just in case. You'll have plenty of time to decide what to do about the book and the reward later on."

He was right, of course. The idea of entering Robin's details into the boxes crossed my mind, but that was never going to be possible. If a serving police officer collects a reward, it's bad enough. It would be even worse if someone who was some form of government cyber-spook (which was how I was beginning to think of Robin) suddenly came into an unaccountable large sum of money.

Never being one to completely trust computers, I downloaded the files from the web page before entering my details into the boxes John had helpfully provided. Once the details had been entered, sure enough, an email message popped into my inbox, complete with four file attachments. I double-checked by entering the twenty-one letter URL into my browser and received the promised message.

BAD LUCK! SOMEONE HAS ALREADY SOLVED THE PUZZLE.

IF IT'S ANY CONSOLATION TO YOU, YOU DID HAVE THE RIGHT ANSWER.

BUT SOMEONE ELSE HAS ALREADY WORKED OUT THE ANSWER AND THERE IS NO REWARD FOR YOU.

"I guess that's the end of the case for me," Robin said – his voice betraying a little sadness, I thought.

"But not for me," I replied and continued with, "My work is not yet done!" The closest I could get to a light remark.

-

It was a strange way to end what had been an amazing weekend in so many ways. Robin and I dressed, and before saying goodbye, I confirmed my promise to visit him the next weekend.

"I'm looking forward to next Friday evening already", I said as we kissed goodbye.

When he had left, I sat in silence for a while (with another large glass of wine, I must admit) and began a long thought process about how I was going to handle the situation I found myself in. My big dilemma concerned the details that were in the book and the puzzle. With the written confession in our possession, I could see no reason for these details to enter the public domain. In fact, I could think of several good reasons why they shouldn't.

So, I wondered, what was the right thing to do?

14. Management Summary

Detective Inspector   Linda Evans   Monday, October 23rd

My meeting with DCI Lancaster was scheduled for 9 a.m. and started on time, but it didn't last long. Once he'd received a brief overview of John Jackson's confession, he immediately decided that we needed to discuss the case with Chief Superintendent Dannatt, since the crimes involved other police forces. He did, though ask me about John's current situation and I informed him.

"So, the bastard is going to croak before we get him to trial," is how he neatly summarised the situation. I confirmed this was probably the case.

He then asked how the confession had been obtained, and I explained that it was one of the files that were encrypted on his office computer.

"You remember I got an ex-boyfriend to help? The one who now works in cryptography for some government department."

"How much does he know about the case?"

"Pretty much everything," I replied.

"And do you trust him?"

"Well, since he works for some department that's so secret, I have to wait thirty minutes for my messages to his mobile phone to be security cleared before speaking to him, yes."

"Multiple messages to his mobile phone? Are you sleeping with him?"

At this point, some of my female colleagues might have taken exception to DCI Lancaster's very personal and very direct question. But I reckon that this is exactly what he would have said to a male DI if the crypto expert had been female, so I didn't find it offensive. I was very tempted to call his bluff and say something like "Well, actually sir, when we go to bed together, we don't seem to find much time for sleep" but I thought better of it. Instead, I just said "Maybe", which was the best way of saying yes without saying yes, that I could think of.

Our meeting with CS Brian 'Dan' Dannatt was scheduled for the Chief Superintendent's earliest availability, 11:30, which gave me just enough time to complete one important errand. I called Stephen Crapnell and asked if he could make himself immediately available since the matter was both important and urgent. He assured me that his diary contained nothing that could not be postponed and would be waiting for me in half an hour – which was all the time I needed to get to his office.

There was one small doubt to clear up among many loose ends that also needed resolving. The rest could all wait, but this doubt could not. If there was one person on the planet who might be aware of John's actions, it would be his only friend, Stephen. He was the only one specifically mentioned in John's book – and I remembered John's apology contained in the final chapter. I needed to make sure that Stephen was the innocent victim that John portrayed him as – and not an accomplice - and was reasonably sure that this could be established in a short interview.

I was quickly able to establish that Stephen was completely unaware that John had been taken into the hospice. The shock and sadness that he showed as soon as he heard this could not be faked. I was sure of that. It made me apologise before delivering the rest of the bad news – that his school friend had murdered six women with no apparent motive. I looked to see if there was anything in his response that showed any reaction to my description of the crimes as motiveless, and there was nothing. Just shock, dismay, and possibly even horror. I made sure he knew that this had to be kept secret until the press announcement which would probably take place the following day.

It's impossible to record what he said as he received the news. It was a series of mild expletives, repeated use of the word no, and words like terrible, awful, and so on. He was in such a state that I had to defer the other reasons for my visit, which were to let him know about the unusual terms of John's will and to pass on John's apology for misleading Stephen in what may well have been their last meeting.

I brought the meeting to a close, knowing that I could find an opportunity to return when John's will was located – presumably amongst John's private papers in his home office. I returned to the station, finally sure that John Jackson had indeed been acting alone as he had stated.

I picked up a large, strong Americano from the coffee shop outside the station before my meeting – I expected that maximum resources of caffeine were likely to be needed.

We entered the Super's office and for the second time that morning, I gave a summary of the situation on John Jackson. DCI Lancaster kept silent as the Super asked a string of questions and took careful notes of my answers. Whilst he was known to everyone as 'Dan', not even his direct reports were able to address him as that to his face. But that was not a problem for me – I just called him sir.

"Six murders, two on our patch, and one each in Kent, Manchester, Wiltshire, and West Midlands?"

"Yes, sir"

"And you have been in touch with only Kent and GMP?"

"Only those two during the investigation, sir. But I spoke to the other two yesterday to confirm the exact details of the victims. I told them only that they would be receiving an update from us today."

"Good"

"And the confession is complete?"

"It contains enough information to accurately identify each victim, although he was not exactly specific about their full names and exact dates of the offences, sir."

"Have you prepared a charge sheet?"

"Yes sir. But he has not yet been formally charged. I believe we need to move quickly on this though. His life expectancy is measured in days, and he could die at any moment."

At the end of the Q and A session, Dan looked carefully at his notes and decided he had enough to go on. He put down his pen, which I noticed to be a fountain pen – the first I had seen since my school days. He addressed his remarks to me.

"Well, obviously this is an excellent piece of police work, DI Evans. I must congratulate you on your sterling effort in solving this heinous crime. The capture of a multiple murderer is a huge feather in your cap – even though it does raise certain challenges concerning areas of responsibility within the various police forces involved, but that is something that I must deal with personally. You were both quite right to brief me before moving forward, and I shall have to consult the other forces before we make any announcement outside this room. In the meantime, I would like you, DCI Lancaster, to formally charge Mr Jackson as soon as possible, and make sure he is kept in his present location under police guard. We three will reconvene in my office first thing tomorrow morning, I assume you have plenty to keep you busy in the meantime?"

The last remark had been directed to me. "Yes sir", I replied, "Still plenty of loose ends to tie up."

"Excellent. One last thing. You will notice that I referred to Mr Jackson as a multiple murderer. I would be grateful if you would make sure that your colleagues use this term when referring to him and his crimes. I am depressed at the developing tendency to use the term 'serial killer'. I find that this term both Americanises and glamourises the dreadful deeds he has perpetrated. While I am unable to prevent members of the press and the public from using the term, I would strongly prefer that it is not used by any member of the police force. Is that clear?"

Both DCI Lancaster and I confirmed that we understood. And I silently wondered if DCI Lancaster agreed with my opinion that we had just witnessed one of the finest impersonations of King Canute trying to turn back the tide that you could ever wish to see.

"Is there anything else?" he asked.

They say that when you are near death the events of your life flash before your eyes. I briefly wondered if the events of my police career would flash before my eyes as my next utterance might well bring that career to an end.

"One more thing, sir. During my investigation, I discovered that John Jackson had one previous interaction with Nottinghamshire Police, but it was not on his record because he had given a false name at the time."

Both men in the room were looking at me with puzzled expressions. DCI Lancaster's face bore the stronger one because he (wrongly) thought that I had already told him everything about the case.

"He used the name of his dead brother, Tom Jędrzejczyk when he was caught up in a raid on a brothel near the M1 Motorway in March this year".

The Chief Superintendent immediately understood the significance of this remark, and instinctively brought his hand to his mouth and briefly pinched the piece of flesh between his nostrils and his top lip. DCI Lancaster retained his puzzled look until the Super turned to him and explained what had happened. He gave him the full story of Police Constable Peake's unfortunate use of a Taser, and the 'management decision' not to make any mention of the incident in his report.

DCI Lancaster expressed his sympathies with the difficulties that his boss had experienced.

"I fully understand the dichotomy you faced, sir," he said in as fine a piece of management-speak as you could wish for.

Turning to me, the Chief Superintendent spoke, more slowly and carefully than before.

"I can see that this information is known to some of the members of the service, but not to others," he said, nodding his head towards DCI Lancaster as he completed the sentence.

"How widespread is the knowledge?" he asked.

"I believe that I am the only one who was not present at the event who knows of its occurrence," I said, "but I cannot be one hundred percent sure of that."

"And do you believe that this information needs to go any further?" he asked, very deliberately.

"Absolutely not, sir. My only reason for bringing it up is that I believe that it might be best to prepare a strategy, just in case it is needed if the full details of the original incident ever were to come out at any time in the future."

"Thank you for your candour, DI Evans. I will bear in mind what you said. Can I trust that there is now nothing else we need to discuss?"

I confirmed that there was not and left the room with DCI Lancaster. Not surprisingly he asked pointedly that we continue our discussion in his office.

"Is there anything else you might like me to know about this investigation before I completely lose my patience with you?" he asked in a manner that made his displeasure clear but could not quite be described as shouting. He expected me to say no, and was therefore taken aback when I replied, "There was also one other thing I would have said to you if you had not brought our last meeting to an abrupt end, sir."

I waited briefly for him to say something, but I must have removed the wind fully from his sales, so I carried on, "John Jackson left a clue at the site of each murder. Something black and yellow. It was a different item at each site, but always black and yellow. I believe he hoped to get himself something of a nickname – he even suggested he might become known as 'The Stinger'. I believe that this showed that he had very limited awareness of how the police deal with these incidents. But it might have become known if we had taken longer to find him out."

"And what do you propose we do with this information?" he asked, his earlier aggression abating.

"I can see no reason to release it, sir. I can only believe that this would give the man more publicity."

"Is this information known to anyone other than yourself?"

I had to think hard for a moment.

"I suppose each service will know about the object that was left at their respective crime, sir, but I am the only person who has read John's encrypted papers that explain that he was doing this and why."

"In that case, I agree with you. Let us keep this to ourselves. And can I trust that I am now fully briefed on the case?" It was not humanly possible to stress a word more fully than he stressed the word 'fully'.

"One other small matter," I continued. "John's private papers also contained information that confirmed he had defrauded the Inland Revenue of a few thousand pounds. I intend to pass this on to HMRC and leave the decision as to how to proceed up to them. I believe that if I delay doing this for a couple of weeks, they will close the case since it will literally be dead at that point. With my current heavy workload, I fear that it will be at least two weeks before I can get around to dealing with this aspect of the case. Do you agree with my priorities, sir?"

He did. And having checked that there was absolutely (another word he stressed strongly) nothing else he needed to be informed of, he ended the meeting.

I did take one additional precaution later that day, which was to write an email to him, confirming that in line with our discussion, I was the only person who would have access to John's private papers and that any information that was extraneous to the detection of the crimes would not be released. And that HMRC would be informed of certain issues relating to the tax affairs of John Jackson when workload relating to the criminal prosecution allowed. Well, we all have to cover our arses sometimes, don't we? I believed that this email would significantly add to the protection that my rear end needed.

And I realised that I had, almost without thinking, made a major decision. Nobody knew anything about John's online puzzle.

15. Operation Firefly

Chief Superintendent Brian Dannatt   Morning, Monday, 23rd October

People sometimes tell me that my role is more about politics than policing. And they usually state it in a critical rather than a complimentary way. And here I am in a position where politics are going to be absolutely crucial if the whole police service is going to come out of this difficult situation in a good light.

Naturally, I'm pleased with the superb police work that DI Linda Evans has put in. Catching a murderer is always a difficult task and their apprehension is a very good thing both for society in general and the police service in particular. Catching a multiple murderer even more so.

But she has given me a problem, even though she seems oblivious to it. She is probably not aware of how the media might react to this. I cannot predict whether the story will be along the lines of 'Our brave boys in blue catch another nasty villain' or "Why did it take PC Plod so long to snare him?' That duality in the way the media reports crime is something we in the police service have little or no influence over. The way they spin it will largely depend upon the politics or even the mood of the newspaper's editor or proprietor. And maybe upon how the narrative best fits with other stories going around at the time.

Over the past few months, some of my colleagues in other regions have come under more pressure than normal because there has been a murder on their patch and months have passed without discernible progress. There will have been criticism from the local press, possibly from relatives of victims, and maybe even activist organisations campaigning on behalf of women's rights or some other cause. All of them are well-intentioned of course, but mostly without the slightest idea of how difficult it can be to find a murderer – especially one who has no obvious connection to the victim as has been the case with these murders. And if another police service now waltzes in and announces that they've found him, then that may make them look worse. It could even lead to them asking questions as to why we have been 'harbouring' a multiple murderer on our territory for so long without either catching him or even communicating with other services about our investigation. It would be a natural reaction of the other service to deflect criticism by blaming our service for deeds done or not done.

Add to that the small possibility that the killer's actions might have resulted from a bang on the head that resulted from police action, and you have a recipe for disaster.

Looking back, I ask myself if I did the right thing by saying nothing about the incident with the Taser. If ever there was a textbook case of being 'damned if you do and damned if you don't' then that was one. If I had gone public with the information about the chief constable's son's error of judgement, then I would probably not be in this situation right now. The reason I would not be in this situation is that I would probably have been moved somewhere else – somewhere a lot less agreeable, I suspect.

So, I have even more reason to want the announcement of this arrest to be handled smoothly. I trust my staff not to say anything about the event in the nightclub. Frankly, I have no choice but to trust them. But I cannot trust anyone outside the organisation if they get a sniff of the story.

We must not allow that to happen. If I do my job in the next few hours, that won't happen, and everyone will come out of it well. If not exactly smelling of roses, at least we won't smell of the stuff you put on roses to fertilise them.

My first call will be with Diane Dowling at Greater Manchester Police. She has had the longest period of an unsolved case from the list DI Evans gave me and so will have been under more pressure because of the perceived delay. Add to that the fact that she heads the largest service outside the Met and has a fearsome reputation for not suffering fools gladly, and I'm sure that if I can get her buy-in to my plan, the others will follow.

After Diane, I'll talk to my opposite numbers in the West Midlands, Wiltshire, and Kent, and with a bit of luck, we will have the whole thing sorted out within twenty-four hours and will be singing off the same hymn sheet. Because we'll have written the hymns ourselves!

Afternoon, Monday, 23rd October

My Call to Diane Dowling, GMP:

"Diane, thanks for taking my call."

"Yes, well, thank you, Diane. And you?"

"Excellent. Diane, we have a situation that affects both you and me, and I'd like to outline it to you and propose a course of action."

"One of my DIs has had a brief conversation with one of your team about a murder in Salford that occurred some five months ago. A waitress I believe it was."

"Yes, that's her. Well, we have now apprehended our suspect and he has confessed to both the murder which occurred on our patch and to the murder on your territory. He's also confessed to three other murders in different parts of the country, as well as causing a death we had previously put down to natural causes."

"Yes, indeed. Some excellent police work. But I'm a little concerned about handling the announcement that we'll be making tomorrow. We've had minimal contact with you, only a little with Kent Police, and none at all with the other two services involved. But I believe it is important to make it appear that we have all been working more closely together in the period leading up to the arrest."

"No problem. I believe the public would prefer to believe that we are all one team, working together, even though you and I both know how difficult that can be in practice. So, if we said that we had a liaison group working on this for the last few months...."

"That's an excellent idea, Diane. A task force sounds so much better. More proactive. Yes, I'll use that description."

"Quite. I'd like to put this idea to my opposite numbers in the other three services today, and hopefully, we can come up with a jointly worded statement that I can deliver at our press conference tomorrow, and which will become the basis for each service to use as a basis for their own announcement."

"Thank you. It will be so much easier if I can tell them that you are on board with the idea."

"Great. I'll have something drafted and in your inbox by the close of play today. If you could get your comments back to me ASAP, I'd be grateful."

"Absolutely – we'll let the necessary people know when we've finalised the text. In the meantime, DI Evans will talk to your team and let them know that they can close their case – details to follow tomorrow."

"Yes. You too."

Evening, Monday, October 23rd

My Call to Michael Tyrrell, Wiltshire Police

"Sorry to call you so late Michael, but it has been a bit hectic here and you've been rather tricky to get hold of today."

"Yes, they're the curse of the job, aren't they, Michael? But if the rumour mill has been working, you'll know by now that we have caught the man responsible for that young woman's death near the care home in Swindon a few months ago."

"Good. I have spoken with Simon in Kent – we have had some contact with them about the young woman killed on the Kent coast, and I believe there has already been some contact between Kent and Wiltshire."

"Yes, that's right. Two on our patch and four others."

"Yes, I have. Everyone including Diane is completely on board with the idea."

"Yes, you're right. He has been flitting around like a proverbial firefly, hasn't he? You know that would make an excellent name for the operation that we're going to announce to the press tomorrow. Mind if I use it? Thanks."

"I'll get a copy of the draft statement to you tonight. I'd be very grateful if you could respond first thing tomorrow – I need to get it all squared away before meeting the press later on tomorrow."

"Thanks."

My call to Simon Harlow in Kent Police was almost identical to the call I made to Michael, so I have not bothered recalling it here.

After some consideration and a consultation with the daughter of the late Eleanor Dunne, I also reached the decision that we will charge John Jackson with Eleanor's murder. Her daughter was only too happy that someone should be brought to book for her mother's premature death. I must admit that I am a little concerned that she might be seeking some form of compensation or recompense but decided that this would be a case where it was better to have her inside the tent pissing out than outside the tent pissing in.

Morning, Tuesday, October 24th

My words to Detective Inspector Linda Evans concerning the planned announcements to the press.

"Linda, thank you for sparing me some time. I wanted to have a brief word with you before we hold the press conference this afternoon. I would like, first of all, once again, to give you my congratulations on a truly magnificent piece of police work. I will certainly be recommending you for a commendation and I have every confidence that my recommendation will be accepted. Well done. And I also want to let you know how we'll be making the announcement to the press today. This is probably the first multiple murder you've worked on, isn't it?"

"Yes, I thought so. Sadly, I've seen a few over the years. Too many, of course. When this sort of thing comes to light there's always a strange reaction from the public. They're obviously pleased that such an evil man is no longer free to roam – but after a while, the papers will stoke them up to say things like 'How come he was able to do all these terrible things for so many months? What are our boys in blue up to?'"

"Yes, quite. But they'll never know just how hard it is to catch one of these evil bastards. Anyway, we'll be announcing the news in a way that does the best job of making the public feel safe. They need to feel confident that we were on to him as quickly as we could be, and that we worked together to catch him as soon as possible – and that the main thing is that he's going to be locked away for a long time."

"Yes, of course. Well, he would be, but his sick mind is encased in a sick body so that won't be the case this time – but we've got him, and he'll not be going anywhere or doing anything from now on. That's the important point."

"No, nothing for you to do. I've been working with my opposite numbers in the other services where his victims were, and there'll be a combined statement at the press conference. Just wanted you to know."

"Yes, see you then."

Afternoon, Tuesday, October 24th

My Speech to the Press Conference concerning the arrest of John Jackson

"Good afternoon, ladies and gentlemen. Nottinghamshire Police Service can today announce that the killer of Megan McCormick, also known by her working name of Suzanne, has been apprehended and has been charged with her murder. His name is John Jackson, and he is a local man. His arrest is a result of Operation Firefly, an operation that was conducted by a top-level task force composed of officers from multiple police services throughout the UK.

As a result of this operation, we have also been able to charge Mr Jackson with five other murders. One of these murders occurred in Nottinghamshire and had at first been described as a death by natural causes, but we have now been able to identify the cause of death as murder.

The other killings took place in Greater Manchester, the West Midlands, Wiltshire, and Kent. All the victims were women, and there was no discernible pattern in either his choice of victim or the methods he used to commit the crimes. I repeat, John Jackson has been charged with all six murders. We are reasonably confident that we have identified all of his victims, but he will be questioned further to confirm this.

The local aspect of this operation was managed by Detective Chief Inspector Lancaster, and a vital role in the investigation was played by Detective Inspector Evans who was responsible for solving the two local cases. DCI Lancaster charged Mr Jackson with all six crimes earlier today. We do not expect any other charges to be made.

I would like to express my gratitude for the hard work put in by DCI Lancaster, DI Evans, and their team in what was a highly complex case. I would also like to thank the many officers from the four other police services who worked with us on this difficult inquiry.

The full details of the victims are included in the press release that is now being handed out to you. I would like to express my deepest sympathy to the families and friends of all the victims and confirm that the thoughts and prayers of all the police services involved in this major inquiry are with them. We have allocated a brief amount of time to answer your questions but trust you will understand that we still have a great deal to do on this case, so would ask you to be as brief as possible."

16. Aftermath

Detective Inspector Linda Evans   Monday, 4th December

The weeks following the arrest of John Jackson has been every bit as hectic as those during the inquiry. Both professionally and personally.

There was a deal of tidying up to be done – more i's to be dotted and t's to be crossed, loose ends to be tied up and various other cliches to be performed.

I accompanied DC Priddis to John's house, and we conducted a second search, this time removing all paperwork from his office and confirming that there was nothing we had left behind that could assist our inquiry in any way.

John's work-related paperwork was all sent to Premier Programming. In his personal papers, I discovered his last will and testament and read the details. The financial arrangements were in line with the information in his book, and there were some personal matters that the executors would need to deal with. There was a separate sealed envelope addressed to Stephen Crapnell.

I made an appointment to see Stephen and took the paperwork with me. He had had some time to come to terms with the shock of John's arrest and the details that had emerged of his activities over the last six months of his life. But he told me he had decided not to visit John. There was very little that Stephen and I had to say to each other about the past, so our discussion centred on the will, which took him only a few minutes to read. He also opened the envelope addressed to him and read the single sheet of typed information it contained.

"He's apologised to me for the work he's left me to do. Nothing about what he's done, though," Stephen said, gesturing to the note in his hand. I accepted his word and made no move to look at it.

"Are you able to shed any further light on this mysterious missing beneficiary?" he asked.

"Not at present, Stephen. But you can be pretty sure that this person will come forward in about a year's time if that helps."

"Nothing else you can tell me?"

"Not right now, no."

"Well, in that case, I'll do the job as executor, settle his bills, sell the assets, set up a trust fund, and make the arrangements, I suppose".

I told him that the police would get involved in arranging the funeral as we would wish to ensure that no details were available to the public for obvious reasons. Stephen understood.

John died two weeks after being admitted to the hospice, during which time I visited him a couple of times. He was in slightly better condition with the aid of the drugs that were being pumped into him and answered my questions to help me clear up some final details of the inquiry. My feelings of anger and disgust abated a little more with each visit as I saw a sad, lonely man, dying alone.

The news of John's death was not released until several days after it happened so that his funeral could take place without intrusion from the press or public. There were only three people in attendance: myself, Stephen, (whether in his role as John's solicitor or his only friend, I'm not sure), and Ralph, his former boss. Stephen and Ralph were the only two people we had notified of the funeral arrangements. I wasn't sure whether to let Ralph know, but in the end, I decided that if any other people wished to attend, then they would be John's work colleagues. Obviously, none felt the need to come.

I was surprised that Ralph bothered to attend, but this surprise was dispelled when he approached me after the brief service to ask whether there was any further action planned on the matter of John's tax evasion. It was obvious that he had only attended in self-interest after all, and I was pleased to let him know that I had passed the matter to HMRC and was unable to tell whether they would be in contact with him or not.

In accordance with the details contained in his will and confirmed by Stephen from John's mother's will (which was amongst the family paperwork in John's files), John was buried with his brother. The headstone was updated with the words "and his brother, John" and the dates of John's birth and death.

I felt that John receiving only a minimal four-word epitaph was somehow right and fitting.

When John's death was announced, a second flurry of press coverage occurred. After that, there was almost nothing in any of the media. The story was over.

As the police inquiry drew to a close, I was 'seconded to the task force' and volunteered to deal with the families of the victims. The personal contact between them and the only member of the police who had been anything like close to John was vital, and I was pleased to be able to speak to them and aid each of them in the difficult task of getting closure after their loss. (Sorry, 'closure' is another cliché, I know.)

I stood by my decision to say nothing about 'The Book' and John's ridiculous puzzle. I remained absolutely sure that if the tabloid press got hold of the story, then it would be spread across front pages in a totally unsympathetic manner. I visualised front page images of a mock Cluedo board, or of that children's game where you identify someone by asking questions and then laying down tiles with pictures of the ones that don't fit the profile. I think it's called Guess Who? Or maybe there would be images of chess pieces or playing cards with victims' faces superimposed on them. And if I'm able to come up with these ideas almost without thinking, there was no telling what the rancid imaginations of the red tops' editorial staff might produce.

I breathed a huge sigh of relief when the end of the month following John's death came around. A whole clear month had passed, and I could now feel confident that the details of the puzzle were not going to be released on the Internet. John had said that he updated the release date for the story each month – so that when he died, the update would not happen, and the story would be released. Once a clear full month had elapsed, this could be crossed off my list of things to worry about. The work that Robin and I had done in completing the puzzle had been successful in preventing its release.

I was also very doubtful that the story would be kept secret if any of my colleagues got to hear about it. Senior officers could almost certainly be trusted. But they had assistants, secretaries, outside advisers, and other potential leak sources. And the more time that passed without me releasing the information, the more difficult it became for me to say anything.

I persuaded my boss to spend a little more of his budget for the services of a forensic psychologist. My justification was that the families of his victims would want some explanation of John's motivation. I also dropped hints that maybe the police would want to know whether the injuries he sustained from his taser-induced fall might have contributed in any way to what happened subsequently.

I've sent her John's blog and my notes on his police interviews and had one telephone conversation with her. She's promised me a full report within the next couple of weeks but was able to state that while his fall probably did cause the headaches and thus his decision to retire early, there was almost zero chance that it affected his subsequent behaviour.

"You're telling me he always was a wrong 'un?" I asked, partly in jest.

"Let's just say he showed signs of abnormal behaviour," was how I think she put it.

And, tying up one last loose end, I bought DS Holden and his wife the slap-up meal I had promised him.

Meanwhile, I spent every weekend with Robin. I owed him a couple of journeys, so I've been down to Cheltenham for three of the last four weekends, discovering his comfortable little house. I thought my flat was tidy until I saw his place. He even washes every dish at the end of every meal and returns them to the cupboard. I knew we were made for each other! I'm pleased to say that his place now looks a little more 'lived in'. We've done many of the things that young lovers are supposed to do – even if we don't qualify on the 'young' part of that label. We're both catching up on lost time.

A few gentle hints ensured that Robin knew that I was getting thoroughly pissed off with the half-hour delay whenever I phoned him. When he reassured me that the wait would reduce to fifteen minutes as I became a frequent caller, he was exposed to my devastating wit – I may have said something about introducing a thirty-minute delay when he wanted to connect with me in any way. He agreed that he would fill out the necessary paperwork the following day to add me to his 'special contacts list'.

And I've formulated a plan for the next year of my life. Formulating such a plan is a complete departure from my norm – I've been much more of a 'one step at a time' girl until now. But circumstances have forced my hand a little in that regard.

The plan results from one important premise. I'm going to leave the police service. The reason is not, as you might think, anything to do with the way I was treated in the public announcements about the Jackson case. I wasn't exactly happy about how my role was portrayed, but not exactly surprised either. I even understood, to a certain extent, the political difficulties that Chief Superintendent Dannatt faced. And I could almost applaud the way he worked his way around the problems. It seems that his strategy appears to have succeeded. The press coverage has been as positive towards the police as we could ever have expected. No, the reason for my leaving the service is much simpler than that.

I believe I've done a good job at being both a woman and a police officer. Many other women succeed at performing these two tasks, fulfilling these two roles simultaneously. But many don't succeed at it, because it's so bloody difficult. There are, I believe, occasions when the roles of a police officer and that of a woman are in direct conflict. I've seen many women who have had to sacrifice one part of their being to achieve this balancing act. They've either become less effective as police officers or lost some of their femininity as a result. That's just my opinion.

What I am not prepared to even attempt is to be both a police officer and a mother. And if nature follows its natural course, I will be one (a mother, that is) in about seven months. So, I'll take full advantage of the excellent maternity benefits I'm entitled to, but I won't be returning.

Telling Robin was one of the more challenging tasks of the past few months – and I think you'll agree I've had some doozies to deal with recently. I spent a whole evening trying to turn our conversation around to a point where I felt it was the right time to tell him. I thought my interviewing skills would make this straightforward, but every time I turned the conversation one way it felt like he was deliberately moving it in a different direction. Eventually, I had to blurt it out.

"Look, I've been trying to turn our conversation around to where I could do this more naturally, but I can't seem to do it, so here it is straight – I'm pregnant."

"The reason you've not been able to turn it around is that I was trying to turn it around to a point where I could ask you to marry me," he replied with a show of frustration that made me burst out laughing.

"And are you willing to take both of us on?" I asked, pointing to my yet-to-show belly, and noting that he was not sharing my mirth.

His 'Of course I am' was said so firmly that it pretty much ended the discussion for the time being.

Later we agreed that I would accede to his desire for a full church wedding –nothing less would satisfy my mum anyway, even though it was not top of my wish list.

"But it will have to wait," I insisted. "If I'm standing in front of all those people and being photographed in a big white dress, then I refuse point blank to appear like a galleon in full sail", I said, making a hand gesture to represent a huge spinnaker spreading out in front of me. Now he was laughing, and I wasn't.

Anyway, we made plans for me to move down to Cheltenham in time for the birth. House-hunting and buying furniture and baby stuff will occupy most of my spare time for the next few months.

As the plan formed in what passes for my brain, (pregnancy has such unexpected effects on cognitive ability), there were some other actions I needed to take to secure my future. The first step was to confirm what had just happened concerning the official description of my role in the Jackson inquiry.

I invited Lorry Hearsum for a drink at the Black Lion. Lorry is a long-time acquaintance of mine and the closest you'll find to an investigative journalist at the local Nottingham paper. In other words, he's a nosy bugger.

Some people believe that his name is a pseudonym, but it's real. Hearsum is the surname he was born with – and it's one of those cases of nominative determinism. An ideal name for a journalist who tries to 'hear sum things' as often as possible.

The 'Lorry' part came from a shortening of his real first name, Lauren. (He remains convinced that his parents were hoping for a girl). He told everyone his name was Laurie and decided to spell it Lorry when he heard someone pronounce Laurie in the same way that you say the surname of that L.S. Lowry bloke who painted the matchstick men a hundred years ago.

Lorry likes to think of himself as someone who drives a truck through obstacles, so he asked for his name to be spelt 'Lorry' in his byline in the local paper, and Lorry it has been ever since.

When he was offered the opportunity for a drink with a police Detective Inspector who had recently been involved in a multiple murder inquiry, he didn't need to be asked twice.

"I need a favour", I told him, and he gave me an expression that said, 'Gosh I am surprised'. An expression filled with true journalist sarcasm.

"But don't worry, there will be something in return for you," I added.

I explained that I wanted to confirm my distance from the 'task force' that had been referred to in Chief Superintendent Dannatt's recent statement. And that once I was distanced from it, I could bring something to light and make sure that Lorry would be first to know about it. He appeared slightly puzzled, as expected, but accepted the offer without question, almost licking his lips in anticipation of the juicy morsel he was sure was coming his way.

"What I'd like you to do is to tell Chief Superintendent Dannatt that you want to run a story about me playing a key role in the operation to catch John Jackson. You know, 'local girl does good' type thing. And then when he tells you that my role was purely local and that I had nothing to do with the national picture, just make sure that your recording device is placed close to the telephone handset and that he confirms it's OK for you to quote him on that."

I paused for him to say something, and he didn't disappoint.

"In return, there's an exclusive on what you're going to reveal?" he asked.

"I'll give you at least a twenty-four-hour start on anyone else hearing about it. That's the best I can promise" I replied.

He accepted my offer and called me a week later asking where to send the electronic recording. I gave him my private email address.

He'll have to wait for the payback though. I'm going to wait until I'm no longer a police officer before I do anything, just to be safe. Then I'll be taking a trip to Messrs Crapnell and Waters with the document that I printed out a few weeks ago and will present my claim for John's estate. And after that, I'll be visiting each of the families of John's victims to lie to them.

I'm going to tell them that John did show some remorse in the end, and that he asked me to give each of them a one-sixth share in his estate. I'll agree with them when they say it will never replace their loss and reassure them that the important thing is to spend it in the way they think best. And I'll agree to keep quiet about it – in fact, I'll insist that they do too.

For the relatives of Gerri and Carol, the money will help cover the cost of bringing up their children. As for the others, I'll tell them it's up to them to decide whether to buy a seat in the public gardens, donate it to a favourite charity, or whatever.

Of course, if I quit my job, Robin and I will not be able to live on his salary alone. I cannot expect to be a full-time mum, even if I want to be one – which I don't yet think I do.

I'm going to have to earn some money – and I plan that the money will initially come from the book. The full story of John Jackson's crimes. The awful way he treated women as puzzle pieces, the lies he told others as well as himself, and the twisted state of his mind (as revealed in his book and his blog). Complete with a detailed opnion from a police forensic psychologist, of course.

I'm sure I can tell the story. And there is no way that the police will be able to stop me. They might be able to if I was revealing information that came to me as a part of my job. But I've got recorded confirmation from a senior police officer that I had nothing to do with the national task force that brought John to justice. And a copy of an email confirming that my boss agreed that the information released about John's crimes and his reasons for committing them should be minimised.

And to top it all, I have vital knowledge of what really happened one night in a brothel just outside Mansfield. Something that might just have played a vital part in the whole story. Something that the police would not want to become the subject of public and press speculation. That part of the story stays with me. I have no desire to dump my ex-colleagues in the shit. Nobody can be sure how much the incident with the Taser influenced what John subsequently did, so I see no reason to include it.

In my humble opinion, John was seriously disturbed all along, and my keeping quiet about the part played by Tom Swift's Electronic Rifle (look up Taser in Wikipedia), will help ensure that there will never be any serious obstacle to the publication of my book. Of course, the families of the victims will all have to receive a copy before it's published. I fear that composing the letter to them explaining why I've done it might take me longer to write than the book itself.

To echo the words of the man that this story is all about, I'll have to think hard about a title for the book. It needs to have the element of murder and mystery, as well as the link to computers and social media. And yet, still be concise. I've thought about "The Twitter Murders", but I'm worried about infringing copyright, as well as linking to a name that might have negative connotations or might have even disappeared entirely by the time I write the book. I'll have to broaden it out to the whole of social media.

Death by SM would confuse people who think that SM stands for Sado-Masochism rather than social media, and I would not want to misrepresent the book (or possibly disappoint some potential readers). There are more catchy titles like "Program of Murder" or "Death@Unknown_Hands" (or maybe "Deaths@... to be more accurate.)

I quite like "The Social Murderer Mystery" but my favourite at the moment is "Social Murderer – The True Story of Multiple Murderer, John Jackson".

Anyway, I've got a year or so to make that decision.

List of Characters

John Jackson

John's Family:

Tom Jędrzejczyk - John's Brother
'Jack' Jędrzejczyk - John's father
Dorothy Jędrzejczyk - John's Mother –
(reverts to her maiden name after Jack's death)
Billy Rodriguez - Dorothy's new partner

Police:

Nottinghamshire:
Chief Superintendent Brian 'Dan' Dannatt
Detective Chief Inspector Tony Lancaster
Detective Inspector Linda Evans
Sergeant Mandy Lewis
Detective Sergeant Roger Holden
Detective Constable Priddis
Constable Christopher "Neppo" Peake
Constable Tweedie

George Woollard – Forensic Pathologist

Other Police Forces:
Chief Superintendent Diane Dowling (GMP)
Chief Superintendent Michael Tyrrell (Wiltshire)
Chief Superintendent Simon Harlow (Kent)
Detective Inspector Widdowson (Kent)
Detective Sergeant Riaz Khan (Kent)

Victims:

Eleanor 'Nelly' Dunne
Gerri Milburn
Carol Prentice
Emily Moss
Ezmiralda Levenaj – known as Macie.
Megan (Suzanne) McCormick

Other characters:

Denis Fittaley - John's literary advisor
Stephen Crapnell – John's schoolfriend and solicitor
Ralph Borshell – John's employer
Robin Scott - Cyber Security Specialist
George Moss – Emily's father
'Lorry' Hearsum – Local Newspaper reporter
Richard Horsenell (@InnCiderTrader) – Twitter Alias
Harriet Hale (@SoShallWorkHer) – Twitter Alias

Copyright © Ian Cummins 2023

All Rights Reserved

Acknowledgements

Concerning the contents of the book: the locations are (almost entirely) real, although there is no Black Lion in the centre of Nottingham (as far as I know), nor is there a league football team called the Bees anywhere in the East Midlands.

I have also taken certain liberties with the structure of secondary education in Nottinghamshire, the location and organisation of Nottinghamshire Police Force and the date of the Messiah from Scratch at the Royal Albert Hall.

The victims, in common with the rest of the people described within the book, are entirely fictitious, although many components of their stories originated in actual posts made to social media.

Concerning the writing of the book: my thanks go first, as always, to my wife for leaving me alone to get on with it. Then to my helpful proofreaders Cliff Antill, Barbara Primrose, and Mikael Westlund and to the Bee Primrose Company for help with publicity.

For their help with the content of the book, I'd like to thank my sister, Susan Folkard, and her husband Dave for information on police procedure; Philip Whitelaw for his advice on wills and probate procedure; and my friend and cyber security expert, Reinhard Wobst, author of Cryptology Unlocked, for his input on cyber security.

All four have provided me with thread, but the embroidery, and hence the mistakes, are all mine.

My thanks go also to the vast army of people who daily expose details of their personal life on X (formerly Twitter), especially those from whom I have 'borrowed' content for this book. Without you it would still have been possible, but more difficult.

Finally, and most importantly, to you, my reader – thanks for buying the book (and even more thanks if you post a review on the Amazon website).

As with my previous books, half the proceeds of this book will go to charities assisting the homeless.

There's more information on my author page on Amazon:

https://www.amazon.co.uk/Ian-Cummins/e/B08LSRKY1Z

And, you can reach me on Twitter: @Accidental_Ian

Other books by Ian Cummins:

An Accidental Salesman: Stories from 40 Years in International IT Sales

There was the time my car ran into a river in rural Suffolk; the time I had the FA Cup in my possession for a whole day; or when I was billeted to stay with a dead woman in Germany; and, of course, the incident with the flight attendant, the elderly hippy, and the gallon of olive oil on the flight from Athens. There are also my thoughts on how Brits can best deal with Americans, and how to sell successfully to customers who don't have English as a first language.

But it's mostly about the stories.

The Wrong Briefcase

What would you do if you suddenly found a large amount of money?

Mark Reynolds is facing the uncomfortable changes of middle age when he mistakenly picks up a briefcase containing a very large amount of cash. Unable to trace its owner, and having received no contact, he decides to keep the vast sum, and discretely invest it - a decision which leads him into an unfamiliar world populated by interesting people.

My Time Again – A Time Travel Novel

How often have you said, "If I had my time again, I would ...."

On the eve of his 70th birthday, Graham Henderson gets the chance to re-live his adult life when he is transported back to his 18-year-old self in 1970 - with all his memories intact.

Must he live the same life the second time around? Will he be able to find a partner to share the re-run of his life? What about changing things for the better in the wider world - is it possible? Surely, he can do something!

Eventually, he discovers he is not the only person to have this experience, and this helps him to find the cause of his jump in time. But it does not solve everything .....

Printed in Great Britain
by Amazon